Don't Look Back

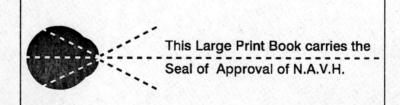

This Large Print Book carries the
Seal of Approval of N.A.V.H.

WOMEN OF JUSTICE, BOOK 2

DON'T LOOK BACK

LYNETTE EASON

THORNDIKE PRESS
A part of Gale, Cengage Learning

GALE
CENGAGE Learning·

Detroit • New York • San Francisco • New Haven, Conn • Waterville, Maine • London

GALE
CENGAGE Learning®

© 2010 by Lynette Eason.
Scripture used in this book, whether quoted or paraphrased by the characters, is taken from the Holy Bible, New International Version®. NIV®. Copyright © 1973, 1978, 1984 by Biblica, Inc.™ Used by permission of Zondervan. All rights reserved worldwide.
www.zondervan.com
Thorndike Press, a part of Gale, Cengage Learning.

LIBRARY OF CONGRESS CATALOGING-IN-PUBLICATION DATA

Eason, Lynette.
  Don't look back / by Lynette Eason.
    p. cm. — (Thorndike Press large print Christian fiction)
  (Women of justice ; bk. 2)
  ISBN-13: 978-1-4104-4254-3 (hardcover)
  ISBN-10: 1-4104-4254-3 (hardcover)
    1. United States. Federal Bureau of Investigation—Fiction. 2. Criminal investigation—Technological innovations—Fiction. 3. Suspense fiction. gsafd 4. Christian fiction. gsafd 5. Large type books. I. Title.
  PS3605.A79D66 2011
  813'.6—dc23   2011033444

Published in 2012 by arrangement with Revell Books, a division of Baker Publishing Group.

Printed in Mexico
1 2 3 4 5 6 7 16 15 14 13 12

This story is dedicated to Christ,
my Lord and Savior,
who allows me to do what I love to do.

The LORD is my light and my salvation
—
whom shall I fear?
The LORD is the stronghold of my life
—
of whom shall I be afraid?
Psalm 27:1

1

Tuesday Afternoon

FBI Special Agent Dakota Richards stared down at the pile of bones unearthed by the backhoe. Jamie would have her hands full with this one.

He looked up to see her coming toward him. She was dressed in a Tyvek jumpsuit she'd donned to avoid contaminating the scene. Underneath, he'd bet she had on her standard khaki capris and a white long-sleeved T-shirt. In her right hand, she carried a pair of blue booties she'd place over her red tennis shoes before entering the area.

As always, Dakota's heart gave that extra little beat in response to her presence. And as always, she held herself at a distance even as she came closer.

"Hey, Jamie."

She offered him a small smile as her brown eyes locked on his. "So you pulled this one?"

"I did." He took in her presence. Petite yet wiry, she had her long blonde curls pulled up into her customary ponytail. He cleared his throat. "This is the third body found near this area. Only this one's a skeleton. Connor called me about an hour ago and said his boss wanted the FBI in on it, and that they might need some of our resources. After looking at the situation, my boss agreed. I knew Serena would request your services." Serena Hopkins, the pathologist and a woman Jamie enjoyed working with. He smiled. "She said you were the perfect person for the job. I agreed."

Her chin rose at his compliment; appreciation shone in her gaze along with a tinge of amusement. "Ha. I'm not sure that means much. I'm the *only* person right now." The other anthropologist she worked with on occasion was on his honeymoon. "You have a partner on this one?"

"Just Connor right now. I'm authorized to call for more help if we need it." Connor Wolfe, former state law enforcement detective, now a detective with the city of Spartanburg, South Carolina, was also Jamie's brother-in-law. Her sister, Samantha, and Connor had married a year and a half ago on Christmas Day, shortly after Jamie's graduation.

"What happened?"

"Two workers were digging a grave and came across a body already buried. Fortunately, that guy over there," he gestured to the Hispanic-looking man sitting on the ground near the backhoe, "saw the bones they'd unearthed and immediately stopped his partner who was driving, so it looks like there won't be any damage to the rest of whatever you might find."

"Bones in a cemetery." She grinned. "Not really unusual, is it?"

"Cute, Jamie."

She turned serious. "Human?"

"You'll have to make that final determination, of course, but yeah, I can see the skull and the outline of what once was a body."

"So, it looks like we've got a homicide?"

"Looks like it. Connor should be back soon. He's talking to the director of the place, but he and I'll be working on this if you concur that it's a homicide. For some reason, they think they'll link the first two they found here to this one. Guess we'll find out." The first two bodies had been found approximately three years ago very close to this spot. "Anyway, we've got a skeleton in a shallow grave. Usually not a good case for death by natural causes."

11

"Usually not. Are we thinking serial killer?"

"Maybe. I wasn't working here when the other two bodies were found, and the detective that did work them is now in another state."

"So you rushed right over. Didn't have anything better to do, huh?" She teased him and he smiled back.

"Naw." They both knew he had an overflowing desk full of cases he was working on.

As Jamie slipped on a pair of gloves, then tugged the sleeves back down to the edge of her palms, Dakota couldn't help notice the brief flash of scars around her wrists. She always wore long sleeves no matter the weather.

But she'd never told him why.

And he'd never told her he'd fallen in love with her practically from the moment they'd met a little less than two years ago when he'd been helping her sister and Connor with the case of missing and murdered teenagers.

Since then he'd been trying to win this lady's heart. Thus far, he'd failed miserably and didn't have a clue what he was doing wrong.

"All right," she turned toward the grave,

12

"let's see what we've got."

Jamie ignored the thumping of her heart that Dakota's presence always seemed to incite and turned her attention to her job. His dark curly hair, keen blue eyes, Stetson, cowboy boots, and Texas drawl combined to make him one attractive man. The problem was, she didn't know what to do with her reaction to him, so she pretended it wasn't there.

They were working in an open field, property that belonged to the mortuary but hadn't been used as graves yet.

Part of the excavation team Jamie worked with on a regular basis had already dug down around the skeleton so that they could stand upright in the grave next to the bones that now lay on a dirt platform.

Normally, they would place the bones on a gurney and transport it to the morgue; however, in this case, the body hadn't been lying down when it had been buried, it had been dropped into a hole sitting up. The bones rested on top of each other, looking like one big lump. And Jamie could see what others couldn't.

Her crew knew the bones were not to be disturbed until she had a chance to see them exactly as they were found. And looking down into the grave, she could see the spine lying facedown. The skull lay just in front of the spine like it had dropped off the end. All of this lay on top of what had probably once been thighs. The ribs were perfectly proportioned, still attached to the spine by some desiccated tissue. The right arm, which included the humerus, radius, and ulna, lay across the back of the spine.

The left arm was missing — the bones that the Bobcat had clipped and pulled out of the grave, to the horror of the workers. It was amazing the machine hadn't disturbed the rest of the skeleton — or completely destroyed it.

Jamie felt someone approaching and stepped to the opposite side of the grave. She liked her space. She shot a smile at the curly-headed crime scene photographer who stood at the edge. "Hey, Chase, have you gotten all the pictures?"

A shock of red hair covered his left eye as he nodded. "I got them."

"Great. Now, I guess it's my turn."

Looking down into the hole was one thing; getting into it was another. She started her anxiety-calming exercises. Abdominal breaths, not chest breathing. One, two, three. Okay.

It had been a long time since the last panic

14

attack and she wasn't about give in now. Time to see what she was made of. Jamie dropped down into the grave. Stood there for a number of seconds, smelling the dampness of the earth, feeling the darkness surround her. Remembered the pain, the mind-numbing fear . . .

Shut it out. Let it go. It doesn't control you anymore. You control it.

She shuddered, then focused on the one thing that would take her mind off her fear.

The bones.

Two hours later, she had her documentation on paper, and with her help, the team brought up what looked to be an entire skeleton jigsaw puzzle. As Jamie supervised the transfer of the bones to various boxes, the rest of the team returned to the grave and continued to sift through the debris looking for any more small fragments or missing pieces.

Jamie picked up a large bone and, using a soft brush, swished it over the piece. "It's a left femur." The largest bone in the body.

"Any clothing found with it?" Dakota said, walking up beside her. She gave a small jump at his sudden appearance, then went back to her bone. He looked over her shoulder.

"A polyester shirt. Remnants of a pair of

pants and some other things that will have to be examined back at the lab."

She set the bone back into the box that would go back to her lab for her to unpack. Then she'd work on putting this person back together to see if they could come up with an identity.

"We're checking the area to see if anything else turns up."

"You don't think this is an isolated incident?"

He shrugged. "I don't know. Since this is the third body to be found under suspicious circumstances, I just want to see if anything unusual catches my eye. I always tend to scout farther than just where the body is found."

Settling a hand on her hip, she scanned the area and said, "Ok, I'll come with you."

They walked the perimeter of the cemetery first, then made their way through it, walking a grid pattern.

"You see anything out of place?" she asked him.

"No."

"Just from my initial observation I can tell those bones have been there awhile."

"That was my impression."

"So you have learned something from me

in the last year and a half or so, huh?"

"I try." He pretended modesty.

She flashed him a grin, then turned to scan the gently sloping grass that stretched out before them. Land that would one day be used to bury the deceased — the way they were supposed to be buried, not someone digging a hole in the ground and trying to hide his crime.

"Any other observations? Anything else that could indicate murder?" He wanted to hear what she thought. Listening to someone else sometimes helped him organize thoughts in his mind.

"Besides the fact that a body's buried in a place it shouldn't be and without a coffin?"

He grinned at her teasing.

She turned serious. "The way the bones were situated says a lot." She described them to him. "The body was dropped into that hole, hands bound behind her."

"Her?"

"The first thing I looked for. The shape of the pelvis and a few other things."

"Right. And the hands were bound behind her?"

Jamie nodded. "I could tell because the right arm bones were lying across the back of the spine and not under it. At least that's my theory until further examination."

She paused and Dakota watched her gaze land on a spot near the edge of the trees. Dread twisted her features as she headed to the area. "Uh-oh. I was wondering if I would see an area like that but hoped I wouldn't."

He followed her and stopped when she held a hand out in front of him.

"What is it?"

She pointed to the ground. "You know as well as I do that statistics show that if a killer kills more than once, he buries the bodies in the same general location. Sometimes, not always. But because the possibility exists, it's always smart to cover your bases."

"Exactly. And?"

"And I bet there's another body buried right here."

"Huh? How do you figure that? Did you go psychic on me now?" In confusion, he stared at the ground. In his many years as an investigator, he'd learned a lot about dead bodies and forensics but hadn't developed the skill of locating graves just by looking at the ground.

When he said he wanted to take a look around, he'd just meant he was looking for a disturbed area, anything that might indicate someone had been doing something they shouldn't, a clue that might lead him to the reason someone buried a body here. Not that he'd really expected to find anything. It was obvious a lot of time had passed since the person in the grave had been put there, but . . .

Jamie gave a small, sad laugh and said, "No, not psychic, just more observant than the average person. I need another grid set up, marked off in twenty-foot sections with string and wooden stakes. We need some more of those workhorses and plywood, too, to set up tables with sifting screens for going through the debris. I'll need my camera guys over here and —"

Dakota held up a hand. "Hang on there. What makes you think there's another body here?"

"The ground."

"Could you explain?"

"It's sunken in right here." She walked the perimeter of the area she was talking about, then pointed to the center. "Then there's another small depression in the middle."

"Uh-huh. And how does that add up to a dead body?"

"Okay," her voice took on the tone of teacher, "say a guy kills someone and he wants to get rid of the body by burying it. He comes out here, sees an open field, digs a grave as fast as he can, then sticks the body in it. It's going to be rather shallow because he's in a hurry."

"Wouldn't someone see that the ground's been disturbed and wonder why?"

Jamie looked around. "We're in a pretty secluded area. Far enough away from the mortuary building that anyone happening to look out a window wouldn't see anything. The perimeter of the entire backside of this cemetery is surrounded by trees so no one driving by can see what's going on." She shrugged. "Who's going to notice? And besides, maybe our killer didn't care if he — or she — was found, although burying the body suggests he didn't want it found immediately." She threw her hands up. "Who knows?"

Dakota nodded. "Okay, but you still haven't answered my question."

"Right. So, our victim is buried and the ground covered back up. What happens to the body over time?"

"It decomposes."

"Right again. As the body decomposes, the ground sinks."

Realization dawned in his eyes. "So, what's up with the second indentation?"

"The body cavity. When all the gases are gone, the ground sinks one more time."

Dakota sighed and stared at the innocent-looking patch of grass. "If there's one body buried around here, I suppose it's possible there's another."

"Hey, guys," the call came from the grave behind them, then a head popped up above the edge, "check this out."

Jamie looked over to see Roxanne, criminalist and grave digger extraordinaire, hold up a plastic bag containing a pair of dirt-encrusted handcuffs.

A chill shot through her as the memory flashed to the forefront of her mind. *He yanked her arms behind her; the cold steel snapped closed over her wrists. His masked faced shoved against hers as he whispered vile things in her ear. A swish to the side, she spun her head. Nothing. No one. Just the man behind her. The brush of rose petals against her cheek, falling to the pillow, the floor. Low, taunting laughter. The whisper, "She loves me, she loves me not . . ."*

Breathlessness came over her as her chest closed in on her lungs. Her heart hammered against her breastbone and the blue sky spun above. She jammed a hand into her pocket and closed her fingers around the small metal object she always kept with her.

A hand on her arm made her jump and it

21

was all she could do to hold in the scream clawing at her throat.

"Jamie!"

She gasped and looked into Dakota's worried eyes. Blinking, she stumbled back and sat on the cool ground. Someone's grave. A grave that could have been hers. She buried her head in her hands and fumbled for an explanation that wouldn't have him calling the men in the white coats to come lock her up in the loony bin.

Sucking in a deep breath, she looked up. "Sorry, I just felt really dizzy there for a minute."

"You looked terrified."

A half-laugh croaked from her. "Sorry. I'm sorry." She couldn't seem to stop apologizing. "I don't know what happened." Yes, she did but wasn't about to explain it. Not now. Maybe not ever. She pulled in a lungful of oxygen and shoved herself up into a standing position. She had a job to do. "I'm all right now."

Uncertainty flickered on Dakota's face as he stepped back without protest.

He now held the bag containing the handcuffs and Jamie shuddered.

She hated handcuffs.

The Hero, as he'd come to think of himself,

gave a victorious smile and lowered the high-powered binoculars to his lap. She still thought of him. Her reaction to the handcuffs proved it.

Only now, he was tired of watching. He'd been watching her ever since he'd come across the article in the newspaper a little over nine months ago. It had been almost nine months old. A paper saved to line the bottom of the bird cage or start a fire in the fireplace.

Jamie had gotten her doctorate and she'd been in the paper holding her diploma.

Jamie. The one who'd gotten away.

Anger tightened his gut. He couldn't believe she'd had the nerve to survive, the strength to thwart him. But no matter. He reined in the anger.

He could hear the voice in his head, chanting. "Stop the pain, stop the pain. Only you can stop the pain." He shook his head.

It was time.

Time for the fun to begin.

Time to let Jamie Cash know her hero had returned and he was ready to renew their relationship.

He put the binoculars away and cranked the car.

The clock on the dash glared at him, reminding him he had an appointment in

23

fifteen minutes. He'd have to hurry. After all, it wouldn't do for someone known for his punctuality to show up late. But after that . . .

He had a stop to make before Jamie got home.

2

Spartanburg Regional Hospital housed the morgue and autopsy room located beneath the Emergency Department. The back door allowed her to come and go as she pleased without running into many hospital visitors who normally came in through the reception area. Jamie preferred the anonymity of the back door.

Once every piece of bone that could be found had been excavated from the unofficial grave, she returned to the lab to get to work on the pieces she had. The grave hadn't seemed disturbed by scavengers, just the backhoe; therefore, the absence of teeth from the skull's oral cavity meant the person had been in the grave for at least a year, most likely longer. The absence of most of the tissue indicated longer. Possibly a lot longer. The evidence of insects would require an entomologist in order to say whether her estimated length of time in the ground for the bones was in the right ballpark.

She kept her phone nearby, expecting to get called back to the scene to examine the second body she was sure would turn up. Then she would help excavate it just like she had the first.

For now, the first body was a good excuse to get away from the area where she'd been so close to succumbing to a panic attack. That hadn't happened in quite a while, but she'd been on edge lately. More so than usual and her defenses were down.

And the handcuffs . . . she'd thought she'd conquered that fear, had put it to rest. Today it had snuck up on her and belted her a good one.

And again, out at the excavation site, she'd felt . . . watched. She'd had the feeling on more than one occasion lately and it disturbed her. But she didn't have time to think about that.

Her jaw ached. Also a common occurrence in her past. She realized her teeth were clenched. Today had opened one too many doors for her to feel comfortable. But she would work through it. Slamming the door on thoughts that would keep her from doing what she had to do, she took a deep breath and told herself to relax.

Focus on the job, she ordered herself. She slid the first box toward her. Reaching in, she pulled out the first bone, a tibia, and placed it on the table beside her. The bones would go to the cleaning room, but first she wanted to see what she had. As she'd explained to Dakota, from the pelvis and the skull, she knew the victim was a female.

For two hours, she worked, examining each piece before placing it in the cleaning container, which held a mixture of hot water and chemicals.

A contract forensic anthropologist for the office of the Chief Medical Examiner for the state of South Carolina, Jamie might be relatively new on the job, but she had already proven her worth in the field of osteology. Putting bones back together to find some way of identifying a person was no easy task.

But one Jamie excelled at.

Her cell phone rang, startling her, causing her heart to jump. She snatched it up. "Hello?"

"Jamie?"

"Dakota. Oh, hi. Well?"

"You were right."

The news didn't thrill her. She'd rather have been wrong. "I'm sorry."

"See you in a few?"

"Yep." She'd known she was going back.

Around seven o'clock, Dakota shut the door to his house and peeled out of his work clothes to toss them into the hamper. After grabbing sweats and a T-shirt, running shoes, and a bottle of water, he headed back out the door and down the sidewalk of his quiet street. Jamie had arrived back at the scene within thirty minutes of his call and had done her thing.

He'd offered to escort her home and she turned him down flat. Something was going on with her, he just wasn't sure what. She'd acted weird all day, jumpier than normal, snappier than usual. And it started when she'd seen the handcuffs.

Dakota pounded his frustration out on the sidewalk, the sweat pouring down his face and soaking through his shirt. It felt good. He thought about the scars on her wrists, her jumpiness, the reaction to the cuffs. He rounded a corner and stopped when he finally realized what it was he'd seen on her face.

Pure, unadulterated fear. No, it was stronger than that.

Terror.

Okay, she'd been afraid. Of what?

With that question spurring him back into

a jog, his thoughts sorted through this bit of information. Now that he thought about it, from their first meeting, the only times he'd ever seen her truly relaxed and comfortable were in her home or engrossed in her work at the lab.

Which is most likely where he'd find her if he called. Working on the bodies they'd dug up earlier this afternoon.

A police car cruised past and Dakota lifted a hand in a wave. Several officers lived in his neighborhood, and he appreciated the sense of community, of watching each other's back.

Again his thoughts circled back to Jamie. And what about the scars on her wrists? He'd never asked and she'd never offered the information.

Maybe it was time to dig a little deeper into the past of the woman he loved.

Yawning, Jamie finally called it a day. Serena had come in to work with her, and between the two of them, they'd gotten a lot accomplished. Serena had left awhile ago, called to a homicide across town. Jamie had told her she'd finish up.

The two older case files on her desk would have to wait. Lower back aching, she straightened, cleaned up the lab, and then glanced at her watch. She nearly shrieked. 9:30. No wonder she was starving.

She looked out the window.

Darkness. Not even a moon to light the way home. It was only a little over two miles to the entrance to her subdivision, and she made the walk to and from work as often as she could. But always in the light. Never in the dark. If she knew she was going to work late, she arranged for a ride from family or a co-worker.

Familiar panic stirred in the depths of her belly. She'd stayed too late, not thinking about the passage of time. The fact shocked her. Normally, she was so careful to make sure —

Out of nowhere, the panic moved up to grip her by the throat and she forced it down, ordering her mind to work, to think.

She couldn't turn back the hands of the clock, so she had to decide what to do. The building teemed with people, and would all night long, but she wanted to be home safe, in her own bed. She looked at her comfortable office chair and grimaced that she would actually consider spending the night in it as opposed to walking home or calling a cab.

Or she could ask for a ride home from someone.

Her cell rang and she grabbed it. "Hello?"

"Jamie? Where are you? Are you okay?"

Samantha's frantic questions raised the hair on her arms.

"I'm at the lab. What's wrong?"

"Oh. The lab. Right. I stopped by your house and you weren't there and . . ."

For the past eleven and a half years, Samantha, Jamie's sister, called almost daily. Since the night Jamie had disappeared, not to be heard from again for a little over two months, Samantha checked on her constantly.

Lately, it grated on Jamie's nerves. Tonight, she felt relieved. "I'm fine, Sam."

"Do you want me to come pick you up? You shouldn't walk home this late."

Hiding her fear at the thought of the walk home, she gave a halfhearted protest, "It's only a little after 9:30. I'll be fine."

"I'm coming to pick you up. Don't leave."

"Sam . . ." But she was talking to dead air. Anger stirred. She wasn't eighteen years old anymore. And yet, she couldn't deny that beneath the anger, relief flowed. Fine, Sam could pick her up and they'd talk on the way home.

Ten minutes later, Samantha pulled up out front in a shiny little red Corvette.

Jamie climbed in. "Connor lets you drive

this?" The car was a special vehicle, willed to Connor when his partner, Andrew West, had been killed in the line of duty a little over a year and a half ago.

"He sure does."

Samantha's straight blonde hair, like their mother's, fell to her shoulders. Jamie had inherited a shinier version of her father's unruly, naturally curly locks that reached to the middle of her back when she didn't have them restrained in a clip or a tie.

"He must think a lot of you," Jamie teased.

Samantha shot her an amused look as she pulled from the curb. "He'd better, he's stuck with me for life. Actually, I had to pry the steering wheel from Jenna with the promise to bring the car right back to her. My car bit the dust this morning and Jenna has plans to see the midnight showing of that new movie that's releasing."

Secretly, Jamie envied her sister's easy-going relationship with her husband and eighteen-year-old stepdaughter. Jamie often despaired of ever having that with a man. Or a family of her own.

Dakota was the closest she'd come, and even in the year and a half that she'd known him, she'd managed to keep him at arm's length.

A transplant from Texas, he'd moved to

the North Carolina FBI branch office. Then after working a case with Connor and Samantha last year, he decided he liked the area so much he'd moved to South Carolina, not minding the occasional hour-and-a-half commute to Charlotte for meetings and briefings. Samantha, who worked out of the Columbia, South Carolina office, insisted it wasn't the area he liked, but one particular person who lived in it. Jamie had a hard time wrapping her mind around the idea that a man would uproot his life for her like that.

"So," Samantha broke into her disturbing thoughts, "I guess you were working on the bodies found this afternoon."

"Yes, and I lost track of time. Speaking of which, I would have been fine walking home, you know."

"I know, I know, I just . . . well, I was just right around the corner and it wasn't any big deal to come pick you up."

Jamie dropped it. Samantha would just start feeling guilty again. If picking her up and taking her home made Samantha feel better, Jamie would let her do it. "So, what are you working on?"

"I've decided to take some time off."

Surprised, Jamie stared at her sister. "What? As of when?"

"Starting today."

"But why? You love your job."

"I do. But I'm married now, and with Connor being a detective and me traveling all over the place whenever the FBI needs a computer expert . . . well, honestly? I just want to be in the same town as my husband, so . . . I'm reevaluating some things."

Before Jamie could respond, Samantha pulled in the driveway. Jamie's little cottage-style house sat in darkness. Not even the porch light burned.

Sam cut the engine. "Why didn't you leave a light on?"

"I did." Jamie frowned and crawled from the car.

"Guess it burned out?" Jamie heard the doubt in Sam's voice.

"You know I change my lightbulbs every month whether they're burned out or not." She didn't ever want to take a chance on coming home to a dark house.

Like the one that now stood before her.

Unease centered itself in her stomach. Something was definitely not right.

Samantha followed Jamie to the door. "The power is on because your neighbors' houses are lit up. Yours is the only one that's dark. I'll just come in with you."

Concerned, but not wanting to show it,

Jamie said, "Samantha, I probably just forgot to flip the switch."

"You don't forget stuff like that."

"And I don't lose track of time either, but I did tonight."

"Whatever, I'm still coming in."

Jamie sucked in a deep breath. "Fine." She swung the door open and flipped the entryway switch. Brightness filled her vision as the high-pitched whine of her alarm system warned her she had forty-five seconds to punch in her code. She did so and looked around.

Nothing out of place. "See? I told you, I just forgot to turn it on."

"I'll give it a quick sweep. You wait here." Samantha's voice came back to Jamie as her sister was already heading into the kitchen to the right, gun drawn and held in front of her. Heart pounding in spite of her brave words, Jamie anxiously studied the den and beyond.

Recently, she'd added the sunroom off the den. Her painting supplies had taken over her bedroom, and the addition of the sunroom gave her the natural light she'd wanted and the space she'd desperately needed. Only when she painted did she crack the blinds to let in the light. The rest of the time the blinds stayed shut tight, just like the ones in the rest of the house.

Examining the rest of the little two-bedroom, two-bath house didn't take long, and when Samantha returned, Jamie looked at her. "You can't turn it off, can you?"

"What?"

"Your FBI cop mode or whatever you want to call it."

Sam gave an embarrassed shrug. "Guess not. It's what I'm trained to do . . . so, I do it."

"Trouble isn't hovering around every corner, Sam. You need to learn to relax."

Surprise lit her sister's eyes before they narrowed. "Who are you and what have you done with my sister?"

Jamie forced a laugh and walked into her den. She didn't feel nearly as lighthearted as she was trying to project for Samantha. In the den, the laughter died a quick death. "That's weird."

"What?" Sam asked coming up behind her.

"Look at my mantel. Do you see anything wrong?"

Samantha studied the mantel. "A picture is missing. The one of you and me before . . ."

"Right. Before the attack."

"Did you move it?"

"No. It was there when I left for work this morning. I think. I mean it must have been. That's where it always is." Feeling creeped out, Jamie grabbed her grandaddy's cane that she kept in the clay pot at the corner of the fireplace. It could be a weapon if she could swing it hard enough.

Gripping the carved oak in her right hand, she left the room and investigated the rest of her house while Samantha finished going over the den.

Jamie couldn't find anything amiss. Uncertainty flickered through her, and she returned to her sister's side to study the mantel. "Maybe I moved it and just forgot."

"Like you forgot to leave the lights on?"

Fear churned within her and she made a concerted effort not to let it get a stronghold on her. "Yes, like I forgot to leave the lights on."

Not.

The Hero watched through his binoculars from his vantage point across the street. He kept his focus on the open blinds. The ones he'd opened and Jamie hadn't noticed yet. He could see her staring at the mantel and knew she'd already taken note of his handiwork. She turned in a full circle, her eyes taking in every detail.

37

Her gaze landed on the window and the Hero almost dropped his binoculars as her widened gaze seemed to stare straight through him. He saw her draw in a deep breath, watched terror and pain flash across her face, then she marched over to shut him out.

A thrill shot through him. The voice whispered, "Stop the pain, stop the pain, you're my hero, only death stops the pain."

Soon. Jamie, soon, your hero will rescue you once more. After all, it was his responsibility to stop the pain. And pain could only be stopped by death.

Soon. Very soon.

3

Jamie grabbed a bottle of water from the fridge and shut the door with more force than necessary. Samantha had called Connor and Dakota to fill them in on the events. Of course they'd rushed right over.

Frankly, Jamie wondered if Sam was overreacting and yet she couldn't come up with a reasonable explanation for the incidents.

Especially her blinds.

She'd never leave them open.

Never.

Hating the thought that someone could see her and she couldn't see them, she simply kept them shut.

Always.

The only thing she sometimes opened to let a little light in was the sheer curtain that covered the long window by her front door. And she rarely did that.

At the back of the house, the sunroom blinds stayed shut unless she had someone out there with her — or she was painting. And then she only opened one set of blinds to let in the light needed.

At the knock on her door, she closed her eyes to breathe a soft prayer. "I don't know what's happening, God, but you've gotten me this far and I know you won't leave me . . . no matter what. Please let there be a reasonable explanation for what's going on and that I haven't finally snapped and lost my mind."

"You haven't lost your mind."

The deep voice made her jump. When Dakota's hands came to rest on her shoulders, she froze. Forcing herself to stay still, ignoring her initial reaction to jerk away, she just stood there — and analyzed the emotions jumping around inside her.

His hands felt . . . comforting. Heavy and strong, but in a good way.

Turning a slow spin, she came face-to-face with the only man she'd allowed to touch her in almost twelve years — not counting the doctors who'd brought her back from the brink of death.

As she turned to face him, he replaced his hands on her shoulders. She let him.

"I'm not?"

"No. Is something weird going on? Possibly. But that doesn't mean you're crazy."

"Then how did someone get in my house without setting off my alarm?"

"I don't know, but we'll figure it out."

Connor stuck his head into the kitchen and Jamie stepped back. Surprisingly, she missed the weight of Dakota's hands on her shoulders.

Something to ponder later.

Connor said, "Hey, guys, Samantha's working the rest of the house. I dusted the mantel and the doorknob for prints and will get the lab to run them for me. It won't be a priority because I'm calling in a favor, so don't know how long it'll actually take."

Jamie gave a rare genuine smile. "I might be able to help that along tomorrow. I've got a few connections."

Connor nodded. "Samantha's going to spend the night here with you tonight and —"

"No," Jamie sighed "really, that's not necessary."

"She says it is and frankly, I agree. Until we know what's going on, you need to stick close to someone who knows how to use a gun."

That stopped her. "What? You think someone's targeted me? That . . . that I've picked up a stalker or something?" The irony of it hit her. She threw up her hands. "Great. I

41

don't leave the house for years and the minute I decide to try and have a life, some sicko wants to ruin it for me." She ignored the tinge of hysteria in her voice and the fact that her volume had notched up a few decibels.

Dakota laid a calming hand on her arm and she shrugged him off. Anger like nothing she'd ever felt before spun through her. Shocked, she stopped, then realized the anger felt good.

Really, really good.

Much better than the fear she'd lived with the past eleven-plus years. She poked a finger in Dakota's chest and said, "I'm not hiding anymore. I'm not going to be afraid anymore. I'm not giving up the life I've just managed to acquire. This time I'm fighting back, got it?"

Whoa. Where did this feisty new person come from? Even Connor stood there looking stunned at Jamie's uncharacteristic outburst.

Dakota held his hands up as though in surrender. "Sure, Jamie. But it might be nothing."

"Right. Tomorrow, you're teaching me how to shoot a gun, okay?"

"Absolutely."

She spun from the kitchen and left silence in her wake.

Dakota finally turned to Connor and asked, "Who was that?"

"I don't know, but I like her." He grinned. "How's the hole in your chest?"

Dakota rubbed the spot, realizing it was the first time Jamie had voluntarily touched him.

He'd take what he could get.

He matched Connor's grin. "It's perfect." The he sobered. "Connor, I don't want you to betray any confidences or anything, but is there anything you can tell me about Jamie that'll help me . . ." He trailed off, not wanting to ask, yet almost unable to help himself.

"She was attacked when she was eighteen years old. She's made tremendous progress to . . . 'get over it' is the wrong phrase. More like *move on* from it."

Dakota blanched, but nodded. "Yeah, I figured something major must have happened to make her so skittish."

"And it wasn't just a physical attack. The guy messed up her mind — big time."

Fury started a slow burn in the pit of his gut. "Like I said, I figured."

"But it's not my story to tell. Jamie will let you in on the details when she's ready.

Samantha told me. Jamie's never mentioned it in my presence. But I'll warn you," he frowned and swallowed hard, "it's one of the ugliest and sickest stories you'll ever hear."

This coming from Connor? A guy who'd been in law enforcement for over fifteen years and had seen every depraved thing there was to see? A sick feeling joined the fury churning inside him, and he vowed to do whatever it took to help Jamie. Whatever it took to keep her safe. "Did they get the guy?"

"That's the worst part. He's still out there."

Jamie caved to Samantha's insistence that she spend the night. Truth be told, Jamie was glad. While she desperately wanted to be independent, to live cautiously but without the paralyzing fear she'd succumbed to soon after she'd awakened in the hospital, she couldn't deny she was . . . uneasy.

She walked into the den and looked at the now shut blinds. The thought of someone watching her made her shudder. How long had this been going on? Was he out there even now?

Jamie swallowed — hard, inched her way

over to the window, and slipped a finger between two slats.

"Are you okay?"

Startled, Jamie whirled from the window, heart pounding in her throat. Samantha.

"Yeah." She winced at the breathless quality of her voice. Clearing her throat, she reaffirmed, "I'm fine." Then paused. "Well, not fine, exactly. A little scared, to be honest."

Samantha walked over to hug her. "We're not going to let anything happen to you."

Jamie pushed a reassuring smile to stiff lips. "I know." And she didn't doubt they'd do their best to keep her safe; however, this person had already been in her house. She'd changed the code to her alarm and felt better, but maybe she should get a dog.

The memories swirled to the forefront of her mind.

He stroked her cheek, stirring the nausea already churning in her belly to new heights. Then he backed off, murmuring under his breath.

Straining against the cuffs, she felt them cut into her, sharp and biting. Blood slicked her wrists.

Then he was back, his low, raspy voice assaulting her left ear. "You're so beautiful, Jamie. Let me be your hero."

Jamie squeezed her eyes shut. "Leave me alone!" The words tore from her throat, raw from her constant screaming.

Movement, sounds. The rushing roar of her blood in her ears blocking everything except the terror. She ignored his low laugh, felt him move away. After a second of tense, dreaded anticipation, she cracked her eyes . . . a shadow to her left. She panted, another scream building, eyes darting, desperation fueling her strength as she pulled, yanked, felt her raw skin tear even more.

The rose petals falling, brushing her face as he dropped them, spread them . . .

"Why are you doing this?" A sob, a plea, a desperate need to make sense of such cruelty.

She felt him pause beside her. "Just call it your therapy." Then he gave another laugh, pain bit at her from all sides . . .

With a jerky movement, she pulled away from Samantha's comfort — and the horrifying memories. "Listen, why don't we send the guys home, order some pizza, and have a girls' night?"

Samantha smiled around the shadows Jamie hated to still see lingering in her sister's gaze. "I don't know, Jamie, it's late . . ."

The phone rang just as Dakota and Connor made their way back into the den area.

46

Jamie grabbed it, grateful for the distraction.

"Hello?"

"Jamie, this is Maya, how are you?"

Maya Olsen, her former counselor turned good friend.

"I'm all right." Not really, but she wasn't getting into it now. "How are you doing?"

"Great, do you have plans tomorrow night? I thought we could catch a movie or something. I'm in desperate need for some girl time."

Forcing out a lighthearted chuckle, Jamie said, "You must be on the same wavelength as I am tonight. Why don't you come over to my house as soon as you can? Samantha's keeping me company tonight. You can join us."

"I wouldn't be intruding on a sisters' thing?"

"Not at all, we'd love to have you."

"All right then, see you soon."

Jamie hung up the cordless phone and turned to find everyone looking at her. "What?"

Dakota frowned. "I don't know how wise it is to invite Maya over until we figure out what's going on with whoever managed to get in your house today."

Jamie gasped. "You're right. I didn't

think . . . I don't want to believe . . . I just can't . . ." She stopped and pulled in a deep breath. "I'll call her back and tell her not to come." She reached for the phone, but Samantha held up a hand.

"Wait a minute. I've been thinking about this. What do we really know for sure? We don't know that anyone was actually in this house. There could be a reasonable explanation for all of the things that have happened and we're just jumping to conclusions because of," she sucked in a deep breath, "your past."

Connor stared at his wife. "How so, Sam?"

Samantha tightened her ponytail and scrubbed a hand across her eyes. "I don't know. Let's think about this. What have we got so far?"

"My picture is missing from the mantel," Jamie stated flatly. She moved over and stared at the blank spot. Her gaze roved over the rest of the area. "Grandaddy's cane is here, all the other pictures are here. Everything looks fine except for the missing picture."

"Right. When was the last time Mom and Dad were here?"

"Last week. For lunch before leaving on their trip to Colorado." Retirees, their parents loved to travel and had most re-

48

cently decided to travel cross-country in their motor home. They'd be back next week.

"Maybe Mom decided to take the picture with her. She was doing some scrapbooking lately, remember? A couple weeks ago, she asked if I had any she could copy."

Jamie sighed. "Yes, I know, but she wouldn't have just taken the picture, would she? She would have asked. I know she would have."

"Maybe she meant to and got distracted. You know Mom, sometimes, she means to do something and forgets."

Dakota pulled out his cell phone. "Well, that's easy to find out. What's her number?"

While he dialed the number Connor supplied, Samantha looked back at Jamie. "What else?"

"All the lights were off. I'd never leave them off."

Uncertainty flashed across Samantha's face and Jamie felt her gut clench.

Samantha said, "Okay, like you said when we got here. Maybe you just . . . forgot. Were you in a hurry to get to work?"

"Yes, in a little bit of a hurry."

"Okay, so you were rushing around. You grabbed your work stuff and headed out the door. It's broad daylight, you're not thinking that you're going to be late getting home and you just . . . leave. Without hitting the light switch."

Jamie bit her lip. Was it possible? Maybe, but . . . "What about my blinds. I never open them. I would have remembered that one."

"Maybe you brushed by them in a hurry and hit them. Or something." She threw her hands up. "Anything's possible."

Jamie realized Samantha really wanted to believe that. "Okay, all of that is possible, I suppose."

Dakota pushed his Stetson back on his head and looked at Jamie as he hung up the phone. "No one's answering. We can try again later. And," he looked over at Samantha, "what you're saying sounds pretty reasonable, but if Jamie's scared, I think it bears looking into."

"I'm not saying we shouldn't look into it, just —"

The door bell rang and Jamie jumped. She gave a self-conscious laugh that lacked humor. "That's Maya. Guess it's too late to tell her to stay home."

Making her way over to the door, she considered everything Samantha had just come up with. Maybe she was just being paranoid.

Gripping the knob, she sighed and closed her eyes for a brief moment. She was over-reacting.

No she wasn't.

She opened her eyes and the door greeting Maya with, "Hey, glad you could make it. Come on in."

Maya, dark hair turning slightly grey, stood at five feet two inches — maybe. She stepped into the foyer and asked, "You didn't sound right on the phone so I ordered a pizza to be delivered here. I'm starved."

Pushing aside bad memories and worries about a possible stalker, Jamie hugged her friend and told herself to relax. Everything would be fine. The bad stuff in her life was over.

Right?

4

Jamie watched Maya pull away from the curb and turned to Samantha as she closed the front door. "She knows me so well. I can't believe she could hear all the stress in my voice . . . crazy. And even though I'll struggle to get up in the morning since it's," she glanced at the clock, "12:15, I'm glad she came over."

Samantha grabbed the pizza box and headed for the kitchen. "It was nice." Her expression stated the exact opposite.

Jamie followed her and watched as her sister tossed the box into the trash. Concerned, she asked, "What's wrong?"

"I'm bothered."

"By?"

"Everything that's happened tonight."

Jamie blew out a sigh and slumped into the nearest chair. "I was trying to forget it."

"Well, I can't!" Samantha's outburst flew from her lips and Jamie flinched, staring at her sister.

She held out a beseeching hand. "Sam, I'm sorry, I —"

"Where's that picture, Jamie?" Desperation flashed before she could cover it up.

Keeping her cool, Jamie stood. "I don't know. I hope Mom has it . . ."

"She doesn't."

Jamie paused. "What? How do you know?"

"She called my cell while I was in the restroom. I didn't tell her what was going on, of course, just asked her if she'd taken the picture from your mantel."

"And?"

"She was indignant that I'd even ask."

Her stomach dropped at that pronouncement. Somehow she'd held out hope that her mother had taken the picture and forgotten to mention it.

Even though she was 99 percent sure she hadn't.

And now that it was confirmed, Jamie felt confused — and scared. "I'm going to bed." Turning on her heel, she left the kitchen, ignoring Samantha's protest.

Ugly fear she'd thought she'd conquered battled to rise up in her, mocking her newfound safety, her determination to succeed and escape the constant reminders of her past.

■ ■ ■ ■

Pain beat through her. Tears leaked from her eyes against her will. Oh God, either save me or let me die! *She wailed silently, refusing to cry out this time. The heavy plaster cast on her lower left leg weighted her down. The handcuffs around her wrist kept her bound to the iron bed. Wetness trickled down the inside of her arm and around to her elbow. The smell of her own blood stung her nostrils. She heard the doorknob jiggle and fought the urge to vomit. Tilting her head back, she stared at the ceiling and caved.*

She screamed and screamed and screamed.

"Jamie?" The soft voice pulled her from her wide-awake nightmare with a gasp. She gripped her head in both hands, then pulled her fingers through her curls.

"What, Sam?"

"I'm sorry," came the heartfelt apology.

Jamie closed her eyes, then turned to hug her sister. "It's all right."

Tears filled Samantha's eyes, then she blinked them away. "I'll be right across the hall if you need me."

"I know. Thanks."

Sam gave her one more searching, apologetic look and walked into the bedroom that she considered hers.

Jamie sighed and dropped onto her bed, staring at the rose-patterned comforter. She knew Sam was apologizing for more than just losing her cool in the kitchen.

A rebellious teen, Jamie hadn't wanted anything to do with authority or rules. At the age of eighteen, she'd been sure she'd known it all, could handle anything that came her way. Almost ten years her senior, Samantha hadn't agreed.

The party had been wild. Jamie had been high on life and something she'd willingly smoked. Then Samantha had shown up.

"What are you doing here?" eighteen-year-old Jamie hissed.

"Saving your hide," Samantha insisted as she pulled Jamie out of the arms of an intoxicated young man, threatening to arrest him if he ever came near her sister again. "The cops are on the way and I'm getting you out of here."

Furious, Jamie flung an arm at Samantha, who ducked and shoved her sister in the car. At first Jamie just sat there, fuming, then she growled, "You are not my mother. Why don't you just stay out of stuff that's not your business."

"You're my sister. That makes you my

business," she retorted. "Look, we're almost home. Sleep it off and we'll talk in the morning."

"I'm not talking to you," Jamie screamed and grabbed the wheel.

Samantha slammed on the brakes and shoved Jamie with a hard hand to her shoulder. She yelled, "Are you trying to kill us?"

Jamie jumped from the car and slammed the door. Samantha cruised along beside her and rolled down the window. "Fine then. Walk home. Maybe it'll cool you off and slap a little sense into your head." She tossed Jamie's heavy coat out of the window and drove off.

Jamie remembered feeling relieved — and cold. She grabbed her coat. Home was only about a mile up the road and she needed the time to herself, to decide what to do about Samantha and her constant interference in her social life. But deep down she knew Sam was right.

Tears clogged her throat. She hated the rift she was causing between the two of them — and the worry she saw in her mother's eyes every time the woman looked at her lately. She really needed to get it together. But she was just so afraid of the future, unsure about what to do with her life. She walked that fine line of being eager for independence and scared of it all at the same time.

Then a stinging pain hit her leg and she knew no more.

Jamie jerked as though she could feel the dart biting into her flesh all over again.

She'd awakened, handcuffed to a bed. Horrified, she'd struggled until the blood flowed from her shredded wrists. And then *he* had entered the room.

Now, sitting on the edge of her bed, she pushed her sleeves up and examined her scars. A minor consequence of her disobedience and rebellion. Her futile attempt at escape. The worst scars were the ones she couldn't see.

On her wrists, the marks crisscrossed each other, the skin healing raggedly, fusing together awkwardly as it had healed only enough to be torn apart once again by her continued fruitless struggles.

Not for the first time in twelve years, she questioned herself again. Why had she struggled so? Almost anyone else would have realized it had been a losing battle and given up.

But not her.

Why not her?

Why had she lived?

Drawing in a shuddering breath, she berated herself for dwelling on the past. "You can't change it, but God can use it. Let him."

Just saying the words out loud brought her a measure of peace she'd never been able to explain. So she didn't try to analyze it, she just accepted it for the gift that it was.

Her Savior. Her Lord. Her strength.

She reached for the Bible she kept on her nightstand. Stacking the pillows behind her, she leaned back, opened her Bible . . .

. . . and screamed.

5

In the back of her subconscious mind, Jamie registered Samantha bursting through her bedroom door, but she couldn't pull her eyes from the picture.

"What is it? Jamie! Why did you scream?"

As though in slow motion, Jamie lifted her gaze to lock onto Samantha's frantic eyes. Her sister had her gun in her right hand as she scanned the room for the cause of Jamie's panicked cry.

Seeing nothing, she lowered the weapon and approached the bed where Jamie still sat, seemingly frozen to the spot.

With shaking fingers, Jamie reached for the picture, then stopped. Doing her best to control her voice, she said, "Get me a plastic bag from the kitchen and a pair of tweezers, will you?"

Questions hovered on Sam's lips, but Jamie stared at her until her sister whirled and left the room. Jamie snapped her eyes back to the picture.

How?

When?

But most importantly — who?

Samantha reentered the room with the requested materials and a demand. "What is it?"

Jamie took the tweezers from her sister and very carefully caught the picture between the ends. She held it up and slipped it into the plastic baggie. Handing it to Samantha, she said, "He put this in my Bible."

"Who? What?" She took the item, looked at it, and gasped. "That's the picture from the mantel."

"Yes, it is." An unnatural calm settled on her shoulders as she leaned back and hugged her arms around her midsection. Shivers danced along her nerve endings and nausea churned in the pit of her stomach.

Samantha looked up. "And you didn't put it there?"

Jamie just stared at her.

Her sister started to pace. "I . . . I mean, you could have decided to use it as a bookmark, right? And then just forgot about it. Or . . . or . . ."

"I didn't put it there, Samantha." Jamie barely recognized her own voice. It sounded flat, devoid of life.

Sam stopped pacing and turned to look at Jamie. "But how? Who?"

"Him."

"But it can't be," came a whispered horrified protest.

"It is. It has to be."

Wednesday

After a restless night even with Samantha sleeping in the bed next to her, resurrecting an old habit Samantha had formed the day Jamie came home from the hospital, Jamie rose and automatically went through her morning routine.

Samantha. What was she going to do about the woman? Her presence beside her last night provoked old memories. Torments, nightmares. Sam had spent every night at her bedside in the hospital as she waited for Jamie to wake up from the drug-induced coma the doctors had put her in while her body healed. Then after she'd been released from the hospital to her parents' care, Samantha had stayed by her side, sleeping next to her in the large queen bed. Only Samantha hadn't gotten much sleep for months. Not with Jamie jerking awake screaming every few hours.

Jamie looked at the scars on her wrists. Deep grooves where the cuffs had cut almost to the bone in some places and healed over with puckered white skin. A vivid, daily reminder of her failure, her weakness. Her inability to escape with one attempt after another until it was almost too late.

With a finger, she traced the area on her left wrist and thought about her past, her tormentor. Her "hero." As those last words filtered through her mind, disgust curdled.

She'd once thought of him that way. After all, he'd made the pain go away. Briefly. Even though he'd been the one to cause it.

And she'd been so grateful. She'd come to look forward to the small things he did to make her more comfortable, was thankful for the food and water he allowed her to have.

He'd bandaged her wrists when he'd realized the extent of her injuries. Given her pain medication.

Taken care of her.

And even while she'd been relieved at the reprieves, with every fiber of her being she'd hated him. And herself. She couldn't understand what she was feeling, why she looked forward to his presence and despised it at the same time.

Stockholm syndrome. Where the victim becomes dependent upon the attacker even to the point of defending him or her.

Jamie hadn't quite gotten to that point, but when Maya explained it to her, she'd been overwhelmed to realize she wasn't crazy, that there was nothing wrong with her.

Then another emotion had forced its way to the surface.

Pure rage.

And it felt good, just like it had yesterday.

Staring at her reflection in the mirror, she set the comb down and made a promise to herself.

If it was him, if he was the one doing this, if he'd targeted her once again . . .

She swallowed down the nausea.

He. Would. Not. Win.

Not this time.

Shuddering, she brushed her teeth and heard Sam stirring. She finished getting ready for work and walked into the kitchen to grab a bagel she wasn't hungry for. Knowing she needed to eat to keep her strength up, she forced it down.

"Sam," she hollered. "I'm leaving."

"Hey, I'll take you."

"I've walked before, I can walk now."

Incredulous eyes stared back at her. "Are you crazy?"

"No. Determined. This guy is not going

to ruin my life again . . . if it's even him."

"That's fine. I understand that, but you still have to take precautions."

Just the thought of walking out of her front door made her want to hurl. And that made the rage rise once again. She would not give up the progress she'd made, would not succumb to the fear again. Would it be caving to accept the help Samantha so willingly offered?

Everything within her wanted to stomp defiantly out the door. Instead, reason overruled her momentary desire for a temper tantrum. If he was the one doing this to her, she certainly didn't want to fall back into his sadistic hands.

"All right," she said. "For now."

Relief at Jamie's easy capitulation flashed over Sam's features, and Jamie felt a twinge of guilt at her own stubbornness. But stubborn could be a good thing.

It was one reason she was still alive.

Fifteen minutes later, she walked into the lab. Her home away from home. Samantha had dropped her at the door, then drove on to the high school to meet Jenna. While school was finished for the year and Jenna had graduated, Sam had volunteered to go with the group of seniors to the lake for the day.

64

Desperate to put last night out of her head, Jamie pulled at the shirtsleeves that came nearly mid-palm, then went straight to the bones she'd started working with the day before.

Then thought about the two old files on her desk. She really needed to look over them. A glance back at the bones she needed to sort through. They were clean and ready for placement on the large metal table.

Yesterday, she hadn't been able to tell much from the bones themselves due to the dirt and other debris still attached to them. Chemicals had remedied that problem. Now, she could begin the road to giving this person a name. The files could wait. Once she had her report on these two sets of bones, she could compare them to the other ones that had been found in the same area.

Ignoring her craving for a cup of coffee, she pulled the femur from the box. Placing it on the slab, she went for the next bone, then the next. Finally, she had the skeleton laid out, each piece placed precisely so. Taking the digital camera from the cabinet above the sink, she took picture after picture of the bones.

And something caught her eye.

Setting the camera aside, she leaned in

and took the arm bone, the radius, in hand. Turning it from side to side, she saw that it had been broken once upon a time. It had healed nicely. Replacing it, she moved to the other arm. The left radius had also been broken. And healed well.

Her stomach flipped as she slowly lowered the bone back into place. She picked up the ulna, turned it. And paused. An epiphyseal line almost fused to the growth cap. The femur told the same story. As a teen aged, the epiphyseal line changed, fused and became an epiphyseal plate. The line indicated this person had never had the chance to advance in age past the late teen years.

She moved to the clavicle, almost afraid to look.

"Hey, Jamie, what's up?"

She jumped and nearly dropped the bone. "Honestly, Dakota, could you whistle or something to let me know you're coming?"

A sheepish smile crossed his face as he shoved the Stetson to the back of his head. "Sorry."

Her heart stuttered for a moment as she stared at him and the feeling confused her. Why was she so attracted to him? She didn't like men — in general — and certainly didn't want to feel anything remotely like attraction for one of them. Not even one she considered a friend.

The knock on the door brought her attention around.

A young man in his late thirties stepped inside. Jamie offered him a short smile. "Hi, George."

"Hi, Jamie. What are you working on?"

"Some bones that were dug up yesterday." She turned to Dakota. "This is George Horton, the department profiler. He joined the team a little after I accepted the job here. So far he's been a great asset from what I hear."

George grinned, flashing a one-sided dimple and white teeth. "Thanks for the praise, Jamie. Dakota and I've met a couple of times."

Dakota nodded and shook the man's hand. "Good to see you again."

"So, did you need something?" Jamie asked him.

"Naw, I was just passing by and thought I'd pop in to say hello. Maybe we can do lunch one day."

With a vague smile, Jamie offered, "Maybe."

Not likely, she thought. As nice as George seemed to be . . .

He left and Dakota looked at her. She tried to sidestep his stare but finally asked,

"What?"

"You know what," he teased with a tight smile. "He likes you."

She grimaced and kept her tone neutral. "I like him too. He's a nice guy."

"So are you going to have lunch with him?"

Just the thought made her shudder. "No." She tried to cover her initial distaste at the thought of anything even resembling a date. "He's one of *those*."

"Those?" Confusion chased the bemusement from his face.

"Yes, a psychiatrist, a *profiler* of all things. You can't trust them. They're way too thoughtful and analyze everything you say. It would be like having lunch with a mind reader or something." She was teasing yet serious about not being interested in George. "No thanks."

Something resembling relief flickered briefly across Dakota's eyes but was gone so fast she wondered if she imagined it.

Then he grinned. "Then will you have lunch with me?"

She smiled back. "No." At his crestfallen expression and wounded stare, she laughed and said, "I don't eat lunch at nine-thirty in the morning. Ask me again in a couple of hours."

He pursed his lips and shook his head. "You got me."

Her heart did that crazy beat-skipping thing again and she turned back to the comfort of her bones. "Yeah."

"So, what have you got on the bones?"

"Female and young."

"How old was she?"

"I'm not sure. Late teens, probably. Eighteen, nineteen. There's only a few teeth so I don't think our odontologist is going to be able to help us out." She sighed. "Give me a little longer and I might be able to tell you more at lunch."

He nodded. "All right, I'm going to go catch up with George, the mind reader. I have a couple of questions for him anyway. I'll be back in a little while."

Absorbed in her work, she didn't even turn as he left.

An hour later, she stretched out the kinks in her back and decided she needed something to drink. Walking into the small office attached to the side of the lab, she went straight to the small college dorm refrigerator and pulled out a bottle of water.

Taking a sip, she let her eyes roam over the familiar space.

And prickles raised the hair on the back of her neck.

Something was off.

Slowly, she took inventory of the area. Everything seemed to be in place, but . . .

What was different?

Her desk. The plant sat where it always did. But it was turned. She kept the words on the pot facing her. "I can do all things through Christ." Maybe one of the cleaning crew had moved it.

Reaching out, she straightened it.

Then stopped. A coldness seeped into her.

The red pen she kept at the top of her desk calendar now lay to the right side.

And the point of the pen stuck out, ready to be used.

She always closed it.

Taking a deep breath, she tried to rationalize it. Okay, so someone had been in her office — and rearranged things a bit. That didn't mean anything.

Did it?

Of course not, she tried to reassure herself. The cleaning crew had just . . . bumped her desk, moved things around a bit.

Only the cleaning crew had never done such a thing before.

A knowing feeling coursed through her and she was certain whoever had been in her office was the same person who'd been in her house.

Him.

Against her will, tremors pushed their way to the surface and she felt that sick, nauseating feeling return. Her right hand slipped under the collar of her shirt and moved to her left shoulder. Tracing the rough edges of the scar that was a permanent reminder of a time she desperately wished she could erase from her memory, she stepped closer to her desk.

Her eyes fell to the calendar and she gasped, her fingers falling from the scar on her shoulder to reach around and grasp her elbow. Her left hand came up to cup her right elbow and she bent double, hugging herself, trying to keep control of the scream bubbling up from within.

"Hey, Jamie . . ."

The scream released and she whirled, one hand flying up to cover her mouth to keep another scream from escaping.

"Jamie! What's wrong?" Crossing to her side, he reached out to grab her and she flinched, backing away from him. He dropped his hands and soothed his voice, controlling the desire to smash the person who'd done this to her. "Come on, Jamie, talk to me. You're safe. You're fine. What's wrong?"

He kept up the chatter, not even sure what he was saying after a few minutes, but whatever it was, it seemed to be working, pulling her from her frozen state of terror.

Her right hand cupped her left shoulder, gripped it so hard, her knuckles turned white. Finally the shaking eased, her hand dropped and she looked him in the eye.

The torment in her beautiful gaze nearly brought him to his knees.

He held out a hand and whispered, "Jamie . . ."

She hesitated, then took it. Slowly, ever so slowly, Dakota pulled her to him and held her in a loose embrace. Tight enough to offer comfort, loose enough that she could slip out of it if she desired to do so.

She said something and he missed it.

"What?" He leaned in closer to listen. Her two words chilled him to the depths of his soul.

"He's back."

6

Jamie pulled away from the comfort of Dakota's arms, almost more shocked by the fact that she let him hold her than the fact that she thought her tormentor had returned.

"I . . . I have to go."

"Where do you want to go?"

"Home. I want to go home." But her safe haven had been breached.

"Let me call someone. Samantha."

"No," the word shot out of her mouth. "No, I don't want to bother her. She's at the lake with Jenna."

"Then —"

"Hey, is everything all right in here? We thought we heard a scream."

They turned at the voice in the doorway, and Jamie flushed, knowing she must look like a scattered mess.

George and morgue security officer Stephanie Hilton looked on with concern.

The woman stood with her hand on her gun. George looked like he wished he had one.

"Sorry, George, Stephanie, I just . . ." She hauled in a deep breath, trying to think of what to say when Dakota jumped in.

"She's fine. I just need to learn to whistle when I come up behind her."

Jamie forced a smile and busied herself with the papers on her desk, hoping George and Stephanie would take the hint and leave.

"Gotcha. Well," an uncertain expression crossed George's handsome features, "I'm just down the hall if you need anything."

"Thank you, George." She appreciated his kindness but wanted him gone. Now.

They left and she wilted against her desk.

"Don't touch anything else."

She froze. "Why?"

"You said, 'He's back.'"

Jamie swallowed hard. "I did?"

"Yeah. Who is he? And why is he after you?"

She ignored his question and said the only thing that she could focus on. "He circled the three." The words felt like they came from someone else, but she couldn't peel her eyes from the desk calendar.

"Huh?"

"The three. He circled it."

Dakota moved around her desk to stand next to her. His shoulder brushed hers, but she didn't move. His breath brushed her cheek and she inhaled.

And didn't move.

She felt safe in his presence.

The three on her calendar still mocked her with its glaring red circle around it; however, she felt herself calming, the terror ebbing slightly.

Because of Dakota.

"What does it mean?"

His question rocked her. "It means . . ." She closed her eyes and let the fear go, pushed it as far from her mind as she could, used every coping technique she'd been taught and some she'd made up. Drawing in a deep breath, she said, "It means he's telling me he's not forgotten me."

"What is the significance of the number three, Jamie?" he asked softly.

"I think it means I was his third victim."

He flinched. "How would you know whether you were his third or eighth or whatever?"

"Because of this." She pushed the neck of her top down to expose the fleshy part of the top of her shoulder.

Dakota paled and swallowed hard. His

finger reached out to trace the raised flesh. "He branded you?"

Dakota ignored his initial reaction of wanting to get the rest of the story from her. That could come later. Instead, he got on the phone and asked for a crime scene team to sweep Jamie's office. He called Jazz, the FBI information expert and part of the Behavioral Science Unit in Quantico, to pull up anybody who'd turned up dead with a number branded into her upper shoulder.

He seriously doubted they'd find anything, but even smart psychos made mistakes occasionally. If this was one of those times, he didn't want to miss it.

While they did their job, they talked to Jamie's boss, Bruno Girard, explaining the situation and the possible need for a little extra security around the building, especially in the area where Jamie worked.

Dakota rubbed his chin. "I also want to look at the security videos from last night through this morning."

Bruno frowned, but agreed. "If there's something weird going on, I want to know about it. No one should have free access to Jamie's office."

"I always lock the lab," Jamie insisted. "No one else is usually in there unless I have

76

students from the university doing an internship or a tour. Otherwise it's just my domain. But I don't always bother to lock up my office. There's nothing in there that would really be considered confidential, and if I do have anything, I lock it in the file cabinet."

Jake Hollister, lead CSI working the day shift, entered the room, and Dakota flashed him a grateful smile as he pulled him aside. "Look, we don't want to alarm everyone in the building, but it looks like Jamie may have picked up a stalker. We believe he could have been in her office. Can you sweep it? See if you find anything that shouldn't be there?"

"Sure, you pull the tapes?"

"Bruno's getting them now."

"I'll get on this then."

Dakota slapped the man on the back. "Thanks."

Jake went to work and Dakota went back to Jamie who'd returned to the bones laid out on the examination table. He whistled a little tune as he approached and she stilled, then turned. "You're a quick study."

He shrugged. "I don't like seeing you so afraid."

She blew out a sigh and closed her eyes for a brief moment. "Trust me, I don't like it either."

"Do you want me to take you home?"

"No."

"But you said . . ."

"I know. But I've calmed down quite a bit and I'm going to stay right here and work."

Admiration welled inside him. No one could accuse her of being a quitter. Strong-willed with a backbone made out of steel was more like it. "All right. It might help to keep your mind off of everything."

Jake popped his head in. "I'm done, guys."

"Anything stand out?"

The CSI shook his head. "Nothing. I'll go run these prints, but if he wore gloves, then . . ." He shrugged and Dakota nodded.

Jamie asked him. "Did you dust the plant and the pen?"

"Sure did."

"Thank you."

He left and Dakota's cell phone rang. Jazz.

"Hello?"

"Sorry, Dakota, nothing on any bodies being branded with numbers."

Rats. "All right, thanks, Jazz. Get back to me if anything turns up."

She promised she would and Dakota turned his attention back to Jamie.

She picked up one of the larger bones.

"Look at this."

"What?"

"This is the radius." She touched his arm lightly to show him which bone she was talking about.

Hope shivered through him. Even with all that was going on and the memories she was no doubt dealing with, she was willing to reach out to him, to touch him. He kept his cool and nodded. "Okay."

"And see this flaw right here?" Her fingernail tapped the area on the bone.

"Yeah, I do. What does that mean?"

"That the bone was broken once upon a time."

"Okay, so we might be able to find medical records on a missing female with a broken arm." He was only half serious.

"Ha. I wish. That would be a needle in a haystack. Although, whoever set it knew what he was doing. She had a good doctor, it healed back almost perfectly." Her voice was low, almost as though she were talking to herself.

"So . . . um . . . what did you mean, 'he's back'?"

She froze for a millisecond, then resumed her positioning of several more bones. Finally, she said, "Surely you know by now I have a rather . . . horrific past."

Softly, he said, "Yeah, I've figured some of it out. Connor gave me the basics without," he assured her, "betraying any confidences." He reached out and placed a hand over hers. She stopped and looked at him. He pressed, "When are you going to trust me enough to tell me all of it?"

Her eyes studied his. "It's . . . a horrid, horrid tale."

"I'll listen when you're ready to tell me." He gave her hand a squeeze and released it.

She rubbed her hands down the sides of her lab coat, then clasped them in front of her. "After I jumped out of Sam's car, he . . . shot me with something and I passed out. When I woke up, I was . . . handcuffed," her voice shuddered over the word, "to a bed."

Did he really want to hear this? Could he deal with what she had to tell him? "You jumped out of Samantha's car?"

She rolled her eyes in self-disgust. "Yes, it was one of those stupid sibling fights that usually blow over and all is well. Only we didn't get a chance to make up until . . . anyway, he grabbed me and . . ."

"The scars on your wrists?"

"Hm. Yes." She turned from him and he watched her shoulders rise and fall.

"It's okay, Jamie, you don't have to tell me."

"I just . . ." Her phone rang, cutting her off. She shot him an apologetic look and fished in her lab coat pocket. He could see the relief on her face as she said, "Let me get this, it's Maya."

"Sure, I'm going to go study the tapes, then be back to take you to lunch."

A soft smile crossed her lips, erasing some of the stress evident on her forehead and at the corners of her eyes. "That'd be great."

He left her to her conversation.

Jamie nibbled a nail as she watched Dakota leave, then turned her attention to Maya. "Hi, Maya."

"How are you doing, Jamie? Samantha called me and filled me in on things."

"Are you asking as my friend or my therapist?"

Maya gave a small chuckle. "Maybe a little of both."

Jamie sucked in a deep breath, then plunged into the conversation she didn't want to have. "I think he's back."

Silence on the other end, then, "The man who assaulted you?"

"Yes," she whispered. "I swear it's got to be him."

"What makes you so sure?"

Jamie told Maya what had just happened in her office. "And he circled the number three on the calendar."

"What else is going on that day, Jamie?"

"What do you mean?"

"That day has special meaning. What is it?"

Dumbfounded, Jamie paused, thinking. Wait a minute, the calendar had been flipped. It wasn't June third circled, it was July third. She gasped. "July third, that's Samantha's birthday! I'd forgotten what month we were in. I was so focused on the fact that the number was circled that I . . ."

"Do you think it's possible that you did that? Could you have marked it to remind yourself it was Sam's birthday?"

"I . . . I . . ." Had she?

"I'm not trying to discount anything you're saying, Jamie, I'm just pointing out it's possible you had Samantha's birthday on your mind, you were distracted, talking on the phone or whatever, and reached over to doodle on your calendar and circled the day."

"I . . . don't think . . . maybe . . . but the pen was . . ." She stopped her stuttering, closed her eyes, and pushed her brain to remember if she'd been the one to circle the number. After all, she'd lost track of time last night — something she never did. Maybe . . . "I suppose it's possible."

Had she put all these people out, looking for something that may not exist? Was she letting her fears overwhelm her again? Causing her to see things that weren't there, interpret things erroneously?

"Just think about it, Jamie," Maya was saying.

Doubt surged. "All right."

She hung up, troubled by the conversation. If Maya was right and Jamie was imagining all of these things, then that meant she wasn't doing nearly as well as she thought she was. The very idea depressed her. With a heavy heart, she went back to the bones and reached for the clavicle, and her breath caught in her throat as she pulled it for closer examination.

Broken. And healed. Very nicely.

Oh Lord, could this mean what I think it does?

7

That question still haunted her when Dakota popped his head back in the lab an hour later. "Hey, are you ready to grab a bite to eat? Samantha can't come because of the field trip, but Connor said he'd meet us at our usual spot."

Flannigan's Fine Food. Ever since Jamie had gotten the job in the lab, the foursome ate at Flannigan's two or three times a week. At least when cases and criminals allowed. Sometimes it was just a partial group — like today.

"Okay. Just let me finish making a few notes and I'll be ready." Bending back over the file she'd spread out over a workspace across from the bones, she put her thoughts on the paper, then clicked the pen. And stopped.

Staring at the simple ink pen, she clicked it again, then again, pulling the ballpoint up into the cylinder, then pushing it back out.

She had *not* left the pen on her desk clicked out.

"Jamie?"

Blinking, she looked up, then shook her head. "I'm coming."

Dropping the pen on top of the folder, she grabbed her purse and followed Dakota into the hall.

Dakota said, "I asked George if he'd go to lunch with us."

"What?" she frowned at him. "Why?"

"I want to get his perspective on the things going on with you. Use his profiling and psychological expertise."

"What if I'm wrong?"

"What makes you say that?"

She blurted, "The third is Sam's birthday. What if I absently circled the three on the calendar? What if I . . ." She stopped, swallowed hard, and averted her eyes. George strolled toward them.

"Jamie . . ." Dakota laid a hand on her arm and she didn't pull away.

Forcing a smile for the approaching newcomer, she said, "Never mind."

Leaning over, he whispered in her ear, "You're not crazy."

Appreciation for this man flooded her and she felt herself relax. A little.

"Hey, guys, I'm ready. Thanks for asking

me to tag along. Being the new person in the house makes for some lonely lunches some days."

Guilt hit Jamie. "I'm so sorry, we should have asked you to join us long before now."

George flashed a grin. "No worries. I've actually been buried under all the paperwork and the act of figuring out what I'm doing that comes with a new job, meeting clients, et cetera. So it's not a big deal."

"All right then, let's get going."

Dakota led the way and the trio headed out of the building and stepped onto the sidewalk. Jamie gave a small gasp as heat and humidity pressed her lungs flat. "Whew! I'm ready for fall."

Two minutes later, they entered the cool interior of the restaurant and Jamie pointed. "Look, Connor's already got us a table."

"Great, I'm starving."

After Connor and George exchanged greetings and handshakes, they seated themselves. The waitress took their order, and Jamie looked around the table. She didn't know whether to laugh or get up and run. She, Jamie Cash, avowed man-hater, sat at a table with three men.

Okay, God, this is just a little further out of my comfort zone than I think is necessary. She examined herself and realized . . . she was fine. No signs of a panic attack, and only the faintest desire to flee the premises and escape to her bed — or the lab. Gladness lifted her and she took a sip of water. *Thank you, God.*

". . . haven't you, Jamie?"

The question threw her. "What?"

Connor's eyes crinkled around the corners. "Are you with us?"

Flushing, she took a sip of water. "Yes, sorry. I was thinking."

"About what?"

She shrugged. "It doesn't matter. What were we talking about?"

George leaned in. "They were telling me a little about what's going on with you. You've got a stalker?" Concern wrinkled his brow and he looked eager to help.

Grimacing, Jamie shrugged. "It's possible. It's also possible that I . . . jumped to conclusions."

"What do you mean?"

"I mean the things that have happened have been things I could have overlooked, forgotten about." She sighed. "Things I could have done myself."

"But you don't think so?" George asked.

Jamie looked away. "I don't know what to think. Everything that's happened has been something that I could have done. Nothing was found by Jake, so . . ." She shook her head. "I just don't know."

"Have you had episodes of forgetfulness? Leaving the stove on when you thought you turned it off? Thinking you put something on the coffee table, then finding it in your bedroom. Little things like that?"

She thought about the picture in her Bible and looked him in the eye. "No."

He blinked and looked over at the other two men. "Then I would say it's a distinct possibility that you have a stalker."

"But how did he get in my house?" Frustration boiled in her voice and she didn't bother to hide it. Dakota reached under the table to grasp her fingers. The warmth of his hand soothed her ragged nerves and she gave him a squeeze.

Connor spoke up, "We checked the alarm wires. Nothing was cut."

Dakota said, "And I had someone come out and change all the locks on your doors and windows."

"You did?"

He looked at his watch. "Yeah. They should be done by now." Fishing in his pocket, he pulled out two keys and handed them to her. "Here you go."

Tears filled her eyes and she blinked them back. "Oh, Dakota, thanks."

The waitress chose that moment to deliver the food, and for a few minutes silence reigned as they dug in. Jamie finally set her fork on the edge of her plate.

"I appreciate you guys believing me." She gave a little humorless laugh. "To be honest, I don't know if I would have believed me."

Dakota rubbed her shoulder and she let him. "Until it's proven different, we're going to treat this as a stalker situation, all right?"

"Thanks."

George spoke up again. "You know, it's hard to come up with a profile of a stalker with so little information, but they generally have some kind of personality disorder, some kind of mental illness. A lot are delusional. Can you think of anyone who you may have come across that might fit that description?"

"Just one," she muttered.

"Excuse me?" George looked confused.

Jamie blew out a breath and stood. "I don't want to talk about this anymore. I need to get back to work."

"Jamie . . ."

"I'm sorry, guys. I know you're just trying to help, but I'm . . ." She laid some money on the table and headed for the door.

Back out under the hot sun, she paused and wondered if she'd be considered rude for walking out, but she felt so restless — and helpless. Like she had no say in the direction her life was taking. And that made her mad. She headed for her lab, wishing Samantha was available for a heart-to-heart sister chat.

A lilting whistle alerted her and she turned to find Dakota walking behind her. She stopped and waited for him to catch up.

"Jamie, would it help to have Maya sit in on any discussions we have of whoever's after you?"

She resumed her walk. "*If* someone's after me. And no, I'm just going to have to find a way to deal with it."

He grasped her hand. "Come on, let's walk in the park."

Fear darted through her. "No. I don't want to go to the park."

"Why not?"

"It's too hot for one thing and I've got to get back to work." *And I'm scared to go there. It's not on my safe-places-to-go route.* But she kept this information to herself.

He watched her for a moment, then acquiesced. "All right. I'll walk you on back."

They walked in silence for a minute or two, then Dakota said, "There was nothing

90

on the security tapes."

"Of course not," she muttered. "Because there was no one in my office, right?"

"I didn't say that."

"You didn't have to."

"Connor and George are still talking about the stalker thing."

"Connor's got better things to do than sit around talking about me. He needs to be working on a case or something."

A faint smile edged Dakota's well-shaped lips. "He is."

Back in the comfort of her lab, Dakota watched Jamie relax for the first time since they'd left for lunch. As she checked out her office for any more indications of an intruder, he watched her methodical movements. He had an idea. "Take the rest of the day off."

Startled brown eyes latched onto his. "Huh?"

"You wanted me to teach you to shoot. Let's go down to the firing range."

In the act of shrugging into her lab coat, she paused. "Really?"

"Might as well." He smiled. "Do you have anything better to do?"

She looked over at the bones laid out on the table. "Actually . . ."

"You might need this, Jamie."

She shuddered. He hated to add to her stress level, but knowing how to defend herself might just save her life. She must have read that in his gaze because she nodded. "All right."

"I'll let Connor know what's going on. He can continue the investigation into the bones and will call me if he needs me for anything."

"All right. Just let me tell my boss and we can go, I guess."

They made their necessary phone calls and within minutes were walking down to the firing range located in the basement of the station.

"Have you ever shot a gun before?" he asked.

"Yes, when I first came home from the hospital, I tried it a couple of times, but I never got very accurate before . . ."

"Before what?" he pressed, seeing the distress on her features.

"Before I ended up too afraid to leave my own house." She pulled her hair up in a ponytail and pinned the escaping tendrils with a couple of bobby pins. She placed the earphones over her ears, the goggles over her eyes, and grasped the gun he handed over.

He brought up a fresh target and said, "Aim for the chest."

"What about his head?"

"Hit him in the chest first. You can go for the head once he's down."

Her jaw gaped a little as she studied him to see if he was serious.

He was. And he let her see it.

Swallowing hard, she nodded and turned her gaze back to the target.

Dakota moved behind her and said, "Now plant your feet apart about shoulder width, get into a comfortable stance."

She followed his instructions to the letter as he explained how to grip the gun, how to aim and pull the trigger. "It sounds so easy."

"It is once you do it for a while."

"What if I miss?"

"That's why you have more than one bullet in the gun."

"Right."

By the time they finished up an hour later, she was hitting the chest area of the target with almost every shot. No bull's-eyes, but she could do some damage if the need arose.

He prayed it never would.

The Hero laughed softly to himself as he studied the pictures in the album. His treasure, his keepsake. One by one he flipped the pages. His first damsel in distress, then the second, the third — the one that got away.

He'd gotten careless with her. She'd begged him not to slit her throat. "Anything but that," she'd wept. "I know you're going to kill me, but do it any way you want, just don't use a knife."

He stroked her cheek with a finger, captured her tears with the digit and watched them drop to the floor. She sucked in such a brave breath and looked him in the eyes, his bright green eyes, the only thing showing through the mask he'd donned. His special mask. The one that turned him into a hero; the man who made everything better. "Then how do you wish to die, Jamie?"

"You're my hero," she whispered, thrilling him with her willingness to say the words without the knife in her face, "you can save me from death."

"But only death stops the pain, Jamie. You have to die in order to be free."

She looked away for a moment, then back. He saw her desperate struggle to keep her terror under control, but she gritted through her teeth, "Fine. Shoot me."

He raised a brow. "I don't shoot women, Jamie. That's simply not . . . acceptable."

A minute passed as she looked down,

swallowed, then looked him in the eye. "Fine. I choose drowning."

That surprised him. He hadn't thought she'd actually choose. But it seemed she surprised him just about every time he turned around. Intrigued with her, he kept her longer than some of the others. But in the end he'd honored her request.

And look where he was now. She'd escaped. And he still didn't know how. Fury rose up in him, hard to contain, writhing to get out.

"Stop the pain, stop the pain. Only you can do it," the voice whispered, pushed him. "Only you can save me. Be my hero."

He slapped his hands over his ears and eventually the voice stopped. Picking up the bottle on the seat beside him, he looked at the label. He must remember to get it refilled. Maybe. Actually, he'd been doing pretty well without it.

The bottle itself was a reminder. He had to keep it together, keep up the façade, or everyone would know. And they must not know.

His mind went back to Jamie. He'd honored her and her request, and she'd not responded in kind and honored him. She'd fought death. Had lived and gone on without him. How dare she? After he'd rescued her? Become her hero? Did his best to make the pain go away?

The rage built and he threw the book across the room. The pictures scattered and one fluttered next to his shoe. He bent and picked it up.

And knew what he was supposed to do.

8

Jamie slipped the new key into the shiny lock of her front door and turned to her bodyguard. "You didn't have to walk me home, Dakota."

"I know. I wanted to." He leaned in a little. "I like spending time with you, Jamie."

She pulled back, her heart in her throat. "Don't . . . don't like it too much, okay?"

"Jamie . . ." He threw a hand up. "When will you trust me? We've known each other over a year and a half and you still hold me at arm's length. When are you going to let me in? Just a little?"

She knew he wasn't talking about her front door.

A long pause followed his outburst. What should she say? What *could* she say?

"I told you . . . I warned you . . ." She bit her lip, wanting to cry — and punch him — all at the same time.

"I'm not playing games, Jamie, I care

about you — a lot."

"And I care about you. As a friend. Okay, more than a friend, but not . . . I don't know if I can do more than friend. I honestly just . . . don't know." Keeping her tone neutral was hard. Almost impossible. She wanted to throw herself into his arms and be normal, like any other thirty-year-old single girl looking to meet someone, fall in love, and get married.

But she wasn't normal.

Thanks to *him.*

"Then let's find out."

She pushed the door open and stepped inside. "What do you mean?"

He followed her in and shut the door behind him. "I don't know. I just . . . I . . ." He let out a frustrated sigh. "Hold that thought. Let's do a walk-through of your house and you tell me if anything looks out of place."

Pivoting on her heel, she let her eyes scan the room, then she walked into the kitchen. Nothing weird here. She followed him through the two bedrooms and the bath she'd had enlarged and turned into a small spa.

"Everything seems fine," she reported. Thank goodness. A chill spilled onto her arms, causing goosebumps to pop up.

Bumps that had nothing to do with the air conditioner. Could she get Dakota out of her house before he went down a path she wasn't ready to explore yet?

"Good, now back to what we were talking about."

Nope, he was determined.

She cocked her head as she walked back into the foyer and set her keys on the side table next to the front door. "You want more."

He flushed and stuck his hands in the front pockets of his jeans. "Yeah. I do."

"I think I wish you didn't."

He froze. Then looked at the ceiling. "Why?"

"Because . . . I . . . don't know what to do with that."

"You don't know or you're scared to find out?"

This time it was her turn to go red. She turned and headed into the kitchen. Dakota followed at a slower pace. Jamie pulled a couple of bottles of water from the refrigerator. She handed him one as she considered his very valid question. "I think it's a little of both."

"Look, Jamie, I know something horrific happened to you. That you were attacked. I understand he hurt you —"

She whirled, cutting him off, the anger rising up like a tsunami. But her voice was barely above a whisper. "*Hurt* me? You think he *hurt* me? He didn't *hurt* me. He *raped* me, then he *tortured* me, then he made me pick which way I wanted to die. Like I was picking out a car. Only instead of the choice between blue and red, I had to choose between having my throat slit and drowning. Only I didn't drown. I lived."

"Oh, Jamie . . ." He reached out a beseeching hand, but she waved him off.

She raised a hand. "Don't. And he's very, very good at what he does. He's like a . . . a . . . ghost or something, a shadow that's always lurking, watching. In spite of what everyone else thinks, part of me *knows* he's back. The other part of me doubts my own mind. But," she grimaced, "the past? It . . . doesn't matter anymore. I survived. God allowed me to live for some reason. And I won't apologize for my . . . issues. God and I are working on those."

"I don't want you to apologize. I'm asking you to consider a relationship with me."

A knot formed in her throat. "I wish I could consider it. I really do. There are things about me that you don't know, that if you did . . ." She couldn't finish.

Feeling trapped, old, horrifying memories

closing in, she walked into the sunroom and picked up a paintbrush. Squeezed paint onto the pallet beside her and dipped the brush. "I don't want to talk about this anymore."

Painting. Her therapy. She inhaled the scent that always calmed her.

Dakota's hand covered hers and she stilled, her heart tripping, beating hard. Because of the topic of conversation? His nearness? The flashes of her imprisonment and torture playing through her mind? Emotions rolled, bumping into one another as they surged inside her.

"Go away, Dakota." The sobs begged for release. She refused to give in. "Just leave me alone right now."

"I don't want to leave you alone. I want to help you."

His soft voice nearly caused a break in her control. She couldn't figure out why he was so persistent. Any other man would have run without looking back by now. "You can't help me. No one can help when the memories . . ." Her breath hitched. "Just go."

More colors on the palate. Her fingers shook as she squeezed the tubes. Panting, her throat squeezed in. She ignored it, having learned she wouldn't die from it.

She just needed to paint.

A fresh canvas.

Bristles dipped in whatever color she could reach first.

Another ragged, whistling breath.

And still, he didn't leave.

Instead, he moved behind her, gripped the brush with her, and held her hand as she slashed the paint across the blank canvas. She registered his presence, vaguely wondered why he didn't leave.

Over and over, he kept his hand on hers and followed her movements as she vented, color after color, with no rhyme or reason to the strokes.

Finally, she let go of the brush, heard it clatter to the table as she sank to the floor. He followed, his arm encircling her shoulders. She let him, leaned into his embrace, exhausted, spent.

She didn't even feel like crying anymore as she let his woodsy cologne wash over her, his presence offer comfort and chase the nightmares away. She lost track of how long they sat there, silent, her panting breaths calming, her heart slowing to a normal rhythm.

Then he spoke. "How often does that happen?"

She sighed. "Every so often."

A pause, then, "Jamie, darlin', I know you have a rotten past, that there are things maybe you can't tell me right now, horrifying things I probably can't even imagine." His voice had gone husky and she heard him swallow twice. "And that's okay. I'm just asking that you let me in a little more. Let me past some of those barriers you've got up. That's all. Let's get to know each other better. Can you do that?"

She didn't answer right away because she didn't *have* an answer. Then she allowed a rueful smile to play across her lips. "I just did."

He kissed the top of her head and her left hand fisted his shirt.

"I care about you, Jamie," he whispered. "Just think about it, okay?"

She nodded against his shoulder, then mumbled, "You know, I don't know that much about you either."

He stilled. "What do you mean?"

"Every time we start to talk about you, you back off."

"I do?"

Pulling back, she stared into his eyes, felt drawn into them to the depths of her soul. Resisting his pull, she said, "Yes. Maybe that's why it's hard for me to open up to you. Because I feel like it would be all one-sided."

"Oh." His brow crinkled as though deep in thought about that one. Then he changed the subject — just as she figured he would. "You've got someone watching your house. You should be fine. I'm going to take off, all right?"

She gave him a sad, knowing smile. "Sure."

"And I'm going to think about what you just said." He frowned as though his mind had already gone to work on it.

"Good."

He pulled himself up from the floor and gave her a hand up. He headed for the door, stopped and turned back. "Would you recognize him if you saw him?"

Closing her eyes, she visualized the face she saw almost every night in her dreams. A face completely covered by a mask. Except for the eyes. "No, not his face. But his eyes. I'd recognize his eyes anywhere."

"What color are they?"

"Green. A weird . . . green. I've never seen such strange eyes."

"Did he alter them? You know, like with contacts?"

She shuddered. "I don't know. Maybe. All I know is I want some more target practice tomorrow sometime."

Dakota admired her spunk for sure. But he worried his heart was getting ready to go splat when she uncurled her fingers from around it and sent him on his way. He rubbed his chest, the area actually aching at the thought.

What was he going to do about her?

The only thing he could do, he supposed. Love her.

And he did. Just the thought of what she'd suffered made him want to get his hands around the throat of the man who'd inflicted those things on her. A rage like he'd never felt before simmered just below the surface.

But was she right? Did he clam up and change the subject if it got too close to piercing through the barriers of his emotional comfort zone?

Probably.

His past wasn't so great either and talking about it wasn't on his top ten list of fun things to do.

His phone rang as he walked back toward the office to get his car. "Hello?"

"Hey, it's Connor. How is she?"

"Hanging in there. By a thread, I think, but she's holding her own."

"I think Samantha's going to head back

over there and stay the night again."

"And you're all right with that?" He already knew the answer to that question but wanted to hear Connor say it.

"Whatever it takes to keep Jamie safe — and comfortable."

Dakota let the relief flow. "Good. I agree."

"Has Jamie found anything more on the bones?"

"I think she's got an idea about them but hasn't really said much." He swerved off topic. "I took her shooting today."

Connor gave a humorless laugh. "Cool. How'd that go?"

"She did a good job. Good enough to cause some damage if she ever needs to."

"Let's do our best to make sure it never comes to that."

"You bet."

"Catch you in the morning first thing?"

"See you then."

By the time Dakota pressed the off button, he'd reached his car. He opened the door and slid in, deciding to drive past Jamie's house. Just to check. Even though he knew she was fine.

After all, she had someone watching her house this very minute. He spun out of the parking lot and onto the street that would lead him right back down the path he'd just walked.

A moment later, he could see the entrance to her subdivision and wheeled in. A couple of turns later brought him to her street. Night approached, creeping in slowly as the sun dipped and the stars started to make their presence known. Shadows shifted, trees danced in the slight breeze that only partially cut the muggy heat.

Jessica Hardesty, the cop watching Jamie's house, sat up to watch as he drove past at a snail's pace. He waved to her and she sat back with a visible sigh and a nod of acknowledgment. Good, she'd been alert, watchful. Jamie was in good hands. Plus Samantha would be here soon.

Movement caught his eye.

What?

Right around the side by the window. The light from the den briefly outlined a shadow.

That of a head and shoulders. He braked and spun his vehicle to the side of the street. Hopping out, he waved to Jessica to join him. She climbed from her car and rushed over. "What is it?"

"I saw someone over there by the den window." He pulled his weapon and headed in the direction of where he'd seen the shadow.

"You want me to call for back up?" she called after him.

"Yeah." Dakota bolted around the side of the house. Whoever had been out there had heard them and realized he'd been spotted. Behind him, he could hear Jessica on the radio giving their location. Ahead of him, he heard pounding feet.

Then silence. The guy was running across the grass now.

Careful not to expose himself in case the suspect had a weapon, Dakota rounded the next corner, gun ready. "Freeze! FBI!"

More scrambling ahead. Dakota gave chase. The darkness pressed in on him. The streetlights didn't reach into the backyards and the lights on the houses couldn't probe the wooded area farther out.

Which was where the guy was headed.

He just hoped Jamie didn't hear the activity going on outside her house and decide to come investigate. He heard the sirens in the distance, caught a flash of movement up ahead. Taking cover behind a tree, he yelled, "Freeze, I said!"

The guy ignored him and darted farther into the woods. Dakota grunted and continued the chase, nearly tripping over the dense undergrowth. He stopped and listened.

Nothing.

Silence except for the sound of the sirens that grew closer. He grimaced as he got on the phone with the dispatcher and in a low voice, identified himself and said, "Tell them to shut off the sirens, I can't hear."

Within seconds, the noise ceased.

He crept forward, eyes straining in the darkness. He didn't dare use a light.

Dakota sucked in a deep breath and willed himself to hear every sound, to notice and dismiss the ones that belonged but focus on the ones that didn't.

He heard nothing. A shiver chased itself up his spine. His eyes probed the area in front of him, then he turned to look over his right shoulder, feeling a spot between his shoulder blades tingle.

Come on, he silently shouted to the trespasser, *move, give me a hint as to where you are.*

A rustle behind him alerted him and he whirled only to catch a brief glimpse of a black mask before pain cracked through his head and blackness descended.

Jamie gripped the paintbrush and stared at the half-finished project. Painting had been her outlet, one of her coping mechanisms when the panic attacks threatened. When she picked up a brush, the outside world faded.

After Dakota had left, she'd returned to her work and immersed herself in creativity.

So when she heard the sirens on her street, it took a moment to register. When they went silent, curiosity prompted her to investigate. Lifting the lid from the can of turpentine, she cleaned the brush, then looked out her window. Flashing blue and red lights pulled up near her house.

"What in the world?" she whispered. Her eyes searched and found the car that belonged to Jessica, the policewoman who'd been assigned to watch her house.

But she couldn't tell if anyone occupied it. Jamie went to the door and her hand hovered above the knob. Anxiety clawed at her and she snatched her hand back. The panic ebbed only to return when she once again touched the doorknob.

Anger at herself swelled. "You beat this, remember?"

Swallowing, pulling in a deep breath, she closed her eyes and swung the door open. Jessica stood on her porch, fist raised as though to knock.

Relief nearly buckled her knees. "Jessica, what's going on?"

"Dakota rode back by here after he

dropped you off and spotted someone around your window. He went after him. I'm here to stay with you."

Dread crawled through her. "Oh no."

"Let's get inside."

Jamie backed up and let the woman in. "What about Dakota?"

"I've got backup on the way."

Jamie could tell the woman was torn between going after Dakota to make sure he was all right and doing the duty she'd been assigned: keep Jamie safe.

A knock on the door had Jamie reaching to open it, but Jessica nudged her aside and took over. She looked through the peephole, then out the side window. Turning to Jamie, she said, "It's your sister, Samantha."

Samantha came through the door like a whirlwind. "Are you okay? What's going on? I saw the police outside your house and nearly panicked."

"You didn't have your scanner on?"

Samantha grimaced. "No."

"Dakota saw someone outside my window and went after him."

Sam's eyes sharpened. "Where's Dakota now?"

Jessica shifted and headed for the door. "I can't raise him on his radio. He's either not answering because he's busy or because . . .

he can't." She disappeared into the night.

Horror caused waves of shivers to rock through Jamie. "Sam?"

"I'll find him. You stay put, okay?"

She left, gun in hand. Officers flooded her yard.

Jamie resisted the urge to go after them, but she knew she would just be in the way. Instead, she paced and stayed away from the windows.

Please, God, keep them safe.

9

Dakota groaned and shifted on the ground. Pain clawed at his head and he lifted a hand to the source. Wetness covered his palm even as his brain clicked through what had just happened. Branches crackled to his left and he grabbed for his weapon only to find it gone.

He rolled to his left and nausea threatened to undo him. Couldn't worry about that now.

"Dakota?"

The soft whisper reached through the ringing in his ears. "Jessica?"

"Yeah." He felt her kneel down beside him. "You're hurt."

"He came out of nowhere."

"I've got an ambulance on the way."

"You see my gun anywhere?"

"Yeah, here."

She pressed it into his hand and he curled his fingers around it, immediately taking comfort in the familiar feel.

He stood, weaving his way to the edge of the trees. His head felt like it might explode any second.

Jessica clutched his arm. "You need some medical attention."

"What I need is to catch that guy."

"He's long gone by now. Come on, we need to let —"

"Dakota!"

The frantic shout turned his attention to Samantha who'd come around the corner, gun ready. He waved at her and immediately regretted the action. "I'm okay."

She lowered the gun a fraction. "I take it you didn't get him?"

"Unfortunately, no. He got me."

Jessica intervened. "I've got the dogs on the way. Let's get you over to the hospital. You need that head looked at."

"I'll be fine. Is Jamie all right?"

"She's worried about you."

"Then let's go show her I'm okay."

The trio made their way back to the house, Dakota moving slowly with Samantha and Jessica staked on either side of him just in case he keeled over. "Guys, relax. I'm fine."

"Right," Samantha agreed. But she didn't move either.

He sighed and stepped through the door to find Jamie pacing the den floor. When she saw him, the relief that coated her face nearly did him in.

"I'm fine," he insisted for what felt like the millionth time since he'd been conked.

Then his heart tripped over itself as she walked over, slipped her arms around his waist, and laid her head against his shoulder.

Samantha's jaw dropped.

Dakota let out a sigh and wrapped his arms around Jamie's shoulders. He held her until an officer stepped inside and insisted on speaking to him.

"I'll be down to file a police report."

"We've got the dogs out and they picked up a scent beyond the woods, but it dead-ended where he must have had a car parked."

Dakota nodded. "He couldn't take a chance parking on this street. He knows we're watching her house. Did you find any prints under the window?"

"Nothing significant. It hasn't rained in a couple of days, so the ground is pretty hard."

"All right." Jamie stepped away from him and headed into the kitchen.

He missed the feel of her wrapped up next to him and wondered when he'd get to hold her again. The thought took his mind off his throbbing head.

The officer motioned to Dakota's still seeping head wound. "You want to get that taken care of?"

"It's . . ." He broke off, refusing to use the word "fine" again. "Yeah, I will. Thanks."

Samantha had followed her sister into the kitchen. She was still behind her when Jamie came back out carrying a first aid kit. In her soft, sweet voice, she said, "Sit down and let me help."

Dakota sat, Samantha stared, and Jamie got busy cleaning and bandaging his wound. "You need a couple of stitches, if you ask me."

"Can you do it?"

She shrugged and bit her lip. "Sure I know how, but —"

"I'm not going to the hospital, Jamie. If you don't want to sew it up, just slap a couple of butterfly bandages on it."

She blew out a sigh and pursed her lips. "Stubborn, aren't you?"

"I've been hanging around you for a while now. It must have rubbed off on me."

Her eyes glinted. "I think I have some extra suture thread left over from an autopsy class. I'll have to sterilize it."

He closed his eyes and grunted. "I'm not going anywhere."

Jamie went to get the required materials while Samantha trailed along behind her once again. Exasperated, Jamie turned. "What is it, Sam?"

"You sure are handling this well."

"Thank you. Now quit dogging my steps, will you?"

Samantha flushed. "I'm sorry, I guess I keep expecting you to fall apart or something."

"Sam!"

"I know, I know! I'm sorry. I'll just go back and check on Dakota."

"Actually, boil me some water, will you?" Jamie turned on her heel and thought about Samantha's expectations. So, she was supposed to fall apart and lose it. She looked at her hands. They shook, a fine tremor passing through them. And yet, Jamie felt in control. Stronger than she had in weeks. And so grateful for the people the Lord had put in her life at this very moment.

Yes, she was scared. Terrified. But she would get through this. She would trust God to get her through it one way or another. Either way, this side of heaven or the other, Jamie knew she'd be fine.

But she really wanted to live.

Taking a deep breath, she found the items she needed, sterilized everything, and found a pair of sterile surgical gloves she'd never thrown out. Another leftover from one of her classes. She didn't actually know why she kept them but at the moment was glad she had.

Returning to the den area where Dakota half sat, half reclined, she arranged her materials on the coffee table. "This is going to hurt."

"I'll live."

She took a deep breath, then let it out slowly. "All right then." And grabbed the iodine, a box of Q-tips, and some bandages.

First she cleaned his wound, inside and out. He flinched several times and the color drained from his face, but he didn't say a word. Samantha grimaced and looked the other way.

A knock on the door jerked Jessica's attention from Dakota and Jamie. She placed a hand on her weapon as she went to answer it. Jamie registered Jessica's movements but didn't look up from her work. In less than two minutes she had a neat row of three stitches just above Dakota's left eyebrow. A nice bruise had already started to form. "I suggest you duck next time."

Dakota eyed her with a dangerous glint.

"I'll try to remember that."

In spite of the seriousness of the situation, Jamie couldn't help the small smile that crossed her lips. Oh how she loved to banter with him. When she let herself. "You probably need an antibiotic and that's out of my realm."

"I'll call my doc and get some."

"He's used to it, huh?"

"Something like that."

"Um, guys?"

Jamie looked up to find Samantha looking at her with an expression that bordered somewhere between amused and annoyed. Jamie raised a brow. "Yes?"

"Can we focus on the fact that someone tried to break in tonight and figure out who that could be?"

Sobering, Jamie busied herself with cleaning up the mess she'd made while doctoring Dakota. "It was him."

"Did you see him?"

"No. I didn't have to."

Jessica intervened. "I'm going back out to the car. Let me know if you guys need anything else."

Jamie nodded. "Thanks so much, Jessica."

"No problem."

She left and Dakota spoke up. "He had a black mask on. The only thing showing were his eyes, but it was too dark for me to get a good look at them. Plus," he raised a hand to his wound, "he was faster than I was."

Jamie dropped three ibuprofen tablets into his palm, then walked over to the window. She stood to the side and pushed the blinds slightly apart so she could look out.

"What are you doing?" Samantha walked over and placed a hand on Jamie's shoulder.

"It doesn't matter, you know."

"What doesn't?"

"How much protection I have. Eventually, we'll slip up or I'll do something stupid."

"You're not going to do anything stupid. We're going to take precautions and be careful."

"I know. But I just have this feeling —"

"Stop!"

Jamie jerked at Samantha's sharp command. "What?"

"You sound like you're giving up. Like you just want to walk out there and say, 'Here I am. Take me.' "

Jamie blinked. "No, that's not what I'm saying. I'm saying . . ." She stopped. She didn't know what she meant. At least not in a way that she could put into words.

Dakota gave a grunt and pulled himself to his feet. "It's late, we've found nothing, so I'm going home."

Jamie walked over and placed two fingers in the center of his chest to push him gently back onto the couch. He obeyed with a questioning look.

She asked, "You have a concussion. Do you have someone you can call to check on you? Wake you up every two hours?"

Regret flashed across his face in a micro-expression that she almost missed. He shook his head. "No, you know my family is in Texas."

"Right."

"Connor can stay with him while I stay here," Samantha volunteered.

"What about Jenna?" Jamie was concerned about Connor's eighteen-year-old daughter. Not that the girl couldn't stay by herself, but Jamie knew she didn't like to do it.

Sam pulled out her cell. "I've got that covered. She can go stay with her grandparents tonight. She loves visiting them at the retirement home. Then I'll call Connor and let him know he's got babysitting duties." She smirked at Dakota who rolled his eyes.

"Jenna just loves going there for the food."

"And the neighbor's cat."

Samantha walked off to make the arrangements and Jamie sat on the edge of the couch next to Dakota. "I'm sorry you got hurt."

Softness replaced the edge that normally lurked just under the surface of his eyes. "Thanks. I'm just sorry he got away."

"You're going to have to take some time to heal, you know?"

The softness disappeared and his gaze narrowed. "Don't try to sweet talk me into taking some time off of this."

"You're neglecting your 'real' cases to protect me."

"Not really, Connor and I were assigned to find out who the dead bodies are. We can't do that without your input."

She sighed. "I know. I just feel like I'm taking you away from . . . something."

He smiled. "I promise you, you're not. And even if you were, it wouldn't be near as important as keeping you safe anyway. Understand?"

Feeling the tears threaten right beneath the surface, she nodded, stood and said, "All right."

Sam came back into the den. "Connor said he's on his way to pick you up. Assuming you live through the night, he'll bring you back to get your car in the morning."

"Good." He looked at Jamie. "That means we get to have breakfast together."

She threw a pillow at him. Gently.

Having to park one street over was a pain, but worth it in order to watch Jamie's house. He couldn't see her from the car, of course, but he'd found the perfect little spot where he could sit on the edge of the woods and see each individual window. When the lights were on, occasionally he could make out the faint outline of her shadow as she moved from room to room. The Hero lowered the binoculars.

Because of the blinds, he couldn't see anything going on inside the house, but he knew they were scared. They'd close in even tighter around Jamie now. But that was fine. He gave a low laugh. It didn't matter how much they watched her, when he was ready, he'd take her and rescue her once more. This time for good.

Stilling, he listened for the voice. Today, it was quiet. But he knew it would be back. For now, he would enjoy the silence.

Starting the car, he wove his way from the neighborhood.

He hadn't planned on the narrow escape he'd had a couple hours earlier. That had been a lucky break on the part of the cop. The Hero still wasn't sure how the man had spotted him, but when he'd realized he was

so close to being caught, he had to think —
and run — fast.

Thankfully, the sirens had given him
enough sound cover to double back and
catch the cop by surprise. He'd tried to hit
him with enough force to kill him, but the
branch hadn't been big enough. Just big
enough to knock him out.

Maybe next time.

10

Jamie looked up from placing the last bone in the body. She now had a pretty complete skeleton. The medical examiner would officially confirm what Jamie already knew. The cause of death. She touched the area where the girl's throat would have been. Her throat had been slashed all the way to the bone. The gouge in the third cervical vertebra left no doubt in her mind.

Jamie swallowed hard and focused.

She'd extracted the mitochondrial DNA from one of the bones and sent it off to be examined and possibly matched with a missing person or a missing person's relative.

A whistle sounded, announcing Dakota's imminent arrival. Jamie smiled to herself and realized how much she appreciated the man. How she wished . . .

"Hey there, Jamie. You making any

progress?"

"Yes." Then she frowned at him. "You shouldn't be here. You should be home resting."

"I've got a whopper of a headache, but no other concussion symptoms. I'm good."

"Hm. I wonder what your doctor would say."

He shrugged. "Same thing he said when he gave me the antibiotics."

She waited. He didn't offer more so she pushed. "Which was?"

"I'll be fine in a couple of days and to take it easy."

Against her will, she felt her left brow arch. "And this is taking it easy?"

"I'm in the air-conditioning instead of the blazing hot sun digging up bones."

She rolled her eyes and shook her head. "Okay, I guess that'll have to do for now."

"Great, so what you got?"

"I've got a female between the age of eighteen and twenty-five, but probably on the younger end. It's hard to tell exactly how long she's been dead. But going by the fact that there's not a lot of tissue left on her body, no hair anywhere, the climate we live in, the ground she was buried in, I'd say she's probably been dead between three to five years. Our entomologist has the insect inclusions and will be able to give you a much better estimate of post mortem inclusion than I. And by measuring her femur, I've concluded that she was most likely between 5'5" and 5'7"."

Dakota took notes in his ever-present notepad. "All right. Let me know when you get the PMI back from the bug guy. I'm going to get Jazz to pull up all of the missing persons reports from five years back that match this description."

"Great. And you might want to expand the search into surrounding areas."

"Yeah, I've thought about that."

"I know it'll make it harder to narrow down, but . . ."

She shrugged and Dakota nodded. He pulled out his phone and stepped from the room.

Jamie turned to the second skeleton she'd finished laying out yesterday. The similarities between the two skeletons chilled her — to the bone.

Did she dare voice her suspicions to Dakota? Would he think she'd totally lost it? That everything that had happened up to this point in her life had finally caused her to crack? If she were totally honest with herself, she would admit she'd wondered it herself initially. And yet . . .

She walked over to the second body and studied the tibia, three of the fingers, both ankles, the left radius. All broken. All healed before death.

More whistling.

Dakota rounded the door and stopped when he saw her. "What is it?"

She shook her head. "You'll think I'm crazy."

Dakota frowned and pushed the Stetson to the back of his head. "No I won't. What is it?"

"I think the same person killed both of these girls."

"Well, that's kind of what we thought when we found the second set of bones in the same area as the first."

"I know."

"So what's crazy about that?"

She looked him in the eye. "Because I think the killer is the same person who took me almost twelve years ago."

If she'd hauled off and slugged him in the gut, he wouldn't have been more surprised. And he couldn't deny the dart of skepticism that shot through him. Still . . .

"Okay, what makes you think that?"

She drew in a deep breath and studied him. He knew she was looking for any sign of doubt. He refused to let any show on his face.

Then she nodded. "Look at this."

He rounded the table nearest him and walked to stand by her side. In a methodical, professional teaching voice, she proceeded to walk him through what she'd learned about each victim. "See the bones? They've been broken. And healed back."

"Okay. People break bones."

"From what I can tell — and later I can give you the scientific rundown of how I know this — but all of these bones were broken about the same time. And all healed back around the same time."

That caught his attention. "Maybe she was in a car wreck or something."

"That's a possibility."

"But?"

"But, look at this victim. I call her Chloe."

He raised a brow. "You name them?"

"Yeah." She shrugged. "I feel so bad for them. They died so young. They deserve names, and until I can find out who they really are . . ."

Dakota felt his heart squeeze with love for this special woman. The dead and the living, it didn't matter. She treated them all with respect. "Who's that one?" He gestured to the other skeleton.

"Bianca."

"Fancy names."

"I know. We girls secretly wish we had exotic names." She led him back over to Bianca. "Look at her vertebrae and the ribs."

He leaned in, wondering what she wanted him to see. As he studied the area, he noticed a gouge in one of the bones. "Wait a minute. What's that depression? Is that supposed to be there?"

"No, it's not."

"So what is it?"

"A knife wound."

Sickness curled inside him. "He cut her throat?"

"To the bone."

"What about . . ." He had to see. He walked over to the one she called Chloe and looked at the same bone. Then he looked up at Jamie. "It's the same, just a slightly different angle."

"I know."

"So why do you think it's the same guy who took you all those years ago?"

"Because of something he said."

Dakota frowned. "What was it?"

She closed her eyes. "He liked to slice and stab."

"Slice and . . . come on, Jamie, make this a little easier for me, would you?"

She fidgeted. Which was odd. He'd never seen her exhibit any sign of discomfort while in her lab. Here, she ruled. She was confident and in charge. She blew out a breath. "He explained how he would kill me. First he would slit my throat and then make the final stab into the rib cage and up into the heart. He wanted to see the — and I quote — 'blood and water flow.' "

He couldn't move. Even though he'd seen just about all there was to see, sometimes the evil snuck up on him and took him by surprise. Surprise at the depravity of human nature. Surprise at what one person could do to another. He couldn't dwell on it for long or he'd go crazy. "Wait a minute. That's a biblical reference, isn't it?"

"You know your Bible?"

"Hey, I'm not a complete heathen."

She gave him a soft, knowing smile. "I know you're not. You just don't talk about your spiritual side very often."

"I know." And he didn't want to talk about it now.

But he had to know about her.

Catching her hand, he stared deep into her eyes, wishing he could see beyond what she would let him. See past the shadows that never really left her. "How did you survive?"

At first, she didn't answer, but she didn't look away either. She licked her lips and said, "God."

Dakota nodded. "I thought you might say that."

"Why?"

"Because it shows in your life. In your words and your actions."

She gave a little laugh. "But I sure wasn't living for him when everything was happening. I was mad as fire at him for a long time."

That surprised him. "Really? I wouldn't have expected that?"

"Why not?"

"Because you seem so . . . so . . . into God."

She smiled. "I am. Now." Then the smile slid from her lips and she shuddered. "But when he had me, I knew I wasn't leaving there alive."

"And yet you did."

"Yes." She picked up one of the bones and traced the broken part that had healed. "I did."

"How?"

She sighed. "Other than giving God the credit, I'm not exactly sure. I've thought about it, of course. When I let myself. And the only thing I can come up with was that eventually my anger overcame my terror. And I was actually able to start thinking. Analyzing. Learning about him. Figuring out what made him tick."

"So what was it?"

"He was 'the hero.' At least that's what he called himself. Hero. He had to feel like he was saving me. Rescuing me."

"From what, for crying out loud? He's the one that put you in the situation in the first place!"

"Yes, well, it didn't take me long to realize this guy was insane. Literally. So, I played along with him. And let him rescue me." A frown flickered. "Only somewhere along the line, I started to believe it." She waved a hand and blinked. "I was really messed up for a while, Dakota. You don't even . . ."

Dare he ask? Did he even want to know? "Rescue you from what, Jamie?"

"The pain."

Jamie wasn't exactly sure why she was opening up so many old wounds. Wounds that had scabbed over and healed, for the most part. Now, she was tearing them open, revisiting a place in her life she never wanted to go back to.

Unfortunately, she didn't have much choice. It was only a matter of time before

133

Connor and Dakota sat her down and made her relive her eight-week nightmare, especially now that she'd let it out of the bag that she thought the guy who'd killed these girls was the same one who'd snatched her.

Her back ached. And she still needed to go over the two older files of the bodies that had been found in the same area as the two skeletons she now had in her lab.

Dakota's phone rang and he walked to the other side of the lab to answer it.

She let herself bend forward and touch her toes to relieve the tense muscles at the small of her back.

Returning footsteps had her straightening. The grimly satisfied look on his face made her frown and ask, "What is it?"

"Jazz found some information about that shirt we found with the first body."

"Oh good."

"With the information you gave her about the label and her computer expertise, she was able to determine it came from an exclusive and well-known retail store and was from the 2005 line."

"So, if our girl bought it new, she died in 2005."

"You estimated she'd been dead about three to five years. That would put her right at being dead for five years. Then Jazz ran a search on missing girls during that time period, using your age range, isolating the geographical area to Spartanburg and the surrounding cities and counties for a sixty-mile radius. I'm thinking that because the graves were found here and the fact that you disappeared from here, this is his home base. He's got a setup somewhere local."

Jamie swallowed. How close had she been living all these years to her attacker?

"Anyway, using your information, she came up with seven possibilities."

"Seven? That's all?"

"Yes. So I've got someone contacting these seven families to see if one of them can identify the shirt."

"What if it was a shirt he put on her?"

"Then we're out of luck on that angle." Dakota paused, then asked. "What were you wearing when they found you?"

She blinked. "The clothes I was wearing the night I disappeared."

"And they found you weeks later. Did you wear the same thing the entire time you were held by him?"

She shook her head. "No, he . . . gave me stuff to wear."

"So he let you loose occasionally?"

Jamie folded her arms across her stomach and nodded. "He let me shower, use the bathroom, take care of personal . . . um . . . issues. He liked me to be clean. I think he had some kind of dirt fetish or something." Why she felt embarrassed telling this to Dakota was beyond her. Then she shuddered. "But I never felt clean even after the showers."

Dakota's throat worked and she wondered what he was thinking. Then he said, "Obviously there was no way for you to escape him or you would have." He stated it with such assured belief that Jamie momentarily went still. He noticed. "What?" he asked.

The lump in her throat took her by surprise. "I don't know. Thank you for saying that. I've wondered if . . ."

"If you should have been able to get away from him."

"I tried to fight him one time, but he was so strong. Unbelievably strong. It was almost like a supernatural strength. He just held me off with one hand and broke my arm. Just squeezed and twisted until it snapped." She bit her lip and pointed to her lower left arm. "And he did it with one hand."

Dakota flinched and looked back at the skeletons on the tables. "He'd have to be strong in order to slash someone's throat to the bone."

"Or in a rage."

"Or that."

She pushed her sleeves up and examined the scars. Dakota's eyes returned to her wrists. "Handcuffs?"

"Yeah." Turning her arm, she said, "I suppose I could have plastic surgery to cover them up."

"Why are they so bad? I've never seen cuffs cause that much damage."

Biting her lip, she pondered whether or not to reveal that to him. "Because I tried so hard to get out of them — one way or another."

"What does that mean?"

A knock on the door made her jump. Jamie pulled her sleeves down in one smooth movement and forced a smile. "Hi, George."

"Hi there." He waved a folder toward Dakota. "I've got that information you wanted. I was passing Lila's desk and she snagged me for the role of errand boy."

"Oh, thanks." Dakota met the man in the middle of the room and took the papers. He told Jamie, "I also asked Jazz to do an extended search, widening the age range a little and going so far as seeing who's gone missing within a hundred-mile radius. She faxed the results. George also provided

137

some great information on a possible profile for this guy."

While Dakota and George discussed his findings, Jamie tuned them out and went back to work on the bones. She desperately wanted to find out who these two women were and offer their families closure.

In the back of her mind, she registered Dakota's phone ringing, George leaving with an absent wave. Totally focused on what she was doing, she jumped when Dakota said her name.

"Oh, sorry, what?"

"We've got another body."

"You mean another skeleton?"

"No, a body. Serena's with her right now." Serena Hopkins, the medical examiner Jamie worked with on a regular basis.

"Okay." Confusion knit her brow. "Well, if it's a body, Serena will take care of it. She doesn't initially need me."

"Not to do the examination, but there's something about this one that you need to know."

Jamie stilled, wondering what he was getting ready to say and fearing she wasn't going to like it. "What?"

"She's been branded. Upper left shoulder. The number seventeen."

11

Jamie stared down at the woman on the slab before her. "How long has she been dead?"

The medical examiner, Serena Hopkins, set aside a tool and said, "Anywhere between four to six months is my best estimate, but who knows?"

"She's very well preserved."

"They found her in the basement of an old warehouse that was scheduled for demolition," Connor said from her left.

"A damp area. I wouldn't expect her to look this good." If you could call it good with a slashed throat and what remaining skin she had in various shades of unattractive color.

On her right, Dakota shifted closer. "This particular basement had been converted into a freezer to store dry ice. The owner also rented out the bottom three floors as storage to various places."

"So, basically, she's been packed in dry

ice for however long she's been dead," Serena concluded.

Jamie nodded. "Well, that would do it. But why is it no one noticed her until today? How long have they been using that freezer?"

"The guy I talked to said he rented half the space. Someone else had the other half, but the only thing in the other half was an old freezer and some meat hooks. He never bothered with it and everyone went about their business."

"Who was renting the other half?"

"A guy who was working on starting his own meat packing company. Only it never got off the ground, so when he realized his business was going nowhere, he went to get the freezer and the few other items in there, figuring he could at least sell them to someone and recoup a bit of his investment. Only when he opened up the freezer . . ."

"He got the shock of his life?"

"Exactly."

Jamie shook her head. "Is Jazz running dental impressions with missing persons reports?" She moved around the table needing to look at the woman's arm.

Dakota eyed her. "Yes."

Deep breath, Jamie. Her throat tightened. Her lungs felt constricted. Just a little farther and she would be able to see . . .

. . . number seventeen.

The raised flesh mocked her, taunted her. She flashed back. *He walked toward her, the branding iron smoking red. "You'll always belong to me now. It's time to release you from the pain."*

"What are you doing?" Terror that never left her increased threefold.

"It's time."

"For what?" she screamed.

"The end. I promised you I would make the pain stop."

She stared at him. So this was it. He'd brand her and kill her. Cold certainty curled in her stomach. This was the day she would die. His eyes glowed with some manic glee. Excitement at her impending death. Slowly, an idea formed.

"Who?" she asked, catching him off guard.

He stopped, some of the excitement fading from those weird eyes. "What?"

"Who made you stop their pain? Who?"

He recoiled, pulled the branding iron away from her, and stared. His lips moved, but no sound emerged. The hand that held his weapon trembled.

Then he left, muttering. Something caught her attention to her right. A shadow? The moon moving behind the trees causing the light to play tricks with the corners of the room?

No time to dwell on it. He returned five minutes later, the iron fiery red once more. "Don't speak."

She'd ignored him and pleaded, "Stop. Don't do this!"

The sizzling iron touched her arm.

"Jamie? Jamie?"

She blinked.

Dakota's hand rested on her upper arm, covering her white knuckles that had been clenched around her own brand hidden by her long-sleeved white shirt under the lab coat.

"Who is she?" Jamie demanded. "I need to know who she is."

Serena's BlackBerry beeped. She punched a button, then looked up. "I think I can help you out there. Jazz just emailed me. Her name is Lisa Dupre. Nineteen years old, she disappeared just after New Year's last year."

"And died a few weeks? months? later," Jamie muttered. "If she died only four to six months ago, he kept her a long time." The thought nauseated her.

Dakota blew out a sigh. "Connor, you want to take the family?"

"I want to be there," Jamie ground out.

No, she really didn't, but this girl's poor family . . . what they must be going through.

"What?"

"I need to be there for them. In case they have any . . . questions. Unfortunately, they won't like the answers."

Dakota and Connor exchanged a look. "Jamie, they don't need to know what their daughter suffered."

She chewed her bottom lip. "Are you sure?"

"Positive. They'll know she had a bad ending, they don't need to know the extent of it."

"Will you give them my card? Tell them to call if they need to? I'll be . . . careful with my answers to whatever they ask."

Dakota paused, then held out a hand. "Sure."

Jamie pulled a card out of her lab pocket. She kept some in there just in case. Dakota took it and slid it into the back pocket of his khakis.

Connor pulled his phone from his pocket. "I'll give them a call and let them know. They may want to see her."

Serena shook her head. "They don't want to see her like this. I'd try to talk them out of that."

While Connor did the dirty work, Jamie

studied the slash on Lisa's throat. Once again he'd used enough force to hit the bone. "So much anger," she whispered.

Serena looked at her. "Why do you have the answers?"

Jamie let a deep breath slip out between her lips. "Because whoever killed her tried to kill me eleven and a half years ago."

The woman blanched, her classically beautiful features twisted with shock. "What?"

"It's a long story."

"Care to share?"

"Not really. Maybe sometime. Does she have any broken bones?"

Serena studied Jamie but didn't push. Instead, she gestured to the wall where she'd hung x-rays. She pointed to the wrist. "Broken in three places. But healed back pretty well."

"He put a cast on her."

Not bothering to ask Jamie how she knew that, Serena moved on to Lisa's leg. "Here. A broken leg. The bone split in a couple of pieces. This part looks like it healed nicely, but there's a chip missing here."

Studying the x-rays, Jamie felt a chill move up her spine. She could have been looking at her own. "He used a baseball bat on her legs. Just enough force to break the bone, not shatter it."

A swiftly indrawn breath from behind her made her look over her shoulder. Dakota's eyes pierced her. "A baseball bat?"

Shoving all of the emotions that wanted to bubble to the surface deep down into a safe place, Jamie nodded. Dakota winced and Connor's jaw went rigid.

Serena continued. "See this? The ulna. Broken in two places."

"She fought him."

Connor stepped forward. "Can you find any prints on her skin?"

Serena shook her head. "No, but I've scraped her for some trace evidence. I've also gone over her clothes with a fine-tooth comb."

"Find anything?"

"Nothing yet. We'll see."

Lila stuck her head in the door. "Family will be here in about five minutes."

A collective sigh echoed around the room.

Then Serena moved to cover Lisa's body. Jamie decided it might be up to her to convince the family they didn't want to see how Lisa ended up.

An hour later, Dakota marveled at Jamie's skill in handling the shattered parents. She'd convinced them they didn't want to see the remains of their daughter, and by the time they left, they'd decided on cremation.

Jamie had stood in the hallway and watched as Mrs. Dupre sobbed into her husband's shoulder. They'd walked to the elevator clinging to one another, grieving the loss of their eldest child. Then Jamie had turned to Dakota and said, "You're right. They're better off not knowing."

"I'll give them a couple of hours to do some processing, then Connor and I will head over to the house to ask them some questions."

They all needed a break from the intense emotions running through the room and had decided to meet at Flannigan's. Jamie declared she didn't really have an appetite, but decided she'd like the company.

Dakota was glad. He felt she needed to get away from the lab for a while. Samantha managed to get away and join them, as did George Horton.

Monica, a waitress they were all on a first-name basis with, approached them with a smile. Her spiky purple hair didn't move in her trek across the floor. Today she had on a nose ring and four earrings in her left ear. "My favorite group is back." She eyed George with a flirtatious smile. "And a newbie. Welcome."

Offering her a small smile, George nodded. "Thanks."

Jamie asked, "How's school going, Monica?"

"It's going. One more semester and I'll be done. I graduate in December."

"That's great. You're going to make a fine teacher."

Monica smiled and took their order. After she left, Dakota turned to George. "Do you have anything you can add to your profile on this guy now that we've got another body? I've got the team at Quantico doing a profile workup too, and everything you've said has coincided with what they think. So far, it looks like we've found three of his victims. If Jamie's right and he's branding each one, we're up to seventeen. That's a lot of missing bodies."

George shook out his napkin and placed it across his lap. He studied his fingers, then said, "I would say this guy is in his mid-thirties to early forties. Probably well educated. Physically strong. He's probably something of a loner but can fit in well in social situations. He's learned to adapt, be comfortable anywhere."

"Why do you say that?"

George spread his hands. "Well, think about it. If he hadn't, there's no way he

147

would still be walking the streets of our fair city. Someone would have caught on to him by now. He would have slipped up and made some kind of mistake." His lips twisted. "From what you're telling me, his crimes have been darn near perfect."

Dakota shifted. "Not perfect. No one's perfect. Which means there's evidence out there, we just have to find it."

"Be that as it may, I think he's going to be a tough one to nail down."

Unfortunately, Dakota felt like George was probably right.

Samantha took a sip of water. "What about his background. How he grew up? His home life?"

"Well," George shrugged, "of course this is all based on an educated guess, but I would say he suffered a horrible childhood, was probably abandoned by a parent, and most likely suffered continuous abuse that messed up his mind."

Dakota snorted. "I understand that children who are abused often follow the pattern and become abusers themselves, but my dad was about as bad as they come and I didn't grow up killing people."

Jamie twisted the napkin between her hands, her eyes on some faraway spot across the restaurant. When her mind registered his comment, she snapped her gaze in his direction. "I didn't know that."

He felt a flush creep up into his neck and jaw. "I don't usually go around announcing it. But my point is, my dad had a pretty heavy hand, knocked me and my mom around. I had some rocky teen years, but that didn't turn me into a killer."

George shook his head. "I'm not talking about that kind of abuse. I'm talking about stuff that you can't wrap your head around but that he thinks is normal."

"Because it's all he knows," Jamie offered with a frown.

Samantha shook her head. "I'm not buying that. If he thinks it's normal, he wouldn't try to hide it. He'd be doing this stuff out in the open. Doesn't the fact that he's hiding his crimes suggest that he knows it's wrong?"

"Not necessarily. He thinks what he's doing is the norm but understands that not everyone holds the same beliefs that he does. He understands the fact that he could go to jail for what he's doing, but he feels justified in going above the authorities' heads, so to speak, in order to accomplish his goals — whatever those may be. It's possible he thinks he answers to a higher power."

Connor nodded. "Okay, so we have to stop him before he finds victim number eighteen."

George glanced at his watch.

Dakota asked, "Are you in a hurry? We usually just kind of take our time over lunch since we all work weird hours."

"No, I just have an appointment in about forty-five minutes."

"You work on a contract basis for the department, right?"

"Right. I do a lot of consulting. And I worked out a deal with the powers-that-be that I could use the office at the hospital to meet with clients I see in my private practice. That way I don't have to keep up with two locations."

"Sounds like a sweet deal to me."

George smiled. "I think so. At least for the ones that don't mind coming into the same area as the morgue. And the ones that do mind . . ." He shrugged. "I manage to work around that."

Monica approached the table with a tray bearing food . . . and a small white box decorated with a black ribbon.

Dakota eyed it, wondering who it was for. The waitress saved it for last, placing it in front of Jamie beside the plate of food.

Jamie looked up. "What's this?"

"Some man asked me to deliver it to you along with your food. Said he wanted to surprise you, that you were very special to him and you'd know who it was from."

Dakota tensed, all senses on alert. He slid out of the booth and stood, eyes darting to the entrance to the restaurant. "Who? Where is he?"

Monica set the tray on the table behind her. A frown pulled her eyebrows to the bridge of her nose. She looked around. "I don't see him."

Jamie still stared at the box as though it were an angry rattler poised to strike.

George set his hamburger down. "What's going on?"

Dakota's eyes narrowed. "Describe him for me."

"Um . . . kind of average looking. You know. Black hair with some gray, probably forty-something."

With that paltry description, Connor motioned he'd go searching while Dakota handled the restaurant.

He raised a brow to George. "Bomb?"

"You think?" He rolled his eyes. "Or it could be some kind of booby trap as soon as you open it. A poisonous spider? A deadly powder?" George frowned. "Don't you think you're overreacting just a bit?"

"Maybe."

Jamie stood, hands shaking, but calm on her face. "Then we need to get everyone out of the restaurant."

At the seriousness of their reaction, George's eyes went wide. "It's not really big enough for a bomb, is it?" he asked as he backed away from the table.

"Who knows? What I do know, I don't like. A mysterious man delivers a package to someone who might have a stalker? That smells hinky to me. Let's evacuate, and if we're wrong, face the consequences later."

Samantha pulled out her leather case that held her badge and FBI credentials. The one-inch blue letters on the upper half of the leather wallet drew stares of all kinds as she started going table to table asking people to leave in an orderly manner; explaining that they had a situation that needed to be handled.

Patrons exited, questions floating on the air, murmuring amongst themselves, several grumbling about having their meal interrupted.

Jamie and George followed the crowd out onto the sidewalk. Officers arrived, lights flashing on the black-and-white vehicles. One officer handed Dakota a roll of yellow crime scene tape and he went to work, sectioning off the restaurant.

The bomb squad arrived and set up shop.

While Samantha and Connor worked crowd control with several other officers, Dakota walked over to Lieutenant Michael Swift, the man in charge of the bomb squad, and explained the package.

"What makes you think it's a bomb?"

"I don't know that it is, but there are circumstances surrounding the package that make me suspicious — and paranoid."

Michael drew in a breath. "All right, Dakota. I know you well enough to know that's all I need to go on." He turned to the man on his left. "Chris, suit up and take Abby."

Chris nodded. "You got it, Loo." He ducked back into the truck. Five minutes later, he emerged, dressed in Kevlar protective gear, with a highly trained German Shepherd at his side.

Dakota looked at Chris. "Abby?"

"Absolutely. The best bomb dog on the squad."

"All right, this way." Dakota led the way to the door of the restaurant, explaining the location of the package. Chris and Abby disappeared inside.

Outside, back across the street, away from

any potential damage, they waited in silence, all eyes on the building.

Then Dakota spotted the waitress. "Hey, Connor, let's get a description of the guy who left the package while we're waiting."

"I was just thinking the same thing." He pulled out a pad and pen and the two walked toward the woman.

Spotting them, she shoved her hands into her hair and said, "I'm so sorry. I didn't know this was going to happen. He just said to give the package to the woman with the white long-sleeved T-shirt on. He even pointed her out. I knew right away he meant Jamie."

"I need you to go over what he looked like again. This time try to get in as much detail as you can, okay?" Dakota asked.

Frightened blue eyes blinked as Monica searched her brain for a description. "Um . . . he was old. Like maybe in his forties?"

"What else? Any tattoos? Anything to make him stand out?"

"He had a scar under his eye."

"Which eye?"

"Um . . . left, I think. And like I said before, he had black hair with some gray in it."

"Height?"

She eyed him. "Maybe a little shorter than you." White teeth came out to chew on her bottom lip. Her nose ring quivered and tears filled her eyes. "He didn't look dangerous."

Dakota placed a hand on her shoulder and looked into her eyes. "Hey, it's not your fault, okay?"

Purple spikes slowly moved up and down in response to her reluctant nod. Then he asked her, "Are there any cameras in here?"

"You mean like security cameras?"

"Yeah."

"Um, one over the door, but I think that one's broken and it hasn't been fixed yet, then there's one in the bathroom hallway. And one in the dining area. I think that's all."

The one over the door was broken. Great.

He hid his frustration and said, "Since the camera's broken, I want you to work with a sketch artist, all right?"

"Sure."

He'd still want to look at the other cameras, but if the guy just walked in the door and handed the package to the hostess, then turned and walked out, he wouldn't be on camera. "All right, check out the crowd. Do you see him?"

Her eyes roved from one person to the next. Finally, she shook her head. "No. No one looks like him that I can see."

Dakota thanked her and walked over to Jamie. "How are you doing?"

"I'm scared. And mad."

"Healthy fear is a good thing. But don't let the mad make you do something you'll regret."

She gave him a long look, then turned as the man in Kevlar came from the building holding an open box in his gloved hands.

12

Jamie held her breath as the man motioned Dakota and Connor over. Both men pulled on gloves and Connor had a plastic baggie ready for the box. Samantha stood by her side, squeezing her fingers. "Well, it didn't blow up."

Jamie gave a halfhearted chuckle that died a quick death. "What are the odds that we'd be involved in two incidents requiring a bomb squad?" Just a little over a year and a half ago, Samantha had made a killer mad and he'd planted a bomb in her car. Fortunately, she'd managed to get out alive.

"I don't think the numbers go high enough."

Pulling in a shaky breath, Jamie let go of Samantha's hand and walked toward the guys. Both of them looked a little sick. The bomb guy eyed her with . . . what? Compassion? Pity?

Dakota swallowed hard and capped the

box. Was that a fine tremor she saw running through his hands? Connor shook his head and stepped toward her. Surely they didn't think they were going to hide that from her, did they?

Stepping next to Dakota, she asked. "What's in it?"

"Jamie, I really don't think you want to see this."

"It was delivered to me. It was meant for me. What's in it?"

"Honey . . . ," Connor began.

"Don't honey me," she snapped, spine going rigid. "I have a right to see it."

"It's a picture."

"Of?"

"You."

"Okay." She raised a brow, trying for a brave front even while her insides quivered. "I'm guessing it's a bad one."

Dakota settled an arm around her shoulders. "Beyond bad."

"Hey, hey." The shout came from the woman who'd been identified as the manager of the restaurant.

Looking relieved at the distraction, Dakota turned. "Ma'am?"

"Can we get back to work here? I'm losing money by the minute."

At Dakota's look, Connor took over. He

pulled the crime scene tape down, demanded order, and patrons filed back into the restaurant. Many asked questions, to which Connor replied, "I can't discuss that right now."

Jamie placed a hand on the plastic bag containing the box and tugged. Samantha stood at her side and George walked up to join them.

Dakota let go of the bag.

Samantha closed in next to her back, Connor drew in a deep breath, and Dakota reached out to cover her now gloved hand. "Think about this, Jamie. It's not pretty."

"I know, I got that." She shot him a look that hopefully conveyed her determination to do this. She couldn't be left in the dark. It was her life and she would not relinquish control of it. Not this time.

He removed his hand with a final squeeze.

Opening the bag, she reached in and slipped the top off the box.

Cold, sick fear curdled in her stomach as she stared down at the picture through the clear plastic bag.

It was her.

What she looked like dead.

Forcing herself into work mode, she desperately tried to look at the picture objectively. *It's somebody else, it's not me. It's somebody else, it's not me.*

But it was.

She lay on a metal table, eyes closed, head straight, not curved as though in sleep, straight as though on the slab in a morgue. Blonde curls surrounded a face she almost didn't recognize. Blue black bruises around her cheeks and chin. One on her forehead.

"He hit me when I talked back to him, told me he'd teach me a little respect for someone in his position," she muttered to whoever was listening.

A squeeze on her shoulder told her Samantha stood beside her.

A sheet covered her from mid-thigh to her armpits. The picture had been taken from the left side, clearly displaying the brand on her shoulder.

"He had an x-ray machine. Before he casted me, he took x-rays."

Samantha stilled. "What?"

"How could I forget that?" she whispered. "No, I didn't forget, I just . . ."

"What else?"

"He never took the mask off. Ever."

"Jamie, what about the x-ray machine?"

Images flickered as though her memories had been threaded through an old super-eight movie reel. "When he broke a bone, he x-rayed it, then cast it. Mostly I remember the casts."

"Plaster residue was found in the second grave," Connor spoke up. Jamie looked up at him and he waved his phone. "The lab sent me a message. The dirt analysis is finished."

She nodded absently and went back to the picture. Her fingers trembled, but she ignored them and examined her legs. Swollen and blue from the knee down, the right leg looked twice the size of the left. "Plaster. That's rather passé these days. Most of the time fiberglass is used." She took a deep breath. "He used drugs. They always made me sleepy . . . and made the pain go away for a bit."

"Your tox screen showed Demorol and Tylox," Samantha interjected.

"Right. Easy street drugs. He didn't have to worry about anyone tracing them back to him." She'd requested her medical information from the hospital about halfway through obtaining her degree. She'd read it from front to back. "Some of that time stands out in my mind so clear. And some of it's just . . . fuzzy, bits and pieces that slip away if I try to focus on them too hard."

George asked, "Can I have a look?"

Dakota slipped the bag out of Jamie's

fingers and passed it to George who let out a low whistle. "Whoa. I'll . . . um . . . need to think about this one. That's pretty far out there."

"Tell me what kind of sick . . ." Dakota couldn't even finish the sentence and Jamie reached out to grasp his hand.

George handed the box back to Dakota, who told him, "You think about it. I'd really like to know how someone could do this to another person and justify that it's okay."

"He thought he was helping me." Jamie couldn't believe she actually uttered the words. "In his sick, twisted, depraved mind, I honestly think he believed that."

Samantha shuddered. "I'd like to help him — right into the depths of hell."

"Sam . . ." Jamie reproved her sister, but understood where she was coming from.

Sam held up a hand. "I know, I know. I'm sorry. If not hell, then at least a high security mental hospital."

Connor said, "All right, people, I guess we need to get this back to the lab to see if someone can get anything useful from it. Bomb squad's gone, everyone's back in the restaurant, and the press are driving me nuts. I can't hold them back anymore, so unless one of you wants to be in the spotlight, I suggest we get out of here."

As one, they turned and headed for the sidewalk that would take them back to the office. The media gave up trying to get statements from them and switched their focus to restaurant patrons who were more than willing to offer their insights on what all the excitement was about.

Jamie grabbed the two files she needed to study and decided she'd pass on the evening news tonight.

The Hero had watched the patrons filter back into the restaurant shaking their heads and wondering what was going on. Now, he climbed into his car, frowning to himself. He'd figured it was only a matter of time before Jamie visited that restaurant again and he'd had his little gift ready.

The only aggravating thing had been all the excitement the cops with her had generated. It made it difficult to get into a good position where he could see her, to watch her expressions and read her body language.

He wanted her to open it immediately, wanted to see her reaction as she took in the picture. But she'd been forewarned that the picture was "shocking," they called it. "Ugly." He thought it was beautiful. Some of his best work. His fingers curled around the steering wheel.

Well, no matter, she'd seen it. He frowned. But she hadn't seemed that disturbed by it. Had she become that good at hiding her emotions? Had she lost her fear of him? The very threat of him? That wouldn't do. Not at all.

Then he remembered the tremble in her fingers as she held the photo. No, she still thought of him. He'd made sure of that. He'd seen her reaction to the handcuffs dug from the grave.

But the picture didn't seem to faze her. Why?

Maybe she needed another reminder. A reminder that he was waiting, but soon his patience would run out and she would once again belong to him.

13

Monday

Burying herself in work seemed to be one way to get her mind off her life and allow her to keep her eyes in front of her instead of constantly glancing over her shoulder. For the last three days, she had worked from dawn till dusk, breaking only for church on Sunday morning. Dakota had insisted and she hadn't had the strength to resist him.

But she returned to the lab the minute she'd finished choking down a lunch she didn't remember ordering. Even painting held no appeal right now.

She was really putting her security team — that is, Dakota, Connor, and Samantha — through it, but she just didn't know what else to do with herself, and the work needed to be done.

Now it was Monday afternoon and she felt dizzy with fatigue. But the time had been well spent. She'd gone over the two older case files, taking copious notes and paying attention to the smallest detail.

Several things stood out. The bodies had been found within a week of each other. The ME's report stated that one had been dead for about three years, the other a week. Both had been found in shallow graves. Both had their throats cut.

And both had been buried with handcuffs that had their first names engraved on the edge. Sandra and Olivia.

The forensics lab still had the cuffs that had come in with her two bodies. Were their names engraved on the edges?

She picked up the phone and dialed Mark's number. " 'Lo?"

"Hi, Mark, it's Jamie."

"What can I do for you, lovely lady?"

Ignoring the lovely lady part, she said, "I need you to look at those handcuffs you've got and tell me if anything is engraved on the edges."

"Aw, Jamie, I'm so backed up . . ."

"This is really important, Mark," she practically yelled at him. Taking a deep breath to calm herself, she said softy, "Please, I just need to know if there's anything engraved. It'll help me identify the bodies."

"All right, give me a couple of hours and

I'll get back to you."

"Thanks, I owe you."

"I'll collect."

"Tickets to the opening Panthers game?" Samantha and Connor had season tickets. Jamie would weasel a pair out of them. They missed most of the games anyway, and Jamie usually ended up going with Jenna.

"That'll work."

She hung up, thinking about what she knew. Those poor women. She had no doubt that the four women had been killed by the same man who'd snatched her so long ago.

The same man who might be stalking her even as she worked. Jamie shuddered. Lately, Samantha had picked her up at the end of the day and stayed with her all night long. Each night, with Samantha in the room across the hall, Jamie fell into bed so exhausted she didn't dream, didn't move, didn't think. Each morning she woke feeling like she'd never slept.

Dakota and Connor spent their days searching for the man who'd left the package at the restaurant. So far, nothing had turned up.

A knock on her door brought her head up from the bone she'd been documenting.

Lila stuck her head in. "Jazz just sent this

stuff. I think you've got a hit on one of the girls. The first one you dug up, I believe."

"Great. Who?"

"Simone Haliday." Lila slipped two pictures from the file she carried and walked them over to Jamie.

Jamie took them and observed, "Simone. A pretty name. Very fancy."

"Comes from a fancy family. Her father is some big-shot financial broker downtown. Her mother recognized the shirt. She said they bought it together for Simone's birthday in 2005."

Jamie stared down at the photo. A picture of a vibrant young woman, sitting on the side of a boat in the middle of a lake, head thrown back and laughing.

The next picture was more formal. A school picture. Reddish blonde hair curled around a heart-shaped face and blue eyes.

Lila cut in on her thoughts. "She's beautiful."

"Yes." Jamie shook her head over the loss of such potential, a young woman's life stolen from her. Anger gripped her at the injustice of it.

Lila sighed. "Her mother said she was wearing the blouse the day she disappeared."

Jamie handed the photos back and stared

down at the one who'd been identified. Simone. "All right. Do they have any DNA of hers left? I've extracted the mitochondrial DNA from the bone, but I need something to match it up with."

"I thought you might. Her mom said she had several baby teeth that she'd saved."

"One will do it."

A light whistle permeated the air and Jamie felt the fatigue of the last three days suddenly lift.

Dakota.

He rounded the edge of the door and entered the lab, stopping short at the sight of the two women. "Oh, sorry to interrupt."

"It's all right." Jamie waved a hand to Simone's skeleton. "Jazz managed to come up with a possible identification for one of the skeletons. Connor did a nice job tracking down the right family. Once we compare the DNA, we'll know for sure."

"Good." He shook his head. "It's such a shame."

Jamie bit her lip. "I know." Pasting a smile on her face, she asked, "What are you doing here? Can I help you with something?"

"Apparently examining your package wasn't on the priority list. I came by to see what was taking so long and stood there while the tech guy finally managed to lift a print off the ribbon on the box. We're running it through AFIS now and if we get a hit, we'll know who left you that nice little package." AFIS, the Automated Fingerprinting Identification System, was fast and reliable. Once the information was entered into it.

"That shouldn't take long."

"Nope, I expect to hear something any minute now."

"Is that why you're hanging around here? So you can pass the info on to me as soon as you get it?" The crime lab was on Howard Street, located off Asheville Highway, a couple of miles from the hospital.

"That and other reasons." His eyes twinkled at her and she felt the flush rise up in her cheeks.

She cleared her throat. "So . . ."

His phone rang and Jamie nearly puddled to the floor in relief. Then frustration seized her. Would she ever be able to flirt like a normal person? Have a normal, intimate relationship with a man chosen by God just for her?

Scared of the answer, yet desperate for it too, she vowed to do her best to conquer that particular fear. She watched Dakota pace and talk as she walked into her office and filed a bone inventory sheet on Simone.

She'd already started to think of her that way since she felt sure the DNA test would only confirm what she knew in her gut.

"Hey, Jamie."

The paper nestled where it belonged, she turned to find Samantha in the doorway sipping on a can of Coke. "Hey? What are you doing here? This place is turning into Grand Central."

Samantha sauntered in and perched on the side of Jamie's desk. "I've got some time on my hands so I decided to come see how things were coming on the bones."

While Jamie filled her in, Samantha's eyes shifted to the picture on the desk, then the mirror on the wall. "Are you listening?"

Blue eyes snapped back to Jamie's. "Huh? Yeah. Yeah."

"What's wrong?"

Sam stood and paced. "Nothing. Maybe. Something. I don't know."

Jamie leaned against the cabinet and crossed her arms. "Spill it."

A sigh blew out of her sister's mouth. "Something's going on with our parents."

Okay, she hadn't expected that one. "What?"

"I think they're avoiding me."

Jamie huffed. "Samantha Cash Wolfe, that's the most ridiculous thing you've said in a long time. Why would they avoid you?"

Samantha tossed her hands in the air. "I don't know! It's been going on for about three weeks now. I call and no one answers. I go over and suddenly they're rushing around saying they have to be somewhere: the church, their exercise class, they're meeting someone for lunch. I haven't been able to have a decent conversation with either of them since . . . forever."

"But you talked to Mom the other night. She called while you were in the bathroom, remember?"

"Because I left a ranting message that it could be life or death and someone had better call me back! Within two minutes my phone rang. They're screening their calls. What is up with that?"

Concerned because Samantha actually seemed to be making some sense, Jamie thought about the last time she'd talked to either one of her parents. It had been a while. She'd left messages and not thought any more about it.

But she hadn't gone over to the house because she'd wondered if she was being watched. She'd been afraid if she went to her parents' house, *he* would follow her. But come to think of it, her parents hadn't bothered to call her back in quite some time.

"Weird."

"What?" Samantha stopped pacing.

"You're right. That is weird. Your birthday's coming up and Mom usually has everything all planned out by now."

Samantha blinked. "Oh, you're right. I'd forgotten about my birthday."

Dakota popped his Stetson-covered head in the door. "Connor forgot your birthday? Want me to beat him up for you?"

"No, silly. *I'd* forgotten."

"Oh, your own birthday? You're weird."

Jamie rolled her eyes. "Dakota . . ."

He held up his hands in mock surrender, then his face turned serious. "AFIS grabbed a hit off the ribbon on your little photo gift."

Familiar fear tugged at her lungs, stealing the breath from her. She forced it away. *Deep breath. You're safe. All is well. God is good. When I am afraid . . .* "Who?"

"A guy by the name of Evan Johannes. We're heading out to his house now. We're taking a hostage negotiator and a SWAT team with us just in case he has a victim there."

"Where does he live?" Her heart slammed against her chest, her breathing felt constricted. "I want to come."

"Absolutely not." Sam reached over and gripped her fingers. Jamie pulled away.

173

"Dakota?"

"No way. You stay put. If this is our guy and he sees you . . . no, it's too dangerous."

"Then let me know immediately what's happening."

"Immediately."

Dakota shoved the earpiece further in his ear and took his position outside the home of Evan Johannes. A small house set on about one acre of land. A fenced backyard contained a dog that started yapping his head off as soon as the surveillance van pulled to a stop across the street.

Two unmarked cars parked down the street along the curb, ready for backup.

Dakota and Connor studied the blueprints of the house that had been provided by the county. Dakota shook his head. "No basement."

"So?"

"How does a guy keep victims inside on an upper level without the neighbors hearing the screams, et cetera? It doesn't seem likely."

"Guess we're about to find out. You ready to roll?"

"Ready."

"I'm going to call his home and see if he answers."

The phone rang and rang. Connor clicked off. "Not answering."

"All right, let's get in there."

Followed by about twenty other law enforcement personnel, the two of them exited the van and headed toward the house. The bulletproof vest felt heavy, the adrenaline surging in his blood a natural high. Excitement and anticipation thrummed through him. They were going to get this guy. And finally maybe Jamie would be free of her past and the nightmares that haunted her.

Connor stood to the side of the door and raised his knuckles to pound on it. "Evan Johannes! Police! Open up!"

Silence.

Dakota shifted. Sweat made a ticklish path down the middle of his back.

Three more times Connor rapped and called out.

Dakota wasn't concerned the guy would slip out the back. They had officers in place all around the property.

Weapon ready, he nodded to the officer who held the battering ram.

A loud *wham* and the door flew open.

He and Connor led the swarm into a living room that stunk.

Bad.

At least a hundred degrees in the house,

the sweat that had trickled before now started to pour. Breathing shallow breaths through his mouth didn't help the familiar sweet sickly stench he'd smelled before. In his gut, he knew what they were going to find.

From his peripheral vision, he saw an officer go to the left. Felt one go to the right. Dakota headed straight down the hall.

"Clear!" he heard from the kitchen.

"Clear!" from the first bedroom.

In his earpiece, "Garage is clear."

He swung around the edge of the door into the next bedroom and grunted. "In here!"

He felt Connor come up behind him. "Aw, man . . ."

"How long you think he's been dead?"

"Couple of days? Serena will be able to tell us for sure after she gets her hands on him."

Dakota approached the body, careful not to touch or step on anything. "Bullet hole to the head."

"That'll do the job if the throat slashing doesn't." He pointed to the yawning gap just below the man's jaw. Flies swarmed the wounds and Dakota grimaced.

"Yeah, I noticed that. Seems a bit of overkill, doesn't it? Either one of those would have killed the guy." Blowing out a rough sigh, Dakota turned to one of the other officers. A kid who didn't look old enough to shave yet, much less be on patrol. "Give the ME and Crime Scene Unit a call, would you?"

"You got it." He whirled and left, looking a little green around the edges. Probably his first homicide. Dakota didn't hold that against him, he was having to work at holding the contents of his own breakfast where they belonged. The smell did it to him every time. It would take days to get it out of his nose.

Connor studied the corpse. "What do you make of it?"

"We need to get a picture from when he was alive and see if the waitress from the restaurant can confirm he's the one who delivered the package."

He looked around the room but didn't see any pictures of the deceased. In fact, he didn't see any pictures at all. "I'll check the den area."

"He doesn't really resemble the sketch the artist did, does he?"

"Too hard to tell. Could be him, but . . ." He shrugged.

"All right, let's get out of here before we contaminate this area any more than we already have."

"I need some air anyway."

They exited the room and headed back down the hall. More flies buzzed around the trash can in the kitchen.

Back outside, Dakota pulled in a lung full of fresh, if hot and muggy, air. His stomach settled, he met Serena and the CSU team as they pulled into the drive. Yellow crime scene tape flapped in the wind. A handful of neighbors stood on their porches watching and wondering at all the excitement.

Several officers began questioning them, trying to see if anyone had seen anything or noticed anything strange over the last few days.

Serena, runway-model beautiful with a mind like a steel trap, greeted him. "Got another one for me, huh?"

"Unfortunately."

"Between you and Connor, I sure do have job security."

"Hey, it's not our fault," he protested. But he knew she was kidding. A little levity before facing such ugly seriousness.

Dressed for the job in a Tyvek suit, gloves, and a mask that hung around her neck for the moment, she nodded. "I'll tell you what I can as soon as possible."

"Thanks."

She left, CSU right on her heels.

Connor had started doing a little questioning of the neighbors himself, so Dakota got on the phone with Jazz. "Can you dig up everything you've got on this Evan Johannes guy?"

"I'm already ahead of you," she said. "Jamie called and asked me to find out more about him a minute after you left. He's thirty-seven years old, was laid off from A-Textiles six months ago. Divorced three years ago, no kids. Ex-wife is now living in England with her second husband and has been since the divorce was final. As far as I can tell, they've had no contact in those three years. Mr. Johannes grew up here in town. Parents deceased, one brother and two sisters. I talked to the brother and it seems Mr. Johannes is estranged from all of his siblings due to an arrest for indecent exposure at a theme park two years ago. No more incidents on record. That was his one and only."

"Bank records?"

"Broke. Getting ready to foreclose on the house."

"All right, thanks, Jazz."

"Not a problem, call me if you need anything else."

Dakota hung up and motioned for Connor to join him.

Connor loped across the lawn and Dakota relayed the information to him. Connor shook his head. "Laid off six months ago. That explains why the power was shut off in the middle of a heat wave."

"This guy doesn't meet George's profile."

"No, he was probably just a pawn. I'm guessing he was paid to make that delivery."

"And was killed for his efforts."

"No witnesses. No one's going to miss a down-and-out jobless man estranged from his family."

One of the CSU team, Jake Hollister, came out of the house, an evidence bag in hand. "Thought you might be interested in this."

Absently, Dakota noticed the ambulance pull up and unload a stretcher containing a black body bag. "What is it, Jake?"

The stretcher passed by him and into the house.

Jake shook the bag. "Two one hundred dollar bills."

"Where'd you find those?"

"Under the bed."

"Loose?"

"Yep."

Dakota looked at Connor. "Okay, that supports our theory that he was paid off."

"Did you find any pictures of the guy?" he asked Jake.

"No, but we're not finished. Julie's working on the den. I'll let her know you need a photo of him."

"Thanks."

Connor wondered. "How do you think our psycho and this guy knew each other?"

"Who knows? Could have been anywhere."

"I'd ask Sam to check out the guy's computer, but the power company said they cut his power off two months ago. I have a feeling that's not the connection."

"Yeah, and no cell phone."

"But he had two hundred dollars under his bed."

"He didn't have time to spend it."

"So, if we're right, this guy was killed the same day he delivered the package."

"That's my take on it."

"Mine too."

"Come on, let's go fill Jamie in."

14

Jamie hung up the phone with a frown. Her nerves felt scraped raw. Had they found him? What was going on? Why hadn't they called?

Refocusing her churning thoughts was no easy task, but standing around stewing about something she couldn't change wasn't doing anyone any good.

Her hand still clutched her cell phone. She'd called her parents' house and gotten the answering machine — again.

After dropping her family concerns in Jamie's lap, Samantha had received a call requesting her computer expertise. She'd protested that she was on leave. The caller said something else and Sam had bolted from Jamie's office with a wave and a "we'll talk later."

With a forceful forefinger, Jamie punched in her parents' number one more time. And got the answering machine. Same story with their cell phone numbers and voice mail.

Rats.

Should she risk going over there? What if *he* was watching and followed her?

She called Samantha's phone.

"What?"

"Have you managed to get in touch with Mom or Dad?"

"Not yet. I'll call you in a little while. I've got a missing kid."

That was the hurry. And why Sam was willing to come off her leave and go back to work. Kids did it to her every time.

Just like they did Jamie.

The girl on the slab, Lisa, was no more than a kid. She may have been nineteen years old, but in Jamie's eyes, that was still a baby.

She returned to Lisa's side and pulled back the sheet. Now that she'd thawed out, the putrefaction process had sped up to the point that the odor was getting offensive. She needed to be placed in the freezer until cremation could be done.

Slowly, Jamie's mind gnawed on the facts as she stared down at the girl whose life had been cut short. Why had she been placed in an environment where she would be found?

"Why that building? Why a dry ice freezer? And not buried like the rest of them. Why deviate from your pattern?" she wondered aloud. She looked at the x-rays still posted on the wall. Broken bones. Healed bones. Branded on the upper left shoulder.

No doubt about it. It was the Hero. Jamie's skin crawled just thinking of him by the only name she'd ever called him.

"Why a freezer full of dry ice instead of a hole in the ground where she might go undiscovered for years? What were you thinking? What was the point? Did you expect her to be found long before now? Did you even care if she was found at all? Or," Jamie drew in a deep breath, "were you hoping she would be found long before now?"

Was she *talking* to *him?*

Maybe.

She wanted to understand. Almost as much as she wanted to bury her head under a pillow and believe that this nightmare would just go away.

But she couldn't do that.

Her phone rang making her jump. Heart pounding out a rhythm to match her ring tone, she snatched up the phone. "Hello?"

"Simone and Karen," Mark said.

"It's the same guy," she whispered.

"What?"

"Nothing. Thanks, Mark, I'll get your

tickets to you soon." She hung up without waiting for his response, her mind already clicking through what she knew and what she needed to do.

Staring down at Lisa, she could well imagine the girl's terror during the weeks leading up to her death. Caused by the man who called himself "the Hero." A sociopath still out there walking the streets, watching her . . .

A disturbing, terrifying thought occurred. "You wanted *me* to see her, didn't you? You knew once I heard about the branding, I'd have to see her for myself." Her stomach turned in on itself as her voice dropped to a mere whisper that echoed in the silent room, "How long have you been watching me?"

A whistle sounded down the hall and her nerves bunched, then relaxed. Then tightened once more. Dakota. With shaking hands, she pulled the sheet back up over Lisa and met him at the door. Still in full tactical gear, the FBI logo prominently displayed, he stepped inside. Grimaced. He didn't like the smell of dead bodies any more than she did.

Jamie moved back a bit to give him some space. Sweat had plastered his hair to his head. His handsome face had a few new

185

grooves in it. And she thought he was the best thing she'd seen all day.

She swallowed hard. "Did you get him?"

"It wasn't him."

A frown pulled her lips downward. "What? How do you know?"

As he explained what had transpired at Evan Johannes's house, Jamie felt a coldness seep into her soul. "Is George still working on the profile of this guy?"

"He is. In fact, I talked to him on the way over here. He's going back over all the facts that we have."

"The . . . um . . . *hero* . . . obviously has access to a lot of medical equipment if he's x-raying broken bones and casting them."

"I know, we're working on that one."

"I can't believe I didn't remember . . ."

"You were under the influence of a lot of drugs, I believe."

"Yes, for part of the time. And other times, I was horrifyingly lucid." She turned away and gestured to Lisa's covered body. "We're waiting on a tox screen to come back on her."

"I'm willing to bet she's got some narcotics in her."

Jamie nodded. She wouldn't be surprised. "If they show up after all this time."

"Anything on the handcuffs we pulled

186

from the grave with the first body?"

A delicate tremor went through her at the mention of the handcuffs. "Not much. A few fibers that matched the shirt she had on."

"What about the second body we found? The one you named Bianca?"

"They found a set of cuffs with her too." And in spite of her revulsion, she'd examined every millimeter of them. Now thanks to Mark, she had a name. "Karen. He engraved the cuffs with their names."

"Oh man." He closed his eyes for a brief moment. "I thought her position in the grave looked similar to the first girl."

Jamie nodded. "There's no doubt in my mind that the same guy killed all four girls. I went over both sets of cuffs and there was nothing but dirt and fibers from their clothing. However, Mark found their names engraved almost microscopically on the cuffs."

"Sick creep, isn't he? So, nothing but fibers or dirt. He washed their clothing and dressed them after he killed them."

"That's what I think."

"As far as the handcuffs are concerned, they're the kind you can purchase online from a ton of dealers. They're Smith & Wesson M&P lever lock cuffs. Virtually impossible to trace. If you had about a hundred people contacting every online seller and every store that sells handcuffs around here . . ." He rubbed his eyes. "All right, here's what I'm going to do. I'm going to put out a lead to every field office in the country requesting information on anyone who's bought multiple pairs of handcuffs in a single purchase." Shrugged. "Might be a waste of time, but . . ."

A puff of air escaped her lips as did a curl from the loose ponytail she'd hurriedly stuffed in a scrunchy earlier. Absently, she pinned it back, then shoved her hands in the pocket of her jeans. Her fingers closed over the small metal item she always kept with her and immediately comfort flooded her.

"What's wrong, Jamie?"

"What?" She blinked. "Oh, nothing, just thinking. I didn't ask Mark what kind of handcuffs they were, but I'd be willing to bet they're the same." She picked up the phone and dialed.

"Mark here."

"What kind of cuffs were they?"

"Uh . . . hold on a second." The line went dead for a minute, then shuffling, a scraping sound, then, "Smith & Wesson M&P lever lock cuffs."

She thanked him and hung up. Looked at Dakota. "The same."

"I'm going to call Jazz and have her ID all online dealers of those cuffs. I should have the results pretty fast. Then I guess we can start contacting them to see if any of them have done business with someone in South Carolina."

A knock on the door brought her head around. Samantha stood there, looking pale and worn out.

Jamie blinked. "Sam?"

"Do you have a few minutes?"

"Sure."

Dakota gave a small salute to the two ladies and exited the room. "I'll catch up with you later."

"Right." Jamie turned to her sister. "What is it? Bad case?"

"The worst."

"I'm sorry."

"A fourteen-year-old kid met up with his online predator. We found him locked in the guy's basement, strangled."

Nausea swirled in her gut and tears found their way to the surface. "Why?" she whispered. "When will the evil end?"

Samantha wrapped her arms around Jamie's shoulders. "When Jesus decides it's time."

"Some days I wish he'd hurry up."

"In his time, sis, in his time."

"I know." Jamie pulled away from the comfort and said, "All right, what else is going on?"

Sam raised a brow, but didn't bother to refute the question. "Can you get away for a couple of hours?"

Jamie looked at the bodies on the table. "Sure. There's not much more I can do here. I'm trying to identify the other girl, but I'm not having much luck. I know her first name is Karen, but that's it. I gave her to Jazz and she's running her through the system. I didn't have a matchup here with the missing girls already pulled. Where do you want to go?"

"To see Mom and Dad."

"You're still not getting any answer when you call?"

"Nope."

"And you want to go talk with them."

"This has gone on long enough. It's time to nail them down and get to the bottom of it. I'm worried."

Jamie blew out a sigh. "I know, I have been too, ever since you brought it to my attention, but I was scared to go over there because of . . ."

"The fact that you might have a stalker,"

Samantha finished for her.

"Yeah."

Samantha hesitated, chewing her lip as she studied Jamie.

"What?" Jamie demanded.

"I hate to tell you this, but chances are, if he's been watching you for a while — and we think he has been — then he already knows where Mom and Dad live."

That familiar sick feeling she got when things spiraled out of control consumed her. "Great."

"That's what's got me a little concerned. They're acting weird and . . ."

Jamie wasn't slow. "And you think he may have contacted them and they're scared. But surely they would have said something."

"Not if he threatened to kill you . . . or me . . . if they continued contact with us."

Jamie slapped a hand on her hip. "But that's crazy! Why would he do that if he's after me?"

"To cut you off from family. To isolate you."

"Has he contacted you?"

"No, I'd tell you if he had. But it could be he's just getting started."

"I just can't see our parents keeping quiet about something like that. Especially Mom. She would have told me or called me regardless of what he may have threatened."

"What if he sent them something?"

"Sent them . . . oh. You mean like the picture he sent me?"

"Right."

Jamie grabbed two water bottles from the fridge. She handed one to Sam. "All right, let's go."

"The guys are meeting us there as soon as they get cleaned up."

"Fine."

It was all she could do to hold back the tremors that threatened to overtake her. Had this guy now included her parents in his circle of terror?

15

Dakota pulled to the curb of the Cash family home and watched a cruiser approach from the opposite direction. The officer waved and kept going. Ever since Sam had discussed her fears with him and Connor, they'd requested more security for the small neighborhood Jamie and Samantha had grown up in.

Until a threat was identified, the frequent drive-bys would have to suffice for now. Dakota had the officer verify that the Cashes were home. Now, he waited for Jamie and Samantha to show up.

Connor spoke from the passenger seat. "You think he's threatened them?"

"I don't know. It's certainly possible. He wouldn't be the first stalker that's gone after the victim's family."

Three minutes later, Jamie and Samantha swung in the drive.

Jamie got out first and Dakota stepped

out to greet her. He wanted to hug the tension from the shoulders she held so stiff. She was saying, "Maybe Samantha and I should go in and talk to them first. Just make sure we're not jumping to conclusions."

"Connor and I discussed it on the way over. You're going to have to tell them about what's been going on —"

"No!" she practically shouted as Samantha joined them next to the car. Connor got out and placed a hand on Jamie's shoulder. She jerked away and turned her back on them. Took a deep breath, then faced them once more. "No, not yet."

"Jamie, I think Dakota's right." Samantha shot him a worried look. "Even if this has nothing to do with who's after you right now, we still have to take into consideration that their safety may be in jeopardy."

The crushing despair that flashed across Jamie's pretty features distressed Dakota, and it was all he could do not to reach out and pull her into his arms. He hated being the bearer of bad news, and it seemed to be the only kind of news he'd been delivering lately.

"What's going on out here?"

The gravelly voice jolted them all to attention.

"Hi, Dad," Samantha called to the tall, thin man who looked like Ichabod's twin.

Not attractive by any means with his gangly arms and legs and hangdog look, the man with the hunched shoulders had obviously felt more than his fair share of heavy sorrow. The wave of compassion Dakota felt for him was mixed with amazement that the man had produced these two beautiful daughters.

"We need to talk."

Charles Cash shifted and Dakota would swear he saw fear flicker in the man's eyes. He looked at Connor to see if he'd caught the expression.

He had.

Charles looked like he wanted to flee. Instead, he cleared his throat and did his best to hide his trepidation. "Uh, this isn't a very good time. We're just on our way out to that exercise class at the gym."

"Is that why you have on your slippers?" Jamie asked.

Her dad flushed. "Well, I was just getting ready to change. You'll have to call before you come back."

Samantha nearly growled. "I've been calling. You're avoiding me and I want to know why."

This time the man's throat bobbed.

"What is it, Charles? Who's out there? Is it her again?"

"Her?" Samantha pushed past her dad to face her mother.

Jamie followed close behind. "Her who?"

The woman went pasty white and Dakota stepped forward to catch her should she keel over. She remained on her feet, placed a hand over her heart, and dragged in a ragged breath. "Oh, Samantha, Jamie. And the boys too. Oh my. Oh . . . well, come in and sit down, I suppose." She ran a blue-veined hand through stylishly-cut straight gray hair that had once been as blonde as Samantha's.

"Claire . . ."

"Hush, Charles."

The man hushed.

The foursome trooped into the den area where Samantha perched herself on the end of the sofa. Jamie took the loveseat, and Dakota made a beeline for the cushion next to her.

Connor quirked a brow at him. Dakota chose to ignore the gesture as he inhaled the scent of the woman next to him. He settled his arm on the back of the small couch and let Jamie's ponytail brush his bare arm.

Samantha started. "Were you expecting

someone else at the door, Mom?"

"Er . . . no. Just a contrary saleswoman who can't seem to take no for an answer."

"Okay, then what's going on?"

"What do you mean, darling?"

Samantha sputtered, "What do I . . . Mother!"

Interrupting, Jamie stood and paced to the other end of the den and back. "Has anyone contacted you about me?"

Dakota watched Charles's eyes flutter. "What? Contacted us about you? No, not at all, why?"

Dakota leaned forward. "Sir, we really need you to tell us if you've been threatened in any way."

"How could you . . . no, not threatened. No one's threatened us. Why?" He frowned, the loose skin around his mouth drawing lines even deeper into the whiskerless face.

His eyes met his wife's and Dakota knew something was going on — and before he left, he'd know what it was.

The Hero watched the house and wondered what was going on. When the foursome had talked on the porch with Jamie's parents, he'd been able to hear a little bit. He'd followed the girls from the lab and they'd never known he was behind them even though he was sure Samantha kept a keen eye in her rearview mirror.

However, stealth was the name of the game and he'd been able to stay close enough to figure out where they were going. Once he'd realized they were going to their parents' house, he'd fallen back and arrived only minutes after they pulled into the drive.

He'd driven past and circled back, avoiding the cruiser. Then parked in a driveway like he belonged. They never offered him more than a cursory glance when he'd pulled into the drive and pressed the button to open the garage door.

After watching the street for a few weeks in the early morning hours before work, he'd figured out most of the residents' routines. The one that interested him the most was the house across from Jamie's parents. A young couple with two small children, both parents worked while the kids went to daycare. They usually left around 7:30 in the morning and returned home around 5:30. After he'd picked the house and learned the routine of its occupants, he came back one morning at 7:25, parked down the street, then made his way to the house. No one noticed him.

After all, he'd learned how to be practically invisible at a young age. His survival depended upon his ability to go unnoticed. Drawing attention to himself was disastrous. Oh yes, he was very good at making sure no one thought anything about his presence.

First the husband left. Then the mother and the two children had piled into their van and she backed out of the garage. Just as she backed out, he rounded the side at a crouch and molded himself to the corner. She was so busy looking in her rearview mirror as she backed out, she never once looked back in the garage.

He knew she wouldn't.

He'd watched her do this every weekday for the past five weeks.

Then the garage door came down and he was able to get the information he needed from the box on the ceiling. A call to the garage door company netted him a remote device to be delivered overnight.

Two days later, he returned and pro-grammed the garage door remote. Just as he figured, the door leading from the garage to the house was unlocked. He made himself at home and befriended the family dog.

A week later, he'd done the same thing to Jamie's house. Only he had to be a little more crafty in gaining entrance to her garage as she was more vigilant and didn't always follow the same pattern. However, as luck would have it, he'd been successful on the first try. Jamie pushed the button to close the garage, stood there and watched it come down, but before it had completed its downward journey, she'd turned and started her walk to work.

And the Hero had placed his foot in the small opening just before the door was to meet the concrete. The door touched his foot and changed direction, the sensors sending the command that something was in the way.

So now he could blend in at either place to watch and learn.

And get to Jamie anytime he wanted.

From the garage window, he watched the house. Once they'd gone inside, he hadn't been able to hear anymore.

Interesting. This little visit with Jamie's parents could only mean one thing. They were warning them about him. Telling them that Jamie's hero had returned and to be on the lookout for him. He chuckled a bit at that. Like they'd know him if they saw him. They could watch for him all they wanted. It made no difference.

The Hero rubbed his chin and pondered the idea of getting to Jamie through her parents. It was definitely a thought. He'd met them once when he volunteered as one of the workers to search the area for Jamie the day after he'd taken her. He'd shaken their hands and offered his condolences. He even gave his handkerchief to Jamie's mother to wipe her tears.

He wondered if she still had it.

He thought of the other girls that he'd rescued and their families. He'd met every single one of them as he silently held back his contempt for them. If they'd loved their children like they professed to the cameras, they'd never have allowed them to be taken. They would have protected them. No, he didn't feel sorry for the families, he felt sorry for their children. Which is why he had to protect them. He was the only one they had.

He was their hero. "Stop the pain, you have to stop the pain." The little voice was back, demanding his attention, his co-operation.

Jamie had to understand that his job with her was unfinished. He couldn't rest until he'd fulfilled his destiny, completed what he'd been called to do as Jamie's hero.

He looked at the item on his front seat, then the handcuffs nestled on the floor-board, ready for Jamie. He'd even had her name engraved on them. They were a special pair, just for her.

But first, he had another gift for her, another message.

Leaving his car parked in the garage, he climbed out, grabbed the leash, and went to deliver the message.

Not only could Jamie see the silent communication going on between her parents, she could practically feel the tension emanating from both of them. She perched back on the edge of the love seat and leaned forward. "Okay, what everyone is dancing around is the fact that we think my attacker is back."

Twin indrawn breaths and one choked cry from her mother had Jamie standing once again. She moved to kneel in front of the woman. "I know it's a shock and I'm sorry I just blurted it out, but we're running short on time and this man isn't stopping. He's still out there killing, ruining lives, families, futures. If he's been in contact with you in any way, threatened you . . . please, we need to know."

Tears leaked down the soft wrinkled cheeks and Jamie raised a shaking hand to wipe them away. Her mother grasped her hand. "Oh Jamie, I had no idea. And no, no one has contacted us or threatened us in any way."

"Then why are you and Dad being so distant and hard to pin down?"

Her mother lifted wet eyes to stare at Jamie's father. Then she looked at the others in the room and sighed. "It's personal, honey. We're not ready to share that with you yet. Can you just accept that for now?"

Jamie exchanged a look with Samantha whose fierce frown said she wasn't having any part in accepting anything. Jamie stood. "Yes, we can. As long as you promise to take precautions and contact one of us immediately should anyone approach you or call you that makes you uncomfortable — or scared. All right?"

Another strange look passed between her parents and Jamie wanted to demand that they spill it right now. However, as long as her parents weren't in any danger, she would respect their privacy.

And Samantha would too, she communicated silently to her sister. Sam's jaw hardened, then her mouth opened. Jamie stared harder.

Sam snapped her mouth shut, but the look in her eyes said she wasn't finished — by a long shot.

An hour later, Jamie was convinced something weird was going on with her parents, but it had nothing to do with her stalker. Still, the more frequent patrols would continue and her mom and dad promised to be alert, vigilant about their surroundings and to call if they noticed anything out of the ordinary.

Jamie hugged her mother. "You promise you'll call if you notice anything at all that seems out of the ordinary."

"I . . . I . . ." She looked at her husband, then sighed. "Yes, if I think I need to call, I promise, I will."

"Okay."

She stepped out onto the porch and headed for Samantha's car, listening to her sister and the guys saying their good-byes. She wanted to get back to the lab and see if there was anything else she could do to identify the remaining set of bones still on her table. Facial reconstruction was a last resort, but one she'd do if it became necessary.

She stopped and turned to say something to Samantha, who walked toward her, back rigid, jaw thrust out. Her eyes blazed with questions. Her tightly clamped lips looked ready to spew them at the speed of light. Jamie closed her mouth and waited.

She didn't have to wait long.

"What do you think you were doing back

there? Why did you want me to keep quiet? Our parents are freaking out on us and you say nothing? I don't get it."

Connor and Dakota hung back, sensing the sisters needed this time.

Jamie sighed and reached out to grab her sister's hand. "Sam, you know I love you, but not everything is your business."

Samantha flinched and jerked away. "Well, thanks a lot."

"No, I didn't mean to hurt your feelings. I just meant that as long as whatever is bugging Mom and Dad isn't related to what's going on with me, then . . . I think we should respect the fact that they don't want to tell us."

Mutiny flashed for a brief moment, then dissolved slowly, like fog on an emerging sunny morning, as Jamie's words sank in. "Okay, I suppose you're right."

"I know you feel the need to . . . hover and protect, but sometimes . . . you just can't."

"She's right, hon." Connor stepped forward to wrap an arm around his wife's shoulders. "You know your parents. They'll spill it when they're ready."

"Okay, okay, I get it." She leaned into him briefly, then pulled away. "Come on, I'm starving."

"You're always starving." He kissed her forehead, and Jamie turned to head back to the car, her mind rehashing the visit with her parents. Opening the car door, she started to slide into the seat and stopped. Blinked. Shock twisted her insides as she stared at the offering lying innocently on her seat.

16

Samantha opened the driver's door, chattering about something that sounded like a swarm of bees buzzing in Jamie's ears.

"What's that?"

The sharp question jerked her, pulling her from the abyss of stunned immobility, and she sucked in a ragged breath. "Another gift from my *hero,*" she spat the words, the terror shooting through her warring with the rage.

"Guys! He's been here."

Samantha's shout pulled Dakota and Connor up short. Without bothering to shut the doors they'd just opened, they covered the twenty yards to Samantha's car in seconds.

Jamie felt Dakota crowd next to her to look over her shoulder. She didn't move. Instead, she took comfort in the fact that he was there.

"A rose?"

"And a note." She hated the shakiness she heard in her voice but couldn't seem to help it.

"Don't touch anything. I'll get a crime scene unit over here."

"Why bother?" she asked woodenly. "There won't be any prints."

"Probably not, but he could have left something else. And we need to get you inside out of sight."

"No."

"Come on, Jamie, you need to be careful. Standing out here in the middle of the street isn't careful."

"I don't care. I'm not going to be afraid anymore."

"That's fine," he agreed as he took her arm to lead her back in the house, "but please, don't be afraid anymore in the house, okay?"

Jamie pulled away from him and walked back the few steps to the car.

Samantha had already completed the call to the crime scene unit and had them on the way.

Her parents appeared on the porch and Samantha hurried up the steps to usher them back inside. Feeling exposed, yet not wanting to give the creep the satisfaction of making her run, Jamie huddled closer to

Dakota who looked surprised. Then he wrapped an arm around her shoulders. "I wish you'd go back inside. We'll see what the note says as soon as the crime scene unit processes it."

"Fine." She cleared her throat, ignoring his request. "Did you see the rose?"

"What do you mean? Sure, I saw it."

"No, I mean did you *see* it?"

He glanced back at the car then moved closer to get a better look at the red rose sitting on the seat. "It looks . . . weird, now that you mention it."

"He used to peel the petals off and . . ." She closed her eyes. Could she do this?

When she opened her eyes back up, his were narrowed on her. "What, Jamie?"

She pulled in a shuddering sigh and saw Connor waving the crime scene guys over. They immediately went to work on the rose and the car while Jamie trembled at the memories washing over her. "He used to stand over me and peel the petals from a rose and let them drop onto the table next to the bed. Then he'd pull the thorns off one by one and place them next to the petals."

He rubbed her shoulder. "Go on."

"Then he'd painstakingly glue the rose back together like it was some piece of art."

"What did he mean by it?"

"I'm sure he'll explain that in the note."

Dakota's fists clenched almost involuntarily as he reread the note left by Jamie's stalker. He refused to call the guy by the name of Hero. Psycho, crazy, possessed, yeah. Not hero.

Connor burst through the lab door. Samantha had gotten sick and he'd dropped her off at home. Now, he was ready to hear what the lab had come up with.

Jamie hovered. "Read it out loud, will you?"

"First of all, there aren't any prints, of course. Second, they found a carpet fiber. They're trying to trace that right now. Also, on the ground next to the car, they found some dog hair."

"That could have come from anyone walking their dog," Jamie snorted in disgust.

"I know, but we still want to cover all the bases."

Connor nodded in agreement. "What's the note say?"

Drawing in a deep breath, Dakota eyed Jamie, who's right eye twitched. Otherwise, her face held the tense, impatient look of someone standing in a long line with no end in sight. " 'Jamie, you're like this rose, fragile, delicate, beautiful. It's my duty to release you from the pain, to put you back together piece by piece until you're free. I will rescue you again. Until then, your Hero.' "

Jamie nearly gagged. "It doesn't even make any sense."

Dakota's jaw clenched and he knew his breathing had kicked up a notch. "Making sense isn't top priority for most psychos. I want this guy."

"We all do," Connor grunted.

"So, what do we have to do to get him?" Jamie murmured.

Placing his hands on her shoulders, Dakota said, "You just have to stay out of his reach. Which means, no more walking to work by yourself, no staying at home alone. Someone is with you at all times, okay?"

Indecision creased the skin of her forehead and she chewed her bottom lip. A ringing phone cut into whatever she had been thinking, and she pulled the device from the pocket of her lab coat. "Hello?"

Connor left the lab, saying he wanted to update George on this latest incident. For a minute, Dakota watched Jamie pace as she talked, then he returned his attention to the note one more time, forcing his gloved fingers not to crunch the paper into a tiny ball and toss it into the trash. Who was this guy? Why did he leave practically no physical evidence behind? How did he know they'd be out at Jamie's parents today, and how did he approach the car with no one noticing him?

Two hours of questioning neighbors had yielded nothing much. Most people had been at work. A stay-at-home mom with three small children had noticed a man walking his dog but said she didn't recognize him. However, she was relatively new in the neighborhood and didn't know everyone yet.

Still . . . a man walking his dog and they'd found dog hairs by the car. Coincidence? Possibly. They had her working with a sketch artist anyway.

Jamie finished her conversation and turned to him. "I've got to leave for a little while. I have an errand I need to run."

"Then I'm going with you."

For a moment he thought she might protest, but then her eyes fell to the letter he still held in his hand, and she snapped her mouth shut. "All right."

"Good. Where are we going?"

"That was Maya on the phone. She has a client she wants me to talk to."

"About what?"

"About what it takes to survive an attack."
He gulped. "Oh."

As Dakota started the car, Jamie patted his arm. "Sorry, I wasn't going for shock value. I'm not a counselor, but sometimes a victim needs to hear from another victim that she'll survive and get past all of the emotional issues that come with being . . . violated."

Her phone rang and she snatched it up, glad for the interruption. Caller ID said it was the lab calling. "Hello?"

"We've got the results on your tox screen for Lisa Dupre."

"And?"

"Tylox and Demerol. And even some morphine."

A cold fist knotted inside her stomach. She'd figured that would be the case. The morphine was a bit of a surprise, but the Tylox and Demerol fit the bill perfectly. "Ok, thanks."

She hung up and told Dakota. He kept his eyes straight ahead as he drove. "All right, so that's just one more piece of evidence against this guy."

"Yes."

"Any luck on figuring out who the other skeleton is?"

"No. I may have to resort to doing a facial

reconstruction on her. She's African American, and all of the missing persons reports that showed up were four Caucasian, one African American that I don't think fits, since his girl measures too short and is too young, and two Hispanics."

"Maybe we need to widen our search area."

"I thought about that but don't even know if that will help. What if she was a runaway or on vacation from somewhere?"

"Even so, it does seem like she would have turned up in the search. Surely someone reported her missing. Let me call Jazz and have her pull records from an extra fifty-mile radius."

Jamie nodded and Dakota got on the phone. She appreciated his help — and his presence — more than she could express. As much as she hated to give up the independence she'd fought so hard for, she couldn't deny she felt much more secure when he was around. On impulse she reached out and squeezed the hand that clutched the steering wheel.

Surprised, he stopped midsentence, then a warm light flared in his eyes as he returned to his conversation. Jamie felt an odd flutter in the pit of her stomach. That strange sensation she often felt in Dakota's presence and never could figure out what to do with it. Curious, she examined it as Dakota turned a corner. Then Maya's building came into view and that feeling turned to dread. Not that she didn't want to help the person who so desperately needed it. She just felt dread at having to dredge up the emotions associated with being raped and lay them out on the table.

But if it would help someone else . . .

Dakota parked and opened his door. She laid a restraining hand on his arm and said, "I need to pray first."

An uncomfortable look crossed his face, but he settled back into his seat and shut his door. "Okay."

"You don't have to say anything."

"I . . . all right."

Taking a deep breath, she closed her eyes. Silently, she prayed. *Lord, you've brought me here to help this young woman who's experienced a terrible trauma. I need you to give me the words, the right thing to say. I need your peace. I need to feel your presence and your unconditional love. And she needs to know that you're the only one who can fully heal her.*

As she prayed, she felt her breathing slow, her thumping heart calm, and her desire to fidget lessen. For several more moments, she just sat as she let God flood her with his presence. Finally she was ready.

She opened her eyes. "Okay. I can do this now."

Dakota stared at her, his blue eyes narrowed, a look she couldn't define shining from their depths.

"What?" she asked.

"What just happened?"

"I prayed."

"I know that. But something happened while you were praying. I watched it."

She frowned at him, not really understanding what he was asking. "I just asked God to cover me with his presence and love. Plus I asked for peace, to be calm, and have the right words to say."

"But you changed physically."

She raised a brow, intrigued. "I did?"

"Yes, it was like . . . something just . . . came over you. All the tension and anxiety that were coming off of you on the ride over here just . . . dissolved."

Jamie shrugged and grinned. "Cool."

He blinked. "Yeah. It was."

Hesitantly, she asked, "You want to talk about it later?"

A slow nod. "Yes, I think I do."

"Great." She squeezed his hand. "Now, I've got to get in there."

"Sure. Let's go."

Three hours later, Jamie felt like her neck might snap from the tension in her shoulders. Yet, she felt good. Relieved. She'd managed to pass on hope to a victim who'd been considering suicide. Jamie's card clutched in trembling fingers, the twenty-year-old college student promised to call if she needed to. Jamie felt sure she'd hear from the girl again. But eventually, she would heal. She'd pressed this point throughout the entire three hours. And she thought it hit home. Finally. And they'd prayed together for a long time, calling on God's healing and peace. The girl had God; she had hope.

Pulling out her cell phone, she punched in Samantha's number. Her sister answered, her voice sounding hoarse. "Did I wake you up?"

"No, I just upchucked everything I've eaten for the last two years."

"Ugh. I'm sorry. You think it's the flu?"

"I guess. I felt a little sick this morning, then after we left Mom and Dad's house, it got worse."

Sympathy for Sam flooded her. "Try to get some rest. Maybe you'll feel better if you can get some sleep."

"I don't have time for this," she grumbled.

"I want to stay with you tonight."

"No way. You need to get better. Plus, if you're contagious, I don't want it."

"Thanks for your concern."

Sam's sarcasm made Jamie chuckle. "Is Jenna there to take care of you?"

"She will be in about an hour. Connor's mom is here and is clucking like the mother hen she is. I didn't want to call Mom."

She didn't have to say anything else. "I understand. Call me later and let me know how you're feeling."

"I will. Who's with you right now?"

"No one. I had an errand to run and Dakota dropped me off. He said to call him when I was ready to leave." Jamie pushed through the double glass doors and stepped out into the sweltering heat — and smiled. "But I don't have to. He's sitting across the street waiting on me."

"Good. I still say he likes you."

There was that dip and flutter in her stomach once more. "I know. I like him too. Talk to you later."

"Bye."

Jamie crossed the street. Dakota got out of his car and hurried around to open the door for her. Smiling her thanks, she slid into the seat.

Once he was settled back into the driver's

seat, he asked, "How'd it go?"

"It went well. As well as can be expected anyway. I think she's going to be all right."

"You're amazing, you know that?"

She felt the flush creep up into her cheeks. "Me? I don't think so, but thanks."

"Not everyone would be willing to do what you just did."

"What's that?"

"Remember."

Swallowing hard, she nodded. "Yeah."

17

Thursday

Two days had passed without incident and nothing else had turned up in the search for the identity of the young girl she'd boxed up and labeled with a case number, keeping the skull out to work on. Why wasn't she in the system? Hadn't she been reported missing? When a person disappeared under suspicious circumstances and the family or friend reported it, the person's information went into an FBI database called NCIC, the National Crime Information Center.

Only Jamie hadn't gotten a hit on Karen. Odd.

And nothing had come back on the car. The dog hairs belonged to a short-haired brown dog. There were several in the neighborhood that fit the description.

The sketch artist had finished the portrait according to the neighbor's input, but no one in the neighborhood who had been questioned seemed to know who he was.

That's because he didn't belong there. The sketch seemed very generic to Jamie. Like it could fit anyone with that general description. She didn't hold out much hope of identifying the man who'd left the rose in her car if she had to rely on that sketch.

With a sigh, she placed the finishing touches on the skull that now had a face, her mind on the fact that she seemed to be waiting for the other shoe to drop. Reconstructing the skull kept her busy physically but left plenty of time for thinking — and imagining.

And praying.

Still, her nerves often bunched and danced under her skin. Looking over her shoulder had become second nature once more, and the slightest odd noise made her jump like a startled doe.

She didn't like living this way.

Fortunately, no new cases had come her way over the past few days and she'd been able to fully concentrate on the task in front of her. The girl had a face and a first name. Now she needed a family to claim her.

Taking the digital camera, Jamie snapped several photos from different angles. Then she changed out the wig, replacing the short afro-styled hair with a longer, smoother piece.

More pictures.

"Wow, that's incredible."

Jamie shrieked and dropped the camera. She whirled, heart pounding faster than a Thoroughbred in a full run. "George!"

"Oh, sorry." He held up his hands. "I'm so sorry. I didn't mean to startle you."

Annoyed, she tamped down her irritation, reminding herself she was much jumpier than usual. She couldn't blame him for her issues. "I'll survive." Bending down, she scooped up the camera. "Don't know if this will, though."

"Want me to take a look?"

"No, I have another one if I need it." She powered it back up and it seemed to be all right. "Can I help you?"

"I wanted to see if Dakota or Connor were here."

"No, they're out questioning Lisa Dupre's family about her last known location, who she was seeing at the time, et cetera."

"Would you be interested in going to dinner then? I have some more ideas about the sicko that's doing this to these girls."

Uneasiness reared. It was nothing personal against George, but she had no interest in being alone with him, not even in a crowded restaurant. She tried to picture doing it. Leaving the lab, walking down the hallway, getting on the elevator . . . nausea waved hello. She swallowed.

"I'm sorry, George, I appreciate the invitation, but I'm swamped right now."

His eyes flickered with something she couldn't define, then he shrugged. "Okay." He started to turn away, then swung back around. "She looks better, more natural with the longer hair."

"Huh?"

"The face. I watched you switch out the shorter hair for the longer. She looks like a long-haired girl."

"Really?" Jamie stepped back to study the girl. She was very pretty.

"Yeah."

"Okay." Jamie left the longer hair on her.

George shifted, turned to go once again, and turned back to Jamie once again. "I don't mean to be nosey, but just for my own clarification, are you and Dakota an item?"

Heat started at the base of her throat and started creeping north. "Um, no, you're not being nosey, I don't guess. I don't know that I would call us an item, but we're definitely . . . ah . . . getting to know each other."

"I see." Another shrug. "That's fine.

Maybe the three of us could do lunch one day then."

A relieved sigh rippled up, but she repressed it and nodded. "Sure, that'd be great."

George left and Jamie let the sigh escape. She had just aimed the camera to take another picture when Serena Hopkins gave a brief knock and entered the lab. "Hey, Jamie, how's it going?"

Jamie stepped back and gestured to the face. "What do you think?"

"Wow. Good job. Have you got the pictures ready?"

"Just about. That's what I'm doing now."

"When you finish, you want to grab some dinner? We haven't done that in a while."

"Uh . . . I'd better not."

Confusion flashed, but Serena just shrugged and said, "All right."

"I just turned George down because I was busy."

Realization dawned. "Ah. Got you. So, he's asked you out too?"

"Too?"

Serena nodded, amusement dancing in her dark eyes. "Yep."

Jamie let out a laugh. "Oh boy. When did he ask you out?"

"About a week ago."

Shaking her head, Jamie chuckled. The man was lonely and needed some friends. Or he was a player and asked out any female he came into contact with. Yet another reason to keep their lunches a group thing. "I'll keep that in mind. I'm not interested anyway."

"Didn't think you would be with Dakota around."

More flushing heat. Jamie wondered if she had any blood left below her neck. "What do you mean?"

"Oh come on. I've seen the way you guys look at each other."

Avoiding eye contact wasn't working. She looked at Serena and tried for a nonchalance she didn't feel. "The way we look at each other? What is this? A movie?"

"No, it's sweet."

"Go away."

A lilting laugh escaped Serena. "I can't, but I can change the subject." Serious now. "Show me the face."

Thirty minutes later, Serena left with the pictures that would appear on the news tonight and Jamie realized she was starving.

And she'd turned down two dinner invitations.

Great.

Picking up the phone, she called Saman-

225

tha. When her mother answered the call, Jamie nearly dropped the phone. "Hi, what are you doing there?" she blurted. "Is Sam worse?"

"Hello to you too, Jamie. No, Sam's much better. I just brought her some grilled chicken."

Ooh, her mother's grilled chicken. "Is there enough for me?"

"Of course, and anyone else you'd like to invite."

Her mother was referring to Dakota. The woman liked him an awful lot, and Jamie knew she had hopes for the two of them. Thankfully, though, she kept her thoughts to herself when it came to that relationship. A fact that Jamie greatly appreciated. She supposed that was one reason she refrained from pushing her mom and dad about what was going on with them. While she was concerned, she had a great respect for other people's privacy. Not that Samantha didn't, but . . .

With a start, she realized she didn't have a ride to her mother's house. In the process of dialing Dakota's number, her phone rang. "Hello?"

"It's me."

"Hey, Sam."

"Is Dakota there with you?"

"No, I was just thinking I'd have to either walk home to get my car or call one of the guys to come get me."

Sam's voice turned sharp. "Don't you dare walk home. I'll be there to get you in ten minutes."

"But you're sick."

"I'm better. Hang tight."

"I . . ." She huffed out a sigh. "Okay. I'll be looking for you."

"See you in a few."

Jamie hung up the phone and set it on the table near the sink in case one of the guys called. She began to straighten the lab, putting away her tools and cleaning up around her work area. She glanced at the clock.

7:00.

Not terribly late, but where were the guys and why hadn't they called?

All at once, the quiet of the place echoed in her ears. She walked to the door of the lab and looked down the hallway. Not a soul in sight.

Weird.

Most of the time, the place was a beehive of activity, slowing down around this time of day, yet still with a few people milling about. Even on the weekends, *someone* was here.

She stepped through the door and headed

toward Serena's office, which was just next door. Jamie knocked and got no answer. Probably went on to supper.

Doing a one-eighty, Jamie made her way back toward the opposite end of the hall and peered through the glass. One empty office after another.

What in the world?

She stepped into the break room.

And saw the notice on the bulletin board.

" 'Retirement party for Harrison Cooper. 6:30–8:00 at Flannigan's,' " she read aloud. She'd forgotten about it. No surprise there. With all the turmoil she'd been experiencing, she'd be shocked if she could remember her way home.

So, was she all alone in the building? Her stomach tightened at the thought. Surely not.

Why hadn't anyone stopped by to ask if she was going? She hadn't planned on it, but she would have left before now to avoid the very situation she now found herself in.

Making her way back down the hall to her office, she decided to get her stuff together and go down to the lobby where Stewart, one of the morgue's security guards, would be sitting. She could wait for Samantha in the comfort of one of the lobby chairs under the watchful eye of Stewart.

Her blue tennis shoes made no sound on the tiled floor. A door slammed shut behind her and she whirled. When no one appeared, she swallowed hard, spun on her heel, and picked up her pace. Her pulse followed suit.

Quick glances over her shoulder told her no one was there, but the uneasiness flowing through her made her heart pound. Her palms grew slick and she rubbed them against her pants.

Behind her, rubber soles squeaked against the floor.

"Who's there?" she called. "Hello?"

No answer.

Someone was back there. Why wouldn't that person answer her?

"I know you're there. Who is it? If this is a joke, it's not funny."

Silence again greeted her call.

Then a low laugh accosted her ears, mocking her, scraping her nerves and making them twitch as though they knew what was in store for them. Her wrists actually ached as though they once again were trapped in the confines of the handcuffs.

And the dam of terror broke, flooding her veins with it, filling her very being with the horrifying memories. Gasping, trembling, she raced to her office on legs that barely supported her. She slapped the door open, then slammed it shut, clicking the lock into place in one jerky movement.

She rested her back against the glass, then moved looking for a place to hide. A phone. She needed to call someone. Her blood thundered in her ears, deafening her to any sound except the sound of her shuddering whimpers.

Oh God, do something. Please, please, please, I'm begging you.

Did she really believe *he* was out there? Her mind said no. Her fear said yes.

Through the glass windows, she watched from behind her desk and waited. Any minute she expected the door to burst open or glass to go flying. No window would keep him from his prey. A thought occurred to her.

Last time he'd taken her by surprise.

This time she knew he was there.

Breaths coming in puffs, Jamie desperately gathered some of her wits together and looked around for a weapon. A pen, a stapler . . . a pair of scissors. She snatched them up. They'd have to do.

The pounding on the door wrenched a scream from her throat. Whirling, she raised the scissors and stopped.

Samantha.

Staring at her in wide-eyed concern, her eyes flitting from the scissors to Jamie's face. "What are you doing? Jamie, open the door."

Wilting against her desk, Jamie dropped the scissors. She honestly didn't know if she had the strength to cross the floor to the door.

"Jamie, come on." Samantha rattled the knob once again.

With trembling legs, she pushed her body from the desk and forced her limbs to walk to the door. Her fingers shook so bad, she almost couldn't grasp the lock to turn it.

Finally, the door flew open and she was in Samantha's arms. Dakota and Connor came up behind her.

"What is it, Jamie, what scared you?"

"He was here."

"What?" Dakota and Connor exchanged a look, then bolted back down the hall, weapons appearing in their hands as though by magic.

It was all Dakota could do to push down the rage he felt at the man responsible for Jamie's continued fear. Using hand signals for communication, Connor noted he'd cover the room to his right.

Dakota held his weapon ready for backup

should Connor need it. He didn't.

All the way to the end of the hall, they searched every possible hiding place.

Finally, they came to the last office on the right. George's office. Dakota raised his knuckles and rapped twice.

Nothing.

But the door swung open.

Stepping inside, he kept his back to the wall. Connor mimicked his moves on the opposite side. A door to the left was cracked. A bathroom?

Making his way over, senses tuned to every nuance in the room, he placed a hand on the door and looked at Connor.

A nod. He was ready.

Dakota shoved the door open. "Freeze! FBI!"

Connor swung around, his weapon trained on the empty room.

Adrenaline pumping, Dakota took in the absence of any threat and lowered his gun. He turned back toward the door and saw movement. He snapped the weapon back up, rushed the door, and yelled, "Freeze!"

George froze, hands held above his head. His throat worked and his eyes looked too big for his face. "Can I help you?"

Connor and Dakota lowered their guns simultaneously. "Did you see anyone out there in the hall?"

"No, no one. I think everyone's at the retirement party."

Dakota motioned to George's hands. "You can put them down now."

George dropped them to his sides. "Is there a problem?"

"Unfortunately, I think our problem escaped."

18

Samantha ushered Jamie back into her office and locked the door behind them. "Tell me what happened." Grabbing a tissue from the box on the desk, she handed one to Jamie.

Jamie stared at it as though she didn't know what to do with it. Samantha took it back and gently mopped up her face.

Staring up at Samantha's concerned blue eyes, Jamie said, "I didn't know I was crying."

"Enough tears to fill a bucket."

"Sorry." She began to calm down, her wracking shudders dissolving into the occasional tremble. Then the anger began bubbling beneath the surface, churning ominously like a tsunami getting ready to make its presence known.

"Where is he? Where did you see him?"

"I didn't see him. I heard him."

"What did he say?"

"Nothing."

A frown creased Jamie's forehead. "Then . . ."

"He laughed."

"Lau—" Samantha cut off the word and waited.

Jamie pulled in a lung full of air and blew it out through pursed lips. "I heard someone behind me. When I turned around, no one was there. I called out and no one would say anything. Then I heard that . . . laugh. That horrible, mocking laughter that haunts my sleep and invades my dreams . . ."

Clamping her lips together, she clung to the anger, the thought of what she'd do if she came face-to-face with the monster again.

The knock on the door made them both jump. Reflexes on high alert, Samantha's hand went for her gun, then relaxed when she saw it was just Dakota. She rose to let him in. Connor followed. "Well?"

Dakota crossed over to Jamie and took her hands in his. Tears filled her eyes again and she looked away, feeling weak — and ashamed.

He settled his hands lightly on her shoulders as though asking permission to touch her. She leaned in. That was all he needed.

He pulled her close and she snuggled up

next to him, hearing his heart thumping in her ear. His voice rumbled up from his chest. "We didn't see anyone, Jamie."

"I don't care if you saw him or not. He was here."

"I believe you."

Warmth flooded her and she pulled back to look up at him. "Do you really?"

His eyes bored into hers with the powerful effect of a laser. "Yeah, I really do."

"So do we," Connor offered, eyeing the two of them with hope. Jamie knew Connor thought of her as the little sister he never had and wanted her to find happiness in marriage.

She walked back over to her desk and pulled another tissue from the box. "I feel like I'm going crazy. Why is he doing this to me? Why doesn't he just grab me and get it over with? Why does he enjoy this mental torture so much? What is the deal with that?"

The questions tumbled from her lips, one after the other, like dominoes.

Samantha squeezed her hand and Connor said, "I don't know, but what do you say we get the tapes from security and see who was in the building."

Jamie shuddered. "You won't see him.

Somehow he knows how to avoid the cameras."

"Maybe, but we have to try." Dakota rubbed her arm, then said, "If we see who else was up here, we can ask if they saw anything — or anyone who didn't belong. Plus I want to talk to the security guard and see if he noticed anyone in the building who shouldn't have been here."

Connor nodded. "I'll go handle that." He left and Samantha perched on the stool looking like she still didn't feel all that great.

Dakota said, "I'm sorry we weren't here. We got caught up in doing some interviews and handling some phone calls. The girl you finished doing the facial reconstruction on went out over the news and we got several leads to follow up on." He blew out a sigh. He flicked a glance at Sam, who had her eyes closed. "I didn't realize Samantha went home sick. I should have made sure someone was with you. I called and you didn't answer your phone."

"I never heard it ring. Sorry." She frowned and reached into her pocket. It wasn't there. "Oh, I left it by the sink in the lab."

Retracing her steps with Dakota next to her, she walked from her office, down the hall a bit, and into the lab. Zeroing in on the sink, she headed for it, then stopped, confusion filling her. "That's odd. I know I left it here because I was cleaning up and thought you might call."

"You didn't put it back in your pocket when you went looking for other people?"

Thinking, she tilted her head and stared at the ceiling. "No, because when I realized I was basically alone in the building," she knew she flushed, but admitted, "it kind of freaked me out."

"Don't be embarrassed. It can be unnerving."

She appreciated his efforts to make her feel better. Too bad it didn't work. "Anyway, I know I didn't get it. I left it right there." Confusion, worry . . . and fear tangoed up her spine.

"All right, is there any way someone could have slipped in the lab unnoticed?"

"No, I would have been able to see . . . wait a minute." She looked at Dakota. "I stepped into the break room."

"For how long?"

"I don't know. Two, maybe three minutes? I read the announcement, then stood there for a bit before coming back into the hall. Then I heard something. I called out and no one answered." She shuddered. "I was scared and ran to my office to lock the door. Then Samantha showed up."

"But you heard him laugh."

"Yes."

"So, there was definitely someone else in the hall."

"Yes!"

"Then we need to check the cameras."

Twenty minutes later, Samantha pleaded a headache and left. The rest of them gathered in the video room. Stewart Hodges, the security guard on duty, did the honors of pulling up the tapes requested.

Connor pointed, "Run it back here."

Stewart complied.

Dakota shifted so Jamie could see a little better. She appreciated his belief in her and the fact that he didn't shrug off her fears — or belittle her for them.

"All right. Right there."

"That's Melissa Ferris," Jamie offered. "She just came out of the break room."

"And headed down the hall toward the elevator."

"There's George. What's he doing?"

"Heading toward the lab."

"Now he's stopping to talk to Melissa." George nodded at something the woman said, then walked on toward Jamie's office. Finding it empty, he moved toward the lab, looked in, shrugged, turned and left.

Jamie spoke again. "Wait a minute, here

comes Lila." Lila stopped and mimicked George's motions. Pause at the door. Look in. Leave.

"Where were you, Jamie?" Dakota asked.

"I don't know."

Another minute passed.

"There you are. Coffee cup in hand."

"I was in the break room. I'd forgotten all about that. That was before I realized everyone was gone. And I didn't even notice the flyer on the wall at that point."

"Okay, so you went in the break room twice. Once to get a cup of coffee and once to see if anyone was in there."

Stewart rolled the tape forward a bit.

Dakota pointed this time. "All right, here is everyone leaving." Workers filtered out one by one, sometimes in groups of two and three.

"Going to the party."

A few minutes later, Jamie's head appeared in the lab doorway. Then she was walking down the hall, checking the offices. She disappeared into the break room once again.

Back out.

Paused and turned to look behind her, her back to the camera. "That's when I heard a door shut." She watched her fingers curl into fists by her thighs. "I called out but no one answered."

In the next clip, she bolted for her office and disappeared inside.

"Okay, let's see if anyone appears."

But there was nothing until Samantha got off the elevator and headed toward Jamie's office.

Jamie wanted to scream. Instead, she held her cool and asked, "So, where did my cell phone go?"

A knock on the door interrupted their study of the images on the screen. Stewart opened the door and George stepped in. He looked at Dakota, "You called me?"

"Yeah, like I told you earlier, we think Jamie's stalker was here and we want your input."

"Sure, fill me in."

They did, then Dakota asked, "Is there a back way into the lab?"

Jamie blinked. "Yes. The emergency door."

Dakota and Connor exchanged a look, then Dakota said, "Thanks, Stewart. We're not getting anything off of this. Can you pull the other videos from the camera that's aimed on the lab's emergency door? Same time frame."

"Sure thing. That door leads to a staircase. Then the stairs lead down to the exit outside. I can check that camera too."

A few more clicks and the back door of the lab and the top three steps leading up to it appeared on the small black-and-white screen. Minutes passed, then the screen went blank. Stewart spoke. "Yeah, that's the one that I had trouble with. I went to check it, but couldn't find anything wrong with the camera. By the time I got back to the desk, the picture was back up." He shrugged. "I logged it in my report, but just figured it was a little blip in the system."

"A little blip called Jamie's stalker, I'll bet. Somehow he covered up the camera and entered the lab through the back door."

Connor agreed. "And found her gone."

"But saw her cell phone sitting there."

"So he took it on the spur of the moment."

"Opportunity."

"He's smart, but also impulsive."

"Which means we might actually get lucky and he'll *slip* up before any more bodies start *turning* up."

George shrugged when they looked at him for his opinion. "It's possible. Yes, I agree he acted impulsively, but now he'll think through his actions before he does anything with it, *assuming* he's the one that took it. If so, he'll disable it so you can't track it. Then again, he may do nothing with it, he may have just wanted something that belonged to Jamie." He spread his hands. "And this is all going on the assumption that he's the one who was in the building and that he has the phone."

"Right."

Jamie blew out a sigh, a headache settling behind her eyes. "Okay, this is enough. Connor needs to get home to Samantha and I need a break."

George looked at his watch. "I've got a late meeting, but give me a call if you need anything else. I want to get this guy as bad as you do."

Not likely, Jamie thought, but kept that to herself. She felt snippy and in a bad mood. George didn't deserve to be her scapegoat. Her frustration at the lack of progress on finding the man responsible for the deaths of possibly sixteen young women wasn't improving her disposition either.

Dakota put his arm around her shoulders. "All right. I'll take you home. We've got a car on your house, the front, and one watching the back where the woods are. You should be safe."

Jamie pulled in a deep breath. "Fine. I need some sleep."

Dakota followed her out. He said, "I'll drive. Hop in."

Two minutes later she was in her driveway. Lights burned all around her house. Dakota stepped out of the car and walked her to the front door. "I don't want you to be alone tonight, Jamie. I promised Sam and Connor I'd make sure you were safe."

She opened the door to her house and stepped in. But this time she noticed something that depressed her. Always before, the minute she entered her home, the stress seemed to roll from her shoulders.

Tonight it didn't.

Because *he'd* invaded her security, her haven, her escape.

Again, she felt the familiar fear mixed with anger surface. She shoved it down. Not tonight.

"Jamie?"

"What?" She blinked. "Oh sorry. I was just thinking."

"About what?"

"About security and how truly fragile it is."

"Agreed."

She set her keys on the foyer table and walked into the kitchen. "That's why we can't rely on humans or security systems or any other thing of this world to be our security."

"Excuse me?" He sounded confused and

she shot him a look. He lifted a brow. "Oh, you're talking about God again."

"Um-hm." Grabbing a bottle of water from the fridge, she looked at him. "Want one?"

"No thanks."

She cocked her head to the side and pinned him with a look. "We never did finish our conversation the last time we talked about God."

"I know. I changed the subject."

Surprised, it was her turn for the eyebrows to shoot north. "Yes, as a matter of fact, you did."

"I've thought a lot about what you said, though."

She wandered into the den area and sat on the couch. Dakota followed and sat beside her. That threw her for a moment, made her edgy.

He must have noticed, because he stood as though to move across the room.

She caught his hand. "No, sit with me."

Dakota sat. She kept his hand clasped within hers, and he thought his heart might very well stop from the sheer joy of having her finally touch him voluntarily.

She was making an effort to overcome her fears, he realized. All that she'd already come through, accomplished in the last twelve years, she was still fighting, still reaching out. This time to him.

He swallowed hard and knew that if he didn't want to have to eat his words, he was going to have to reciprocate. Settling back against the couch he looked beyond her and stilled. "Is that your latest painting?"

She followed his eyes to the sunroom. Her latest project finished in the middle of a sleepless night sat drying, the oil glistening in the lamplight.

"Yes." She shot him a look. "A little different than the one you 'helped' me with." She wiggled her fingers around the word.

An empty beach in the middle of a thunderstorm. Waves pounded the shoreline, a lone figure stood staring out over the water, her hair whipping in the wind, arms upraised.

"What is the person doing?"

"Marveling at God's amazing power even in the midst of the worst storm you could ever imagine."

"Does that parallel with your life?"

"Absolutely." She cleared her throat. "Now, tell me about your childhood."

Ouch. Aw man, anything but that. He'd rather talk about her storms than acknowledge his tumultuous upbringing.

Ignoring his initial response, he dug deep. He was in love with this woman for all the right reasons. She'd already shared quite a bit of her ugly past, he could do no less — not if he wanted things to go where he was pretty sure he wanted them to go. A white dress and a tux flashed to mind.

"All right. My dad was a cop and so was my grandfather."

"Is that why you became one?"

He rubbed his chin. "Oh, part of it, I suppose, but I've always been fascinated by law enforcement. Of the good guys defeating the bad guys. All of that."

She nodded.

He brushed nonexistent lint from his pants and took a deep breath. "Anyway, my . . . uh . . . dad had some anger issues. I guess the job just got to him. He started drinking shortly after a really bad case had gone wrong. I was about twelve at the time and remember seeing it on the news. There'd been a hostage situation and a shoot-out. My dad was a part of it. Somehow in the crossfire a pregnant woman and her two-year-old daughter were killed. Internal Affairs investigated and said the bullets came from his gun. He was never the same after that."

Jamie winced but didn't move from his

side. Her fingers clutched his tighter.

"The drinking got worse and my mom begged him to get help. But he wouldn't. And the more he drank, the meaner he got."

"I'm so sorry."

"I am too. He started coming home drunk every night after cruising the bars with his buddies. Then the physical abuse started. At first it was only when I wasn't around. My mom would have bruises and broken bones after I'd been gone for a while, and she always had some kind of story about why. Then he lost his job. Was fired from the force."

"Oh no."

"That's when things got really bad. He started in on me. I think that was the final straw. I think it was either the fourth or fifth beating that landed me in the hospital with a concussion. My mother lost it."

"Oh Dakota, I'm so sorry. I can't imagine . . ."

"One night she waited for him to get home, then bashed him over the head with his prize guitar. She caught him by surprise and beat him senseless. After he passed out, she grabbed the two suitcases she'd packed — and me — and we left."

The compassion shining in her eyes nearly undid him. Swallowing hard, he took a mo-

248

ment to get it together.

She asked, "Where did you go?"

"We wandered around from relative to relative for a couple of years, then we went back home."

"What happened?"

"We got back and found the place deserted. From all appearances, he left not too long after we did. I haven't heard from him since."

"Where's your mother now?"

"Living in Texas with her sister."

"Is your father why you don't believe in God?"

"Oh, I believe in God, I just don't know that I believe all that stuff about Jesus loving us so much that he was willing to die for a bunch of sinners."

"You've never had anyone in your life you'd be willing to die for?"

Her question punched him in the gut. Stunned, he just stared at her.

And he knew for certain he'd die for her.

The realization threw him, knocked his world from its axis and gave him something to process — later. Clearing his throat, he said, "Maybe."

For a long minute, she just sat there and stared at him. Then slowly she wrapped her arms around his neck. His hands came up to settle at her waist and he kissed her forehead. Then he buried his face against her shoulder.

For several moments they just sat there, then Jamie said, "Thank you for telling me."

"It's not a pretty story."

"No, it's not. But ugly stories don't scare me much anymore." She cocked a half smile at him.

"I don't like reliving it. Thanks for listening."

"Anytime." She pulled back from his embrace and stood. His arms ached with emptiness, but he let her go, humbled by what she'd just done.

He didn't want to make a big deal out of it, but it was . . . at least to him. No one in his life had ever done such a selfless act — for him. Not even his mother. She'd checked out on him shortly after their return home to find his father gone. Checked out mentally if not physically. He still talked to her occasionally, but mostly focused on his work . . . and Jamie.

"Here."

He blinked. Jamie had left the room and gotten him a soda.

His favorite. She kept these in her fridge? For him? His love for this woman expanded.

"Thank you." He took the proffered can

and popped the top. The carbonated liquid burned a path down his throat and he sighed. "I needed that."

She smiled. "I thought you might."

"It's getting late. Do I grab the couch or do you want to head to your parents?"

Her smile turned upside down. "I don't want to go to my parents. I'm worried if I stay there, whoever this guy is won't care. I'm afraid that he won't hesitate to go through them to get to me."

"I understand that. The couch it is then."

"Oh Dakota, you don't have to do that."

He stood and grazed a finger down her cheek. "I know I don't, I want to."

He saw her swallow. "Thank you."

"Go get some sleep."

A smile trembled on her lips. "All right. I have a clean toothbrush in the guest bathroom."

"You mean Samantha's bathroom?"

She gave a short laugh. "That'd be the one."

"I'll find it."

She disappeared down the hall.

His phone buzzed and he pulled it from his pocket, his emotions in a freefall. Then he saw that it was Connor.

"Hey, what's up?"

"Are you still with Jamie?"

"Yeah."

"I'm on my way over. One thing we've kind of swept under the rug is how this guy got in Jamie's house. It's been bothering me. I know we went over her house when it happened, but I'm just thinking we missed something. Plus, Sam wants me to see if I could talk Jamie into coming home with me."

"Well, come on then. I was going to sleep on her couch tonight. She didn't want to go to her parents' house."

"Worried he'd follow her there?"

"You got it in one."

"All right. I'll be there in about ten minutes. Let's see if we can figure this out."

"I'll let you in."

The Hero watched Connor's car pull into Jamie's drive. It looked like she was going to have a lot of company tonight. And that was fine. It would give him time to move on to the next phase of his plan. Make his presence even more personal. And begin to remove those who might be barriers to accomplishing his goals.

He backed out of the driveway where he'd parked. Security was pretty tight around her house and he'd had to be even more careful about concealing himself. But it seemed luck was on his side. He'd learned the routine of the cruisers that drove past Jamie's house, and as far as the police were concerned, his car belonged in the neighborhood now.

Turning left out of the neighborhood, he wondered if his luck would hold. Connor was at Jamie's, as was Dakota. Opening the glove compartment, he looked at his weapon of choice. The knife gleamed in the dim light.

He shut the box.

"Stop the pain, you have to," the voice whispered.

"I am," he said aloud. "I am. Now shut up."

The voice fell silent.

He turned right, then another left.

And pulled across the street from Connor and Samantha's house.

19

Dakota opened the door and Connor stepped in, relief at the air conditioner's coolness evident on his features. "It's too hot to think."

"I know, but we're going to have to force ourselves."

"Right."

"So this guy gaining entrance to the house has been bothering you?"

Connor went into the kitchen and came back with a water bottle in his hand. "Yeah, it is."

"Any thoughts on how he got past her security system?"

"Not really. Short of getting her code, I don't see how it can be done."

"We checked the wires, nothing was cut, her phone was working fine." He spread his hands and shrugged.

"I know. And all the windows are wired."

"Then he had to have the code."

"All right, let's go with that thought for a minute. How'd he get it?"

"He watched her punch it in?"

"But the panel is on the inside."

The two men fell silent, each lost in his own thoughts. Dakota offered, "Then he can see in her house some way. Uses high-powered binoculars or something."

Connor blew out a sigh. "That seems a little far-fetched."

"You got a better idea?"

Grimacing, Connor shook his head. "No."

"So, let's think outside the box."

"Get creative?"

"Right. If I wanted access to this place, how would I go about doing it?" Dakota stood and paced over to the fireplace, pondering his own question.

"Find a way past the security system and —" Connor's words slowed, "— make sure I could come back if I wanted to."

"Do you think he somehow has access to the company's security codes?"

A shrug and a sigh. "There's no way to know. No way to really investigate that. It's a well-known company with call centers all over the country."

"True, but our guy is right here." Dakota pulled a picture off the mantel and looked at it. Jamie as a teenager in her carefree days when smiling came naturally and the world was a safe place. Samantha stood beside her making bunny ears above the back of Jamie's head.

"What are you guys talking about?" Jamie appeared in the doorway dressed in comfortable-looking sweats and a T-shirt that said I MAKE NO BONES ABOUT IT, I JUST DIG THEM UP.

Connor said, "Hey, sorry if we woke you up."

"You didn't. I was reading."

"Connor decided we needed to pay more attention to how this guy bypassed your security system."

"Oh."

Dakota felt his heart twitch. "It's one of the reasons I didn't want you alone in your house. I'm afraid if he's done it once, he can do it again."

She grimaced. "I've thought about that."

"Even with the cops outside, I still don't feel comfortable with you here alone. The captain agrees we've got enough evidence that someone is after you so he's good with the protection for now. Unfortunately, I can't keep those guys out there indefinitely."

"I know."

"Look, Jamie," Connor stood, "I know you're worried about staying with your parents and I agree. But why don't you come stay with Sam and me just until we get this guy."

She frowned. "But what about Jenna?"

"I've explained the situation to her. She wants you safe, and after her experience with a killer last year, she's willing to do whatever it takes to make sure you have the protection you need. She's staying with my parents even as we speak."

Through no fault of her own, Jenna had fallen into the hands of a killer Connor and Samantha had been trying to capture. Connor had found her just in time, and father and daughter now reveled in their second chance at renewing their relationship.

"I guess that would be all right." Her jaw clenched and Dakota figured she felt that she was allowing this guy to win, to disrupt her life once more.

"Jamie, don't get mad, let's just do what we have to do to get this guy behind bars. You've worked hard to get where you are. Staying safe isn't taking a step backward."

Shock made her blink. "You read me pretty well, don't you?"

He shrugged and Connor smiled. Dakota didn't budge as he gave a short nod in the direction of her bedroom. "So are you going to go pack or do I have to do it for you?"

■ ■ ■ ■

Only one light burned in the main part of house that he could see. It filtered through the living room from the den area. A light over the sink sent out a deceptively comforting glow. The garage door fit snug against the concrete and the driveway was barren. The daughter, Jenna, must be out. Connor was at Jamie's. That left Samantha alone.

That would work.

The Hero opened the glove compartment and pulled out his weapon of choice.

To kill or just do some damage? That was the question.

He'd make up his mind as the opportunity arose. He might just be here to observe. Could he enter the house without Samantha being aware?

He'd have to act fast, decisively. She was trained in self-defense, how to take care of herself. He'd have to catch her off guard, render her defenseless.

The knife clenched in his right hand, he walked the perimeter of the house. Samantha lay on the couch, asleep from all appearances. He'd heard she hadn't been feeling well. Tonight, maybe he'd do her a favor and help her feel nothing at all.

His heart raced as he thought about what he was about to do.

"Do it, do it. Please stop the pain," the voice begged.

"I am, I am," he whispered.

He shook his head to get the words out of his mind. He couldn't afford any distractions. Creeping closer to the window, he peered in. No animals to warn of his presence. An alarm system — not armed, he noticed.

Would the door chime if he opened it?

Maybe a window.

He looked at the French doors and made his way over to them. Pressed down on the handle.

Locked.

The garage?

Closed.

The front porch light was on. He'd avoid that.

He looked back at the garage.

A window slightly cracked. Hmm.

Keeping an eye on the neighboring house, he molded himself to the shadows, his steps full of stealth and purpose. Placing a gloved finger under the bottom edge of the window, he raised it slowly. It lifted smooth and easy.

Fortunately, the window wasn't that high off the ground and he was able to hoist himself over and in. He landed on concrete with a quiet thud. Giving his eyes a second to adjust, he stood there, then took in his surroundings.

Empty, yawning space greeted him. Samantha's car sat closest to the door. Leaving the window open in case he needed a quick way out, the Hero stepped lightly, his black-soled shoes silent on the cement floor.

At the door he twisted the knob. Locked. He grinned behind the mask. No matter, this was still his lucky day. He'd come prepared. Reaching into his back pocket, he pulled out a small tool and inserted it into the deadbolt.

He'd practiced this over and over on his door at home until he had the movements down. Approximately six seconds later, a slight click sounded.

Yes!

The knob took a little longer, but finally it, too, succumbed to his deft fingers.

Now, if the door wouldn't squeak or chime, he'd be in.

Slowly, he pushed and without a sound, it opened. His heart thudded in his chest, perspiration beaded under the mask, and he stilled, gathering his thoughts, praying to his god.

The air conditioner hummed, a clock

ticked. Sounds seemed amplified, the atmosphere thick as though lying in wait. For a moment he wondered if they knew he'd come. Was it a setup? A trap?

Anxiety slicked his palms. Encased in the black gloves, the fingers of his left hand curled into a fist; his right hand gripped the handle of the knife.

He listened.

Nothing.

Gradually, he relaxed, his confidence creeping back in. No, there was no way they'd know he'd be here. There were no cops ready to descend upon him and halt the work he did — and was here to do.

He crossed the kitchen and slowly pulled the phone plug from the jack.

Then he peered around the corner to see Samantha lying still, her slumber undisturbed by his entrance. He made his way forward, into the den, intending to watch her sleep for a few minutes.

Until her eyes opened.

Jamie loaded her overnight bag with the things she would need for tomorrow. Friday. Maybe she would take the day off. She'd already identified all of the bodies and no new cases had come in as of today. She'd worked almost two straight weeks. It was time for a break.

Throwing the strap over her shoulder, she grabbed her laptop and made a mental note to buy a new cell phone tomorrow. She didn't want to cancel the one she felt sure *he* had taken on the off chance that they might be able to trace it.

But she needed a phone.

Just the thought that he had been in the lab made nausea slither through her. He'd invaded every aspect of her life and it infuriated her — and made her feel helpless.

However, she raised her chin and stared at her reflection in the mirror. Just because she felt helpless didn't mean she had to act that way. For the last half a dozen years, she'd been proactive in getting her life back together. No one was going to do it for her — although several had tried. It was up to her.

And she'd be actively involved in finding the man who was terrorizing her. Yes, she was scared, and no, she wasn't going to do anything dumb. But she wasn't going to sit by and be a victim again either.

She wondered if Connor or Dakota had a gun she could keep with her.

"You ready?"

Dakota's voice jerked her from her thoughts and she turned from the mirror to look into his handsome face. "Yes, I think I'm going to take the day off tomorrow."

"Really? Why?"

"I need a break."

He took her overnight bag from her. "Well, if anyone deserves one, you do."

"Thanks." She followed him back into the den where Connor looked to be deep in conversation with someone.

While they waited for him to finish, Jamie went about the business of locking up her house. It didn't take long. She looked around and shook her head. "I don't get it. How did he get in?"

Dakota sighed. "Beats me. And that scares me."

Connor finished his call and Jamie shut off the lights and set the alarm.

An indrawn breath made her look up. "What is it?"

Dakota pointed. "Look."

She and Connor looked in the direction indicated by his finger. Nothing looked out of place. Her front door stood open, her table with the small mirror above it on the wall opposite the door seemed innocent enough. "What?"

"The mirror," Connor breathed, excitement mixed with horror evident on his face.

"What am I missing, guys?" she asked in

exasperation.

"He watched you punch in your code."

Stunned disbelief punched her. "He did? How?"

Dakota moved outside the front door. "Okay, after you shut the door, program the alarm."

She did as instructed.

A shadow moved outside the side window covered by the sheer white curtain.

Then Dakota opened the door and looked at Connor. A frown drew his brows together. "I couldn't see it very well. I mean, I could see the mirror perfectly, but Jamie was standing in the way."

She thought for a moment, going over her daily routine. An idea dawned. "Wait a minute, do it again."

Connor lifted a brow and Dakota shrugged, stepped outside once more, and shut the door. This time Jamie slipped into the kitchen and approached the alarm box from a different angle. The one she normally used when coming in the back door from her garage.

She punched in the code.

Dakota opened the door. "Bingo. The curtain is too thick to see the numbers, but I saw the motion of your hand on an outline of the pad. It wouldn't be any big deal to copy it on a real key pad."

"All he had to do was wait until you came through the garage. He probably stumbled upon that information by accident. Maybe he was trying to see in the window, see what you were doing, and got lucky."

"And sometimes I open that curtain."

Dakota raised a brow. "You do?"

"When I wasn't leaving my home, it's the only thing I felt comfortable opening to let in a little natural light. I still do it upon occasion."

"Well, either way, I think we know how he got in without setting your alarm off."

She took a deep breath. "I want to change the code again. I don't know how many times I've used the new one since we changed it after he made his first appearance. He could have the new code as we speak."

Jamie moved to the box, punched a few buttons, and then the sharp whine sounded indicating the code had been changed. "There, that ought to do it."

Dakota nodded. "Let's go."

Something occurred to her. "Do you mind if we make one stop on the way?"

"Where?"

"The lab. I need to look over a couple of files on my day off."

20

The Hero watched her blink. Then the fear ignited behind her pretty blue eyes. She bolted upright and went pasty white. The blanket fell to her lap. He just stood there and waited, watching, ready for whatever move she decided to make.

Somewhat to his surprise, she did nothing. Except swallow hard. And remain silent.

He frowned.

And waited.

Her eyes narrowed, her mouth opened. Then shut.

Why didn't she say something?

He shifted and her gaze flicked to the knife in his hand. A deep breath lifted her shoulders, then her eyes latched back onto his.

How many minutes had passed?

Uneasiness made him edgy. He'd never had one of his girls act like this. She unnerved him. He didn't like that.

A step forward.

And still she didn't move, just watched him.

What?

Why didn't she scream? Try to run? *Say* something?

He cleared his throat. "Hello, Samantha."

"You."

One word. Filled with a loathing that nearly singed him. Again, he was taken aback and hesitated.

And that made him angry.

"Yes, me."

She sat straighter, one hand clutching the blanket, knotting it into her fist. "You nearly destroyed my sister."

"No, I almost set her free."

"You're sick."

The disgust on her face just cemented his knowledge that he was the chosen one, the blessed one. The one to end the suffering and pain. "I'm chosen."

"What do you want?"

"To release Jamie from her pain and show her who her hero is."

"That makes absolutely no sense. You *cause* the pain."

She moved. An object clipped the side of his head and he ducked in reflex. She was off the couch and around the side of the den in a flash.

He ducked the other way that led back into the kitchen as she beat a path through the dining room. As she raced for the door he'd entered only moments before, he cut her off, snagged her arm, and threw her against the refrigerator.

A huff of breath and a pained grunt met his ears. She stumbled away, fingers grasping for a weapon. He kept his stance and watched her. There was no way out, he had her backed into a corner.

Her hand grasped her abdomen where it had connected with the handle of the appliance. Pain twisted her face.

He stepped forward. Two tears leaked from her eyes and trickled their way down to drip from her chin.

So, she wasn't quite as fearless as she appeared.

"It's all over, Samantha. I'll be sure to tell Jamie you put up a good fight."

They heard the sound at the same time.

A key in the lock.

"Connor!"

She moved, the Hero parried. She lifted a leg and her heel caught him in the solar plexus. Gasping, he stumbled away. Then with a roar and a lunge, he caught her.

The knife sliced home.

■ ■ ■ ■

Jamie heard Samantha scream Connor's name. A scream that twisted terror through her. Under the light of the porch, Connor's face went stark white. Shoving the door open, leaving the key in the lock, he burst inside with the order for Jamie to "Stay behind me."

A light burned in the den. Connor went straight for it. Jamie hit the light in the foyer and headed for the kitchen, disobeying Connor's command. The scream hadn't come from the den. And the sweet smell of fresh blood assaulted her nose from the right. "Connor, I think she's in here!"

He doubled back as Jamie slapped the kitchen light on . . .

. . . only to see Samantha's lifeless body lying in an ever-widening pool of blood.

"Connor!"

Horror flooded her. She couldn't move as Connor stepped around her to see what had her frozen to the spot. A swift indrawn breath and his harsh cry jolted her. She moved with trembling steps to the phone where she grabbed it and punched in 911. And realized it was dead.

Her eyes fell on the disconnected plug,

and with hands trembling, she grabbed it, pushed it into the jack, and dialed the numbers again even as she watched Connor working on his wife.

"Is she . . . please, Connor, tell me . . ."

"I've got a pulse, but she's bleeding pretty bad." He muttered to Samantha, "Come on, baby, hold on." To Jamie. "Her pulse is weak. Take care of her, I've got to make sure he's not still here waiting to ambush us."

Jamie gave the information to the operator, who ordered her to stay on the line. Carrying the phone with her, she dropped it to her side and knelt by Samantha. She shook so hard, she didn't know if she'd be any good to her sister.

Control, Jamie. Deep breath. Help Samantha. Control. You have the training, you can do this.

With that mantra playing in her head, she blocked the fact that Samantha might very well die on her kitchen floor and assessed the wounds. A stab wound to her side. Blood everywhere, including under her legs.

What was that from?

Connor returned in a flash. "The house is clean, he's gone through the garage, I think. I'll have to worry about that later. How is she?"

Reaching out, he placed a hand on Samantha's throat. His hands shook almost as bad as hers as he monitored his wife's respirations and pulse.

"Connor, get me a towel, a thick one, and some duct tape if you have it. We'll have to improvise. The wound doesn't look terribly bad, but I don't know how long she's been lying here bleeding — or what the knife nicked inside her . . ." Panic flamed. She whispered, "There's too much blood. Where's it all coming from?"

Tortured eyes met her, but he nodded and went to get the items she needed.

The EMS could take over when they got here, but it was up to her to keep Sam alive until they arrived. And that meant controlling the bleeding.

A towel appeared in her hand. "Do you have any sterile gauze and alcohol and scissors?"

Seconds later he opened the packets of gauze and poured alcohol over her hands. She hoped it would kill as many germs as possible. With trembling fingers, she pulled out the gauze and packed it into the wound as best she could, then she took the towel. "I need some scissors."

He handed them to her and she cut a strip, folded it, and duct taped it over the wound. So far the blood wasn't seeping

271

through.

Sirens sounded outside, feet pounded up the steps of the porch. She blinked.

Rough hands pulled her away.

Professionals took over.

Her job was done. She'd kept Samantha alive until help arrived.

Jumping back into the action, she explained who she was and what she'd done. Connor hovered, cell phone to his ear as he shouted at someone on the other end.

Dakota probably.

An IV hanging on the pole fed much-needed fluids into Sam's pale, still body. Efficient hands loaded her onto the gurney, and before Jamie felt like she could blink, Sam was in the ambulance.

"Hold on," Connor called. "I'm riding with her!" His hand gripped hers. "I'm going with Sam. Can you drive my car and meet us there?"

"Yes, yes, go."

He went.

Jamie grabbed the keys that had been left in the door and bolted for Connor's car.

Ten minutes later, she followed the ambulance into the emergency room parking lot.

A parking spot yawned right in front of her. She snagged it and raced for the entrance. Dakota stood just inside the door.

Slowing her pace a fraction, she went to his side and looked up at him. Words wouldn't come, she could only stare at him, asking for something, but not sure what it was.

Immediately, his arms came around her and he pulled her into an embrace.

Sobs wracked her and she let the tears fall.

21

Dakota hated hospitals. He knew Jamie wasn't exactly fond of them either.

She shifted on the hard plastic seat beside him and her head nudged his shoulder. His heart sighed with a love that scared him. Made him wonder if she would ever be able to return it.

Finally losing the battle between worry and exhaustion, she'd drifted off. He wrapped an arm around her and gently pulled her into a more comfortable position against him. Leaning his head back against the wall, he shut his eyes.

God? I haven't talked to you much lately, but Jamie believes you're there. And she's about got me believing it too. I don't know why all this is happening. If you're so loving, why don't you do something? But I guess I can recognize my own limitations. I don't know your mind or the way you work. But if you could give Jamie some comfort — and a

*whole lot of protection — I'd be grateful. And
let Sam be okay, please? Jamie needs her to
be all right. We all do.*

He waited to see if he felt different for
having prayed.

Nada.

Disappointment swelled within. Did that
mean God wasn't listening? Discouraged,
he closed his eyes.

He must have drifted off, one ear tuned
to his surroundings, because when he felt a
hand on his shoulder, he jumped. His left
arm was asleep because of the awkward
position, and he felt weighted down in
quicksand. Jamie sat up, dislodging his arm
and rubbing her eyes with the palms of her
hands.

She spoke first, "Connor? How is she? Is
Sam going to be all right?"

For the first time, Dakota noticed Jamie's
parents sitting in the chairs facing him.
Anxious, they had their eyes on Connor, as
desperate to hear news about Sam as Jamie.

Connor closed his eyes, then opened
them. Tears reddened them and Dakota's
heart dropped to his toes. *Oh God, no.*
"Connor?"

"She's uh . . . she's still alive, hanging in
there, but she's lost a lot of blood." He
looked at Jamie. "You saved her life tonight."

She blinked and looked away. "If it wasn't for me, she wouldn't be in this situation," she whispered. Then she cleared her throat. "Where did all the blood come from, Connor? There was so much of it and I couldn't see where it was originating? And then the paramedics were there . . ."

Grief clouded Connor's features and Dakota knew. "She was pregnant, wasn't she?"

Jamie's mother gave a soft cry and her father grasped her hand.

A gasp and a whimper from Jamie. "And the baby?"

A nod from Connor. "The baby is still hanging on too. She's about three months along. Her due date's around the beginning of December. But the doctors have already said not to hold out hope. Sam's been too traumatized and the blood loss . . ." He swallowed hard and looked at his hands. "So, I'm trying to prepare myself to prepare her . . ."

"Where's your faith, man?" Dakota asked.

Connor snapped his head up, sucked in a deep breath, and just stared.

Jamie reached out and grabbed his hand. "Dakota's right, Connor. We have to have faith. He has a purpose for that little life in there."

Connor nodded and rose to his feet and hugged his in-laws. "I'm going to go back and check on Sam and give Jenna a call to fill her in. Why don't you guys go on home?" He looked at Jamie. "It might be best if you stay here at the hospital, actually. I can arrange for that."

Relief that Samantha was still alive warred with the grief that she might lose a baby Jamie knew she wanted very much. Her parents looked worn and weary, the stress of whatever was going on in their personal lives now compounded by Samantha's run-in with a serial killer.

Her mother laid a hand on Jamie's arm. "Come home with us, sweetie. There's no reason for you to stay here."

Jamie gave her mother a hug. "If I thought you would be safe, I would. But after what's happened tonight, I just don't dare . . ." She bit her lip. "I can't. I'm sorry."

Dakota snapped his phone shut. "It's arranged. Sam's condition is considered critical, so she's going into ICU for the night but will probably be moved to a room tomorrow if everything goes well. With special permission, we can set you up a cot in Sam's room. Connor said he'd crash in the doctors' lounge."

"Thank you."

He nodded, his eyes soft with concern, compassion. "My guess is, as long as you and Sam are safe, Connor's going to want to be hunting this guy down."

Jamie nodded. "All right. Mom, Dad, I'll stay with Sam and call you immediately if there's any change."

"We'll be praying," her mother said as she leaned over for one more hug. "Also, when Samantha has recovered, there's something your father and I need to talk to you about."

Curiosity and dread hit her. "Something good or bad? Because I don't think I can handle any more bad."

When tears filled her mother's eyes, Jamie's heart nearly stopped. "What is it, Mom?" Eyes beseeched her dad.

The tall man shifted his lanky frame and cleared his throat. "It's good, Jamie. It's all good. It'll be something happy to save for when Samantha's ready, okay?"

"Fine." Something to look forward to. It must be a doozy, though, to induce happy tears in her mother at this tragic time.

After her parents left to check on when they would be able to see Samantha, she turned to Dakota and whispered, "We have to stop him."

He tugged her into his arms. She went

willingly, grateful for his strength to lean on if only for a few minutes. Then he set her back from him. "What do you need from your house?"

She looked down at her bloody clothing. Sam's blood. "Another change of clothes would be nice, since I didn't pack enough. I wasn't planning on . . . this."

"I'll get Jessica to go in and get you some."

"She'll need the alarm code."

"I'll give it to her."

"And the bag in my bathroom. Tell her just to throw everything she sees on the counter into it."

"Got it."

Jamie watched him make the call while her mind churned. As soon as Samantha was awake, she'd be inundated with questions about what had happened at her house.

Closing her eyes, she leaned against the wall and waited on Dakota to finish his conversation. *God, I want to pray, but I don't even know what to say. I know this isn't of you. I don't want to blame you. I stopped blaming you for all the bad stuff that happened to me a long time ago. I guess I'm just upset because I don't understand. I don't get how you could let this happen to Sam. But,* she hauled in a breath, *I refuse to doubt you. I will believe that you know best. I made that decision a long time ago. Your character hasn't changed just because of this situation.*

"You're doing it again."

Praying ceased and she jerked her eyes open to blink up at Dakota.

"You're praying, aren't you?"

"Yes."

"I could tell."

"I'm still not sure I understand exactly what you mean."

"And I don't know if I can explain it. But it's like . . ." He waved a hand, "something happens on your face."

She shot him a perturbed look. "Okay."

"Ah, man, I'm just saying that while you looked disturbed and maybe almost angry when you were praying, you also had this relaxed, peaceful . . . um . . . countenance? I guess that's the right word. It's really odd. I've never seen anything like it."

An idea of what he meant softened her. "I think I understand, but don't ask me to explain it either. It's just God, I guess."

"I prayed."

That stilled her. "You did?"

"Yes."

"And?"

He shrugged. "I don't think anyone would have accused me of changing physically dur-

280

ing my prayer."

"That doesn't mean God didn't hear it."

"Hmm."

The double doors whooshed open and Connor stepped through. "They're taking Sam up to ICU. A crime scene unit is going over my house and officers are interviewing neighbors. Hopefully someone will remember something that will give us a heads-up on this guy."

"Great. I'll go with you. Do you have an officer on Sam's room?"

"She'll be here shortly."

"Has Samantha woken up yet?" Jamie wanted to know.

Eyes clouded as he nodded. "Yes."

"Does she know about the baby?"

"Her first question."

"Did she say anything about what happened?"

Connor clenched his jaw. "Not yet. The doctor didn't want me pressing her."

Jamie paced away three steps, then back. "She's a cop. She's thinking about everything, processing it. She'll tell you soon."

"I know." He blew out a breath. "All right, let's go see if she's ready."

The trio made their way up to Samantha's room. Jamie pushed the door open and had to bite her tongue on a gasp. Samantha looked awful. Pale and wan, bruised and battered.

If only Jamie hadn't stopped at the lab. They would have gotten there in time. Regret kicked her and she took in a shaky breath.

Eyes closed, Samantha breathed deep, even breaths. Peaceful, narcotic-induced sleep. Questions would have to wait.

A cot graced the opposite wall near the bathroom. "Connor, if you need to stay here, I can check into a hotel."

He just looked at her. She gave up. Not that she couldn't be stubborn when the occasion called for it, but right now didn't seem to be the time.

Dakota handed her a cell phone. "I got this for you. An officer delivered it while you were sleeping on my arm."

Wide-eyed, she reached for it. Her fingers brushed his and she shivered at the contact. A good shiver. She was almost getting used to the feelings he induced in her. A fact that thrilled her and scared her all at the same time. "Thanks."

Connor's phone rang and he snatched it up. "Wolfe here."

Jamie tucked the phone into her pocket and walked over to Samantha's side as Connor talked. Then Dakota's phone buzzed and the soft chatter filled her ears.

Focused on her sister, she took in every detail. Her heart hurt. "Oh Sam, please get better fast. I need your constant nagging and overprotectiveness more than I ever thought I would."

"Thanks a lot, sis," came the whispered response.

For a moment, Jamie wasn't sure she'd heard it, but a quick glance up confirmed Samantha's eyes were open. "Hey, how are you feeling?"

"Like I ran into a knife."

Jamie grimaced and Samantha squeezed her hand. "I'm so sorry."

"Not your fault."

"He got you under your rib but missed almost everything vital — including your uterus."

"The baby's still okay, right?"

"Yeah. He's fine."

"He?"

"Uh-huh." Jamie forced a grin. "Too many girls in our family. We need a little boy around to shake things up."

Samantha laughed, then gasped. "Please don't make me laugh. It hurts. You don't think things are exciting enough already?"

Jamie grimaced. "I meant a different kind of excitement."

The guys quit talking and joined Jamie around the bed.

The door opened and they all turned as one.

The nurse narrowed her dark eyes on the lot of them. "What do you think you're all doing in here? This is an ICU room."

Between badge flashes and explanations, she quieted her protests and left. But not without shooting them all a dark look and the promise of "I'll be back."

"Don't leave me here with Nurse Arnold," Sam begged in a whisper.

Jamie choked on a surprised laugh and the guys exchanged smirks. Then seriousness descended. "Sam, do you feel like talking about what happened?"

Samantha grimaced and Connor stroked her hair, his fingers lingering on a bruised cheek. "You don't have to right now if you don't feel up to it."

"No, I need to. You need to get this guy." She licked her lips and Jamie handed her the cup of water from the tray. Sam took a sip and said, "I was asleep on the couch. Something woke me up and he was standing there watching me."

A shudder.

Connor's muttering under his breath.

Dakota's hand on her shoulder.

All of it registered through the roaring in her ears. Jamie knew exactly what Sam was talking about. She used to wake to the same nightmare.

"I think the terror just froze me, so at first I just sat there. I wasn't really sure what to do. I didn't have my weapon, so I waited for him to make the first move." A frown fluttered between her brows. "That seemed to throw him off."

"Why do you say that?" Connor leaned closer.

"I'm not sure, just a gut feeling." She sighed, shifted, and groaned.

Connor said, "That's enough."

"No," she protested, "just give me a minute."

Jamie tried to calm her churning stomach. Dakota slipped an arm around her waist and she shot him a grateful look.

Samantha continued. "Then I . . . I sensed something from him. Like he was getting ready to do something, so I threw the remote control at him. It hit him in the head, distracting him long enough for me to make a run for it." She gave a weak humorless laugh, leaned back and closed her eyes. "Guess I didn't run fast enough."

The door opened. The nurse who said she'd be back. "All right, you people really need to leave. Mrs. Wolfe can't get her rest if you keep making her talk."

Dakota raised a hand. "I'm leaving." To Connor, "I've got a couple more calls to make. I'll wait for you downstairs."

"I'll be there in a minute."

Dakota left and Jamie wilted onto the cot that had been set up for her.

Sam whispered something. Jamie glanced at Connor. "What did she say?"

He shook his head and leaned over Samantha. "Say that again."

Rousing herself, words slurring, she said, "He was going for my throat."

Jamie sucked in a breath.

"But I kicked him and he got me in the stomach."

Then she was out. Asleep. Or passed out from the drugs, Jamie wasn't quite sure.

Lasering a look at Connor, the nurse left the room.

"He's escalating, Connor."

"I know."

"He's not following his pattern. Going to kill Sam in her own home . . . that's a message. He wasn't interested in carrying out his sick fantasies with her, he wanted to . . ." She couldn't speak past the lump in her throat.

He hugged her close. "We'll get him, Jamie, we'll get him."

22

Dakota and Connor arrived back at the house where the investigation was still going strong. Yellow crime scene tape bordered the property. Connor had called Jenna on the way over to tell her not to come home anytime soon.

Despite being almost midnight, several neighbors stood at the edge of their lawns to gawk.

Deciding exhaustion could be considered his new best friend, Dakota shoved it aside and climbed from the car. Surveying the scene, he asked Connor, "What do you think about insisting Jamie go to a safe house until this is all over?"

Flashing badges, they ducked under the tape and made their way inside the house where Dakota figured Jake Hollister, lead CSU, would be processing the kitchen.

Connor sighed. "We might have to. The only problem with that is, he'll just wait us out. And possibly find another victim while he's waiting for her to come out of hiding. She can't stay in one forever. But we can ask George his opinion."

"If this keeps up, she's going to have to do something, if only for a break from the constant stress. I don't know how much more she can take without snapping."

"Jamie's strong. Stronger than I think any of us realize."

"I know, but with her past . . . I just think we need to keep a really close eye on her."

Connor paused and studied Dakota. "We will."

"Right." He looked at Jake. "What do you have for us, Jake?"

Jake looked up. Compassion flickered as his gaze landed on Connor. "A lot of Samantha's blood. A few hairs that I suspect will belong to people you know — or else be unidentifiable. Who knows, though? Maybe we'll get lucky and get a hit on somebody in the system." His look said he didn't hold out much hope on that one. Standing, he nodded to the open kitchen door. "He got in through there."

Frowning, Connor strode to the opening. "Samantha didn't have the door locked? I can't believe that."

"Unless this guy's got some lock picking

skills, that door wasn't locked. There's no way for me to tell just by looking at the lock. Plus," he motioned them on out into the garage, "that window there was wide open. No sign of forced entry."

"That's impossible. There's no way we would have left the window open. Not with everything going on."

Dakota blew out a breath. "And yet, Sam didn't have the alarm set."

Connor went still. "No, she didn't. Why not?"

"Were you expecting Jenna?"

"No. At least not unless she called Samantha to let her know she was coming home, and Sam didn't say anything about expecting her."

"Call Jenna and see what she has to say."

Connor immediately got on his phone and placed the call.

Dakota turned back to Jake but didn't get a chance to ask his question before the vibration of his phone grabbed his attention. "Hello?"

"Dakota, this is Jazz. I got a hit on that facial reconstruction. The girl named Karen."

"Who is she?"

"I ran her through NCIC using different search parameters. Four years ago, she was here in Spartanburg from New Jersey visiting relatives when she and a cousin got in a fight. Sharlene Karen Fuller took off and was never heard from again."

A strikingly similar story to Jamie's. Interesting.

"Have you contacted the family?"

"Working on it."

"All right, thanks, Jazz. Anything else on the other girls? Their last movements, the last people to talk to them, anything?"

"Not much, but I can fill you in when you come in tomorrow."

"I'm not going to be able to make it to the office tomorrow. Can you send me an email summary? It'll come straight to my phone."

"Sure, I can do that. Also, those handcuffs? We're working on the online dealers, but so far nothing. And none of the field offices reported anyone buying cuffs in bulk."

"Yeah, I kind of figured that's the way it would play out. You're still a doll."

Dakota hung up the phone and turned to find Connor still in conversation with Jenna. His voice sounded normal enough, but the white-knuckled grip he had on the device didn't look good.

"It's all right, Jenna. No, Sam's going to be fine. I'll talk to you later."

He lowered the phone, jaw clenched, breathing accelerated.

"What?"

Connor pinched his nose then said, "Jenna snuck out of the house two nights ago. Due to the odd hours Samantha and I keep, we don't have the chime on the door activated." Alarm systems allowed owners to choose whether or not a warning sounded when doors opened and closed. "But all of the windows of the house will set it off. The garage windows won't."

"So, she slipped out the door and then the garage window?"

"Yeah. Obviously not wiring the garage windows was a gross oversight on my part. First call tomorrow will remedy that."

"Let me guess, she didn't shut it all the way on her return trip."

"Nope."

"I thought you guys were past all that sneaking out stuff." Jenna had gone through a rough time last year. In an attempt to get her father's attention, she'd excelled at rebellion, including sneaking out of the house on a regular basis. But they'd worked through their issues and had seemed to be doing great. Especially since Connor and Samantha's wedding.

"I did too. She said she'd explain when

she saw me, so it looks like a father-daughter conversation is a priority on the to-do list." He sighed. "Although I have to be honest and say I don't think it would have mattered if the window had been locked and wired. He would have figured out another way in." He paced two steps forward, three back. "All right, so we know how the guy got in here . . ."

Jake nodded and slipped something else inside a plastic bag. Labeled it. Added it to his stash. "He took his weapon with him and went out the way he came in." He pointed to the trail of blood that had dripped from the knife.

An officer stepped into the kitchen. "Excuse me, Dakota, Connor, may I have a word?"

"Sure." Connor looked up. "You got something?"

"Yeah, maybe. One of the neighbors reported seeing a guy running through the neighborhood. Another one said a blue Honda sat across from his house for about an hour. Thought it was a little strange because it was parked in front of a house that's for sale and empty."

"Didn't happen to get plates, did he?"

"Nope, of course not."

Dakota tapped his lip. "Okay, we have

more than we did five minutes ago. A blue Honda. Make?"

The officer consulted his notes. "Um, thought it might be an Accord."

"What shade of blue?" Connor asked.

"He said it was a light blue. A car passed by on the street as he was looking out his window. The headlights flashed on the Honda for a minute, and the guy said he got a pretty good look."

"But no plate."

"No, sorry."

"Did you guys check out the inside of the house?"

"Absolutely. Empty. With no signs of any recent occupants." He flipped his notepad closed. "I also called the realtor and got her on the phone. She said the last time she showed the house was a week and a half ago. Her background check came back clean. Same with the owners who were transferred to Canada three months ago. They're clean too."

Connor nodded. "All right. Good job. We'll just have to work with what we've got. It's better than nothing."

Dakota's phone rang. "Hello?"

"Hi, it's Jazz again."

"Shouldn't you be headed home by now?"

"Not if I want to keep up with everything.

How's Samantha?"

He heard the subtle anger in her voice. "She's hanging in there. Should be fine eventually." If she didn't lose the baby. But that wasn't his news to share.

"Oh good. When I heard . . ."

"I know, Jazz, it's shaken us all up."

Jazz coughed and he wondered if it was to mask tears. Then she said, "I managed to track down Karen's family. Anderson, South Carolina."

"I thought they were in New Jersey."

"They were, but when Karen went missing, they moved down here with their relatives to be close to the investigation. Even when the case went cold, they stayed. Made a life there."

"About an hour away. I feel a road trip coming on."

"I sent the directions to your phone. I also emailed you that other stuff. It's not much. Some statements from possible witnesses. But the one thing that stood out was that two mentioned a blue Honda being in the area when Karen disappeared."

Dakota went cold, chilled all over, then flushed hot.

This was their guy.

"Jazz, you're amazing. I can't tell you how much this helps. Now go home and get some rest."

"Yes sir. On the way now."

Dakota hung up. Turned to Connor and filled him in. "Feel like a drive to Anderson?"

Connor hesitated. "I don't want to get too far from Sam."

"She'd kick your tail if she thought you had a lead you didn't follow up on because of her."

A faint grin creased the corners of Connor's mouth. "I know." Then his eyes hardened. "But she's my priority."

"And she should be. I can handle it myself. You stay with her."

Connor nodded. "Yeah. You go on if you want." His phone rang. Dakota watched his friend's face bleach white and he bolted for the door. "I've got to go. Sam's started bleeding again and they're having trouble stopping it."

23

Blinking back tears and muttering pleading prayers, Jamie watched them wheel Samantha down the hall. Her sister had been sound asleep but had awakened with a gasp of pain in her abdomen. Suspicious, Jamie had jerked back the sheets to see a large circle of blood spreading quickly.

Bolting for the door, she'd grabbed a passing nurse who called in reinforcements. There was mention of an ultrasound, a D and C procedure, then Sam was whisked out the door, her hands in a protective cup over her stomach.

Sure that the baby was already gone, Jamie began praying for Samantha's emotional well-being as well as a quick recovery.

At almost forty, she knew her sister had pretty much given up on the idea of having a baby, feeling she was too old. Jamie had laughed and began finding information about women having babies well into their forties.

And now to find out Sam had been so close . . .

She'd called Connor to give him the bad news. Now, guilt pressed in on her. Questions ate at her. Had there been any way to prevent this? What could she have done differently in order to make sure this guy didn't attack her family? Why hadn't Connor had someone watching his house? After all, they'd entertained the idea that someone might come after Jamie's parents. They'd taken steps to protect Jenna.

But they'd never considered he might come after Samantha.

Why not? Because she was a cop?

Possibly. But also because Samantha had been the protection, not the one who needed it.

Jamie's mind whirled in between her prayers. Left alone in the room, exhaustion dragged at her. The little bit of sleep she'd gotten on Dakota's shoulder hadn't been enough. Her head ached.

The door burst open and Connor flew through. "Where is she?"

"They took her to ultrasound and possibly . . . a D and C." She held the tears in check.

He swallowed hard. "Okay, I'm going to go find her. You try to get some rest, she's going to need you."

Nodding, Jamie blew out a breath and watched the man who loved her sister beyond anything she'd ever seen, exit the door as fast as he'd entered.

Knowing there was nothing she could do but also knowing rest was out of the question, she settled on the cot to wait for Samantha's return. Her eye fell on the nightstand. Slowly, she reached for the Bible, opened it up, and began to read.

Friday Morning

Dakota woke with a jerk. He'd caught himself dozing at his desk around three in the morning and decided to head home. After making Connor promise to call as soon as he could, he'd fought the exhaustion, determined to do more research into the lives of the girls Jamie had ID'd. At 4:30, he gave up knowing that he couldn't go without sleep indefinitely.

He looked at the clock. 9:07.

Bed covers flew as he scrambled from the bed and into the bathroom.

Five minutes later, he was on his way to Anderson, South Carolina. After Samantha's relapse last night, he knew he'd be making this trip alone.

Two officers watched Jamie's parents' house, two stood guard on Samantha's room. Which meant Jamie had protection too. His mind slightly at ease, he punched in the speed dial number for Connor's cell phone.

"Hello?"

"How's Sam this morning?"

"Sleeping right now. They needed her ICU room for someone more critical, so she's in a private room with constant supervision. They were going to do the D and C last night . . . er . . . this morning . . . whatever . . . and when they did the ultrasound, the baby still had a heartbeat."

"Wow. Man, that's fantastic."

"I know. The doctors are still saying she's going to lose it, but we're putting our faith in the God who heals — and who still performs miracles."

Dakota felt something shift in his chest. Faith? Hope? The desire to believe what his friends believed? "I'll . . . uh . . . I'll be praying too."

Silence from the other end of the line, then a thick, "Thanks, friend," came from an obviously moved Connor. "We're in room 455."

Change the subject. "I'm on my way to

Anderson. I want to talk with Karen's family and see if they have anything to add to what little we already have." A spur-of-the-moment thought hit him. "Ask Jamie if she wants to go with me. It might do her some good to get out of this city for a few hours."

"Hold on."

Muffled voices in the background, then, "Yeah, swing by here and get her."

A U-turn had him going in the right direction. The thought of spending the day with Jamie lifted his spirits right through the roof. In spite of the reason for the trip.

While he drove, he called the family, requesting some of their time this morning. To his surprise, he found out Karen's mother and aunt were on the way to the morgue to take possession of the remains.

He called Lila. "Tell Serena not to let them leave until I get a chance to talk to them, all right?"

"Sure."

At the hospital, he took the elevator up to Samantha's room to find her resting comfortably. Jamie and Connor stood by the window talking quietly. Connor shook his hand, then Dakota turned to Jamie. "Karen's parents are downstairs in the morgue. You still want to join me?"

She winced, but nodded. "Yes, Serena will

be there, but I probably know more about the case than she does."

A knock on the door. They swung as one toward it. Samantha blinked her eyes open. Connor walked over to open it and admit George.

"Hey, sorry to interrupt. I came to see if Samantha felt up to talking. I wanted to try and add as much as I could to the profile I'm building on this guy."

Sam rolled her head over to look at George. "Hi, George."

"Hi, Sam. Sorry to see you this way. He must have been a pretty tough character to get the best of you."

"Not so tough," she muttered. "If I had been feeling better, he wouldn't have had a chance."

A raised eyebrow and skepticism showed for a brief moment before George smoothed his face into impassive lines. "Tell me what you can about him."

"He knew what he was doing. He had a plan, was organized and carried it out." She touched her bandaged side. "Well, most of it."

George settled himself against the sink and folded his arms across his chest. "What was his conversation like?"

"What do you mean?"

"Did he talk to you?"

"Yes, a little. He was very . . . controlled, I guess is the word."

"Anything else?"

"He seemed mad when I didn't immediately start talking to him. When I didn't get up and run."

A brow furrowed. "Who was the first one to speak?"

"He was."

"What did he say?"

"He said, 'Hello, Samantha.' "

"That's it?"

"Then I think I asked him what he wanted."

"Did you exhibit any kind of revulsion? Disgust?"

"Yeah." She stared at George. "A lot of it."

"He was angry because you forced his hand. Altered the way things were supposed to go down. At least in his mind."

"Tough."

George turned to the others in the room. "Our guy is a psychopath as opposed to psychotic."

"What do you mean?"

"Psychopaths are smart, average to above-average intelligence. My guess is he's near genius-level IQ. Psychotics are disorganized with below-average intelligence. This guy is still exhibiting all the qualities I talked about before. The only interesting thing about him is that he's stuck around this area for so long. Most psychopathic killers are transient. They may change jobs or leave town abruptly. But all of the other factors . . ."

Dakota narrowed his eyes. "You sound almost like you respect him."

George lifted a brow. "I respect his intelligence. I suggest you do the same. He's very smart and you'd be wise not to underestimate him."

A thoughtful nod, then, "What kind of car would he drive?"

"A nice one because he can afford it. And I don't necessarily mean flashy, just nice and dependable. He fits in with those around him and is socially competent. Most likely no one who knows him would even suspect he does the kinds of things he does. He's also following this story very closely in the news. It excites him to see the chaos he's created. He wants to hear about how the police are stumped and have no leads. He thinks the police are stupid and he's far superior to the authorities." He looked at Dakota with a small smile. "Hence the need to respect that he is smart. I'm not saying you have to like it, but . . ." He spread his hands and shrugged.

Dakota grunted. "Makes you want to do a background investigation on everyone you come in contact with, doesn't it?"

Jamie nodded, her eyes still on Samantha. "She's getting tired."

George stood. "I've got another client coming in. I need to get back. Let me know if there's anything else I can do for you."

Dakota patted the man on the back. "Thanks, George." He looked at Jamie. "You ready to head downstairs?"

"Let's go."

24

Jamie walked into the morgue behind Dakota and nodded to Serena. This part of the job she could do without. She didn't have to be the one to break the news to the family on a regular basis; however, she was often in the room when family members identified the body. She watched their grief and her own heart broke with theirs.

She'd never been able to develop a layer so tough that she could view someone else's heart-wrenching pain without empathizing. She supposed that was a good thing.

Dakota approached the two ladies. "Mrs. Fuller?"

"I'm Doreen Fuller." A heavyset woman in her late forties stepped forward. "This is my sister Clarice Freemont."

"Ma'am." Handshakes and greetings concluded there, Jamie introduced herself and explained her position. Serena let Jamie take the lead.

"So, you think the bones belong to my Karen?" The double chin quivered, but she held herself together.

"Yes, ma'am. I did a facial reconstruction that several people called in tips on. The majority of them named her as Karen Fuller. Plus, the DNA samples you provided when she disappeared finally came back as a match with the remains."

The woman pulled in a deep breath. "All right, let me see this reconstruction."

Jamie led the two ladies into the viewing room where she kept the reconstructed skull. Lifting the cloth covering it, she turned it to face them.

"Oh my." Hand to her chest, Mrs. Freemont breathed deep. "That's almost scary." She looked up, a mixture of amazement and grief contorting her features.

Silent tears dripped down Karen's mother's face. "That's my baby. Right down to her eyebrows. The left one was higher than the other. Even the hair . . ." She reached out to touch it, fingers lingering, loving. As though it really were her daughter's hair.

"I'm so sorry, Mrs. Fuller. I wish it wasn't her."

"Well, if it wasn't, it would be someone else's grief, wouldn't it?" Quiet, low words. A mother's pain for a lost child. "How did

307

she die?"

Jamie cut her eyes to Dakota.

He frowned.

Placing an arm across the woman's shoulders, Jamie asked, "I'll tell you if you insist, but I have one question first. Was Karen a Christian?"

"Yes, she loved her Lord. Gave her heart to him when she was nine years old."

"Then you know where she is now."

"I figured all along that's where she was. All parents in my situation want to hold out hope that their child is still alive — even after four years. But," she patted her ample chest, "somehow you know deep down inside that your baby's not coming back." Her voice choked on the last word and she swallowed to regain her composure. "So, what you're saying is I need to rejoice in where she is, not dwell on how she got there."

Shrewd dark eyes pierced all the way through to Jamie's soul. "Yes, ma'am. That's exactly what I'm saying."

"It still hurts." Fat tears rolled down her cheeks.

"I know it does." Jamie squeezed the woman's shoulders. "We're not made to say goodbye. God didn't make us that way. We're eternal beings meant to live with him and those we love forever. So when we have to part with a loved one for a while because of death, it hurts."

Grey hair trembled with her silent sobs. Jamie held her. The aunt looked on, anger glittering. Serena shook her head and pointed to her watch, indicating that she needed to leave. Jamie nodded that she had everything under control.

"Don't let this make you bitter," she whispered. "Make something good come from Karen's death. If she was the kind of girl you say she was, then she wouldn't want her death to cause any more pain."

Mrs. Fuller straightened. "You're right. She wouldn't. Thank you for that reminder." She took the tissue from Dakota's outstretched hand and mopped her face. "All right, tell me what we need to do."

Once plans for Karen's remains had been made, Dakota and Jamie escorted the women to a small waiting area.

Dakota began, "Do you mind if I ask you a few questions? We still don't have the man who murdered your daughter."

"What do you need from me?"

"I've read the case file. And I've read through all the interviews. But I'm hoping if you tell me about it one more time, maybe you'll remember something."

A heavy sigh, a snort from the aunt who, up until this point, had been mostly silent.

Dakota eyed her. "I'm guessing you think we're all pretty incompetent."

Mrs. Freemont leaned forward, derision marring her face. "You bet I do."

"I can understand how you would feel that way, ma'am, and I'm truly sorry nothing has come to light, but to be honest, this guy doesn't leave any evidence. And Karen's not his only victim."

"What do you mean?"

Dakota flicked a glance at Jamie. "I mean, we believe she was one of many that this man has killed."

Mrs. Fuller fanned herself. "Oh my. Oh my."

The aunt jumped in. "You mean there's a serial killer out there? Is that what you're saying?"

"Yes, ma'am. Unfortunately. That's why I need you to put your anger aside and answer my questions. Maybe I'll ask one that the detective who was on Karen's case four years ago neglected to ask."

Another snort from the aunt. "Now that wouldn't surprise me any. That other man was an incompetent fool."

"I don't know about that. I do know he didn't know what he was up against. We do."

"Oh you do, do you? And just what makes you think you know any more than the idiot before you?"

Jamie stood and paced to the window. "Because he broke into my sister's house last night and stabbed her."

Complete silence. Shocked faces. Subdued attitude.

"What questions do you have?" Mrs. Fuller finally asked.

Jamie turned, wondering what had compelled her to blurt that out. But the look on Mrs. Freemont's face told her it was something she'd needed to hear. Compassion now softened the features that had been granite only seconds before.

Dakota jumped in. "I know you were visiting relatives when Karen disappeared."

"Yes, and she'd gone to a party with my nephew. They were at a friend's birthday party and she —"

"Sorry to interrupt, but where was the party?"

"Here. In Spartanburg." Mrs. Fuller snatched another tissue from the box on the table beside her. "I didn't really want her to go, but she was eighteen. Her cousin was twenty." She shrugged. "They were grown. What could I say?"

Mrs. Freemont finally spoke once more.

311

"Unfortunately, my son wasn't nearly as innocent as my niece. I didn't realize it at the time, but the birthday party was more like a keg and drug party."

"Ah."

"Karen wasn't really into that kind of thing, but my nephew didn't tell her everything. So, she went, thinking she was going to visit and meet some friends that went to Wofford."

"She was planning on going to college there. Had already been accepted and had an academic scholarship. It's where my son went." This time Mrs. Freemont spoke to the floor. "I've felt so guilty . . ." Her lips trembled and she pressed them together, then said, "I don't understand how he let this happen. He should have protected her. Watched out for her . . ."

Karen's mother covered her sister's hand and closed her eyes. "There is no blame placed except on the one who killed Karen. Josiah couldn't have known. He was young, a little wild. No different than any other young person sowing a few wild oats. He's a good man now."

"I know." Sniffle. "I know."

"Anyway, apparently the party got out of control. Karen wanted to leave and Josiah didn't. She called me. I told her to call a cab and I'd pay for it. She went outside to wait for the cab and that's the last anyone saw of her."

Dakota blew out a sigh. "Someone reported seeing a blue Honda in the area. Do you know anyone with a car like that? Someone Karen would have trusted to give her a ride?"

"No," Mrs. Fuller said. "We were visiting from New Jersey. There was no one."

"He probably drugged her." Jamie spoke from her position by the window.

"This doesn't fit his profile, though," Dakota spoke up.

Mrs. Fuller shifted and focused on him. "What do you mean?"

"From what we can tell, he stalks his victims, watches them, learns their patterns, then strikes when the opportunity presents itself. Karen was from New Jersey, visiting Anderson. There's no way he would have had time to do all that."

"She was a crime of opportunity. An impulsive one too," Jamie offered.

Dakota gave a slow nod and flicked a glance at the two women. "So, when she called you, she sounded . . . ?"

"Mad. She was furious with Josiah."

"And that's one thing I don't think he'll ever get over." Mrs. Freemont grabbed her own tissue to dab her eyes.

"She wouldn't want him to feel guilty about that," Jamie said softly. "They would have smoothed things out if they'd had the chance."

"I know and I've told him that numerous times, but it still haunts him."

"But she wasn't scared," Dakota redirected.

"No." Karen's mother. "She just wanted to get home and away from that place. She was just plain mad." She gave a little laugh. "Ooh, that girl could get mad." Then sadness covered her once more.

Dakota blew out a sigh. "Did she have a cell phone on her?"

"They found it outside the house, tossed into the bushes."

"That wasn't in the report." He shot a disgusted look at the ceiling.

"I think they found it later. The family that owned the house had a yard service. When they were trimming the bushes, it fell out."

"And of course he picked it up, getting his prints all over it."

"Yes, and when he asked the owner if it belonged to anyone in the family, they said no. The guy realized it could have something to do with what had happened to Karen, so he took it to the police."

"Did they find any prints or anything on it?"

"Just the man who turned it in and Karen's."

"Probably had her toss it," Dakota muttered. He stood. "Thank you, ma'am, Mrs. Freemont. I guess that'll be all for now. I appreciate your willingness to answer my questions. I know it's not easy dredging this back up."

She took his hand, looked earnestly into his eyes, and pleaded, "Please find this killer. Not just for Karen's sake, but before he kills someone else."

"We're doing our best, ma'am, I promise."

Jamie and Dakota escorted the ladies out of the room, and Dakota said, "So Karen Fuller was in the wrong place at the wrong time."

"He was probably on the prowl for another victim, saw Karen standing by the curb, had his knockout drug with him, and snatched her."

"She never knew what hit her."

He rubbed her shoulder. "I'm sorry. I know that was difficult for you to listen to."

"Not as hard as it was on her mother and aunt."

25

The Hero watched the door to Samantha's room. Two guards had been posted on either side. No matter, he was finished with her anyway. He had no doubt that Jamie had gotten his message loud and clear.

It was getting close to the time to bring the games to an end.

He almost hated to stop. It was so much fun watching everyone run around like little ants scurrying to rebuild what he was slowly destroying.

Their confidence, their faith in the system, their security. Their families. He hated families. It was all such a sham. Hypocrites, all of them. Well, he'd prove it to them, show them how miserable they really were and teach them not to hide behind the façade of happiness. He would expose the truth — that happiness and love don't exist.

They'd identified Karen. She'd been number fifteen.

"Stop the pain. Only you can do it. You'll be my hero."

Only Jamie still needed him. He'd failed her. Failed in his duty. But he would rectify that soon.

Soon, Jamie, soon.

Monday

Somehow, the weekend passed without incident. Monday morning, Dakota did a little more digging into the cases of the newly identified women looking for common factors. Jamie had found the physical similarities in the bones. Now he needed more information.

Five victims. Six if he included Jamie.

Using a map, he decided to bring George in on this and do a little geographic profiling. George said he could be at the station in ten minutes.

Dakota pulled up the software known as Criminal Geographic Targeting on the computer, and it shot a supersized image to the wall opposite him, giving him a twelve-by-twelve screen on which he could build his profile.

Geographic profiling was an information management system and investigative tool that evaluated the locations of connected crimes that were thought to be serial in nature. Once he input the data related to time, distance, and movements to and from the crime scene, the analysis would give him a three-dimensional model. A jeopardy surface. Meaning, where everything took place. Then the system would spit out the most probable area of residence, workplace, and leisure areas for the offender.

Did it work?

Sometimes.

Was it worth taking the time to do?

He hoped so.

George knocked on the door and Dakota gave him a nod. "I'm getting ready to input all the data. Once I do, I want your opinion on where we need to be looking for this guy."

"Sure. What made you think of this?"

"Just an idea."

"How familiar are you with the program?"

"I took the class that was offered but haven't done much with it. That's why I wanted your help."

"No problem. Why don't you read me the information from the files and I'll do the inputting? I just took a refresher course on this last month."

"All right." Dakota grabbed the nearest file and they got started.

After a few false starts with George muttering to himself about modern technology, they finally figured it out. By the time they were finished, the jeopardy surface contained height and probability codes. Now all they had to do was superimpose the image onto a map of the area.

George clicked and dragged.

Dakota sat back and studied the image. "Does it say anything to you?"

"Not really."

"Any connecting factors?"

George blew out a sigh and stared at the wall. "The five girls all disappeared from various locations. There doesn't seem to be a pattern there. Eastside, westside, all over."

"Right. I agree. But they were all buried in the same spot. Except for Lisa Dupre. He changed his MO there and we suspect there are other bodies out there that we haven't found yet. Put our victims' residences in and let's add that as a factor."

As George typed, a knock on the door had Dakota swiveling in his chair. "Jamie? What are you doing here?"

"I hitched a ride with an officer coming this way. I would have walked but figured you'd have a fit if I did." The morgue was only a couple of blocks from the police department.

He frowned. "You know it. How's Sam?"

"She's doing all right. No more bleeding, the baby's heart rate is even stronger this morning so we might get our miracle after all." Blinking back tears, she moved to his side. "What are you working on?"

"A geographic profile."

She studied the screen. "Do you mind if I help?"

"Sure." He handed her the files. "Why don't you go back over all the medical stuff? And if anything else pops out at you, let me know. I also had Jazz go back and pull all of the missing persons cases in the city for the last fifteen years that match the demographics for our victims. I want to compare their stories to the ones we already have."

Jamie took the stack. "How many were there?"

"Twenty-two that raised a red flag. That's not counting the ones we already have identified."

She winced. "That many? All right."

Three hours later, Dakota gave up. "Let's keep this information and take a break."

Jamie looked up from the file she was reading. "Can I take these back to the hospital?"

"Sure, I can sign for them." Dakota grabbed his pen.

She nodded. "I just can't help feeling

we're missing something. Something that would blow this whole thing wide open. A connection that's obvious and we're just not seeing it."

Dakota stood. "Take the files. It's no problem. Come on, I'll walk with you back over to the hospital. I want to check on Sam anyway." He turned to George, who still had his gaze fixed on the multicolored wall. "Thanks for your help."

"You're welcome. Let me know if there's anything else I can do for you."

"Will do."

Dakota and Jamie headed out from the station. "I have to admit, I'm a bit stumped."

Jamie feigned shock. "The big bad FBI man?"

He laughed and cut his eyes at her. "Watch it, woman."

She shifted the files and he reached for them. "Let me have those." When his fingers brushed hers, tingling awareness zipped through him. Jamie flushed and he knew she'd felt it too.

As soon as this case was over, he promised himself. As soon as it was over. Definitely incentive to make it happen.

Carrying the files, he smiled as Jamie avoided his eyes and picked up the pace.

She cared about him whether she liked it or not. And one day, God willing, she'd be able to admit it.

Slow, steady progress had already been made with her, in his opinion. He had patience perfected, as far as he was concerned. No matter how long it took to win her heart, he had the time.

Jamie dropped the last file onto the window seat. Samantha must have heard the soft slap the file made against the vinyl covering because she turned her head in Jamie's direction. "Hey."

"Hey there, how're you doing?"

"Ready to get out of here and get home."

"Mom and Dad were just here. They went downstairs to get something to eat but should be back in a bit."

"Good." She licked her lips and reached for the water cup Jamie had just refilled. A long sip and a sigh. "I can't seem to wake up. I just want to sleep and sleep and sleep."

Jamie gave a low laugh. "Well, that might be a combination of drugs and pregnancy."

A maternal smile covered her sister's face and she placed a protective hand over her small bulge. "Yeah. I can't believe it."

"Is that why you didn't say anything to me?"

"Partly." Sam's blonde hair fell over her face and she pushed it back to look at Jamie. "And partly because it was such a delicious secret to keep all to myself."

"I can't believe you didn't tell."

"I know. It was hard — and easy too. It was just weird. Connor and I've only been married a little over six months. And then there's the whole Jenna factor." Concern marred Sam's forehead. "I wasn't sure how she would handle having her dad's attention diverted from her just as she's gotten it back."

"Jenna's a big girl. She's finally got her head on straight. She'll be in love with that baby the minute he's born."

"You're still stuck on 'he,' huh?"

Jamie grinned. "You bet."

A knock on the door pulled Jamie's attention from Sam to her parents who were entering the room.

Upon seeing Samantha awake, they hurried to her side for gentle hugs and kisses. Then her father pushed the files Jamie had been reading aside and settled himself on the seat beside her. Samantha moved her feet and her mother sat on the end of the bed. The woman reached out to massage a foot. "How are you feeling, honey?"

"Much better. Sore, but that's to be

expected. I'm going to be on bed rest until the next doctor's appointment, but that's all right too. As long as this baby's born healthy, nothing else matters."

Her parents exchanged a look. Jamie pounced. "What is it? You guys are just dying to tell us something, so why don't you go for it?"

Immediately tears filled her mother's eyes and her dad cleared his throat a zillion times. Finally, her mom took a deep breath and said, "I don't really know where to start." She looked at each of her daughters. "There's so much you don't know. So much." She looked away, then back. "I've thought about how to tell you this and there just isn't an easy way."

"Mom! Spill it." Sam, the impatient one.

"Your dad and I went through some hard times back before you were born, Jamie. Sam was about nine years old, so she probably remembers some of it."

Samantha shook her head. "No, I don't remember any hard times."

"Well, they were there, whether you remember them or not. Anyway, your dad hurt his back real bad one summer. He climbed up on the roof to repair a shingle and fell off."

"Oh, wait! I do remember that," Sam declared.

"He was on a lot of medication. But the pain was horrible. And he was afraid to have surgery. So, the doctors tried to keep him comfortable with painkillers. Lots and lots of painkillers."

"He got addicted, didn't he?" Jamie whispered, looking at her dad. He nodded and clenched his jaw.

"Yes," her mother cleared her throat. "He did. I knew it and so did a lot of other people, but your dad wouldn't admit he had a problem. Even after the surgery that he finally consented to have, he couldn't seem to kick the drugs. His back healed, but he was never really completely out of pain."

"So he kept taking the painkillers. Where did he get them?"

"He just doctor hopped. Saw one doctor after another. Since he rarely turned anything into the insurance company, nothing was on record. And back then, they didn't have the kind of computer tracking systems they have now. So, it wasn't hard to get his hands on the pills."

Her mother's throat bobbed and Jamie's dad took up the story even while she wondered where they were going with this. "One day I was in a mindless, drugged daze, not feeling any pain, that's for sure. I left a few pills out on the table, intending to pop some more. The phone rang and I went to answer it, leaving the pills on the table."

A quiet sob from her mother echoed in the room.

"Sam, you were old enough to know better, but you'd had a rough day at school. A bully had pushed you down and said some mean things to you. You grabbed a few of those pills, popped them in your mouth, and swallowed them before I could blink. I threw the phone down and tried to make you throw up. You just looked at me and said, 'But Daddy, I had a bad day. I want to feel better just like you.'"

Sam gasped. "I don't remember that."

Tears dripped down her mother's cheeks. "We had to rush you to the hospital to get your stomach pumped."

Her dad stood. "I felt like I'd been slammed with a ton of bricks. The fact that I had taught you that a few pills could make you feel better, and then I couldn't stop you from —" He broke off, swallowing hard.

"He left that night and I didn't hear from him for two years."

Jamie sat straight up. "What? Wait a minute. I happened somewhere in those two years. Are you saying," she gulped, "Daddy's not my daddy?"

"No," her mother rushed to say, "he's definitely your daddy. Neither one of us knew I was pregnant when he left. I didn't find out until about a week later."

Jamie and Samantha stared at their parents in stunned disbelief.

Then Jamie shot to her feet and faced her mother. "Why are you telling us this now? There's more, isn't there?"

"Yes," a sob, a sniffle, then, "there's more." She looked at Samantha. "Are you okay with me telling you this? I didn't want to do this now, but she wants to meet you and is insisting on sooner rather than later."

Samantha leaned forward, wincing. "I'm fine, it just hurts to move."

"Who wants to meet us?"

Another glance exchanged between her parents, then, her father said, "Your sister."

26

Ever since her parents' had dropped that emotional bomb, Jamie had been like a zombie. All day, she'd gone back and forth between work and checking on her sister. The one in the hospital, not the one she'd just learned existed.

She had another sister somewhere in the world. How insane was that? And not just any sister, a *twin.* Someone who looked exactly like her. Maybe. What if she was a fraternal twin? Jamie hadn't thought to ask. Her mind had buzzed like a horde of swarming bees.

After her parents finished their incredible tale, they'd left, leaving Jamie and Samantha to talk about it, to deal with this life-changing news.

She had a sister who'd discovered she was adopted when her father delivered the news on his deathbed. After his funeral, she'd started the search and found her family,

Jamie's family, in a matter of minutes.

While Samantha and Jamie sat there stunned, absorbing the information, good news had come in the form of the doctor. Samantha could go home as long as she promised to stay in bed and keep her feet elevated.

Jamie volunteered to take care of her. Having identified all of the bodies, she could take some time from work until something else came in. If an anthropologist was needed while she was out, the one from Charlotte would help out as well as the one in the neighboring town of Greenville. That had been the arrangement before Jamie took her current job a year and a half ago. It could be done again in an emergency.

Between the two of them, Jamie's duties were covered.

Safely ensconced in Samantha and Connor's newly wired, heavily secured home, Jamie sat at the kitchen table reviewing the files of the missing/dead girls once again. She glanced at the clock. Nearly midnight. She should be exhausted. But her mind hummed, and Jamie knew if she went to bed now, she'd toss and turn for hours.

So, she might as well work.

Pushing aside thoughts of a sister who wanted to meet her, she focused her attention on the details in the files.

Concentrate, she ordered her scattered brain.

Connor and Dakota had gone to check on something two hours ago. Samantha was sleeping, and Jamie wanted to jump out of her skin. She needed to go home. And as soon as Connor walked in the door, she would.

Her life had been upended, her security stripped away from her, and a panic attack threatened to undo her. She needed her home. But her home wasn't safe anymore.

It didn't seem to matter. The urge to flee nearly strangled her. Hands shaking, she picked up her new cell phone and punched in Maya's number. Should she call her this late? Jamie had before and Maya never seemed to care.

"Hello?"

"Hi, Maya, sorry to call you so late." She managed to get the words out around the tightness in her throat. Surprisingly enough, she thought she sounded almost normal.

"Hey, stranger, that's okay, how are you?" A rustling sound filtered through the phone, and Jamie pictured Maya sitting up in bed and turning on the lamp on the nightstand.

"I'm not so good right now."

Maya's voice took on a more professional

tone, yet still tinged with the concern of a friend. "What's going on?"

"I'm on the verge of a panic attack. My coping strategies aren't working."

"Why not? Why the attack now?"

"A lot of reasons I don't want to go into right now. I just needed to . . . to . . ."

"You need some security."

"Yeah."

"You know I'm here for you."

"I know." The pounding of her heart eased a bit. Still, her air felt cut off, like she couldn't fill her lungs up full enough.

"Talk to me."

"I'm trying."

"How's Samantha?"

"Pregnant."

A gasp. "What? You're going to be an auntie!"

Maya's squeal of excitement fed Jamie's. She pictured holding Sam and Connor's baby. Then the baby wasn't Samantha's, it was hers. And Dakota's. Her stomach did a little flip at the thought and the constriction in her chest loosened. "Yeah, I am."

"When?"

Pant, suck in air, pant. "Around Christmastime, I think. She's only about three months along. Twelve or thirteen weeks."

"What a wonderful Christmas gift."

"I need to go home, Maya."

"Why?"

Anxiety twisted inside her once again. "I'm not sure. I just need to be there. I need to feel safe again." Tears dripped down her cheeks to splat onto the file in front of her.

A hand settled on her shoulder and she jumped and whirled, heart pounding at full gallop once more.

Dakota stepped back, hands held in front of him. "I whistled, I promise."

Sam stood behind him. "You're supposed to be in bed," was all Jamie could think to say.

Samantha jerked a thumb at Dakota, who stood in the doorway. "Had to let him in. Plus, I was up anyway. I have to go to the bathroom — again." She disappeared, hand held tight to her wounded side.

Jamie turned back to the phone. "I'm sorry, Maya, I need to go. Thanks for listening."

"Dakota's there?"

"Yes. I'm going to get him to take me home."

"Trust him, Jamie, lean on him. I truly believe God has put him in your life for a reason."

Pausing, Jamie let that sink in. "I sure hope so."

Saying goodbye, she hung up the phone. Her hands shook and she felt like her lungs still strained for air.

Dakota took her hand and cradled it between his palms. "I'll take you home. Can you wait until morning? Connor is here now, and I can come by first thing. As early as you want."

As much as she wanted to go . . . "What if it's not safe?"

"I'll make sure it is. I promise."

She studied him. The reassurance she saw sent relief flowing through her. "Okay, I don't know why I'm doing this. I don't want to give in to the anxiety."

"You're worn down. You've been through so much and now you find your attacker is back. Give yourself a break, Jamie."

His compassion nearly did her in. Sucking in a deep breath, one that finally hit her lungs full blast, she closed her eyes and drew on the strength she hadn't been able to find only moments ago. "All right. I'll be all right."

"You will, I promise."

"Why are you doing this, Dakota? Why do you care so much about me?"

His intense gaze bored holes into hers. Then he whispered, "I think you know why."

"I don't want to lose you," she whispered back.

Then his eyes smiled. "Not a chance, lady."

Standing on tiptoe, she pressed her lips to his, then stepped back.

Dakota didn't move. He didn't dare. She'd just taken a huge step forward and he didn't want to make a wrong move. Lips still tingling, heart so full he couldn't speak, he didn't really have to worry about making any kind of move. The word *frozen* came to mind.

Then she pushed out a nervous little laugh. "Did I just do that?"

"Uh-huh." He blinked.

"So, say something."

"Um . . . how do you feel?"

"Like I can breathe now."

"I'm glad *you* can."

She caught his meaning and breathed a little laugh. Then she blinked up at him. "You'll take me home first thing in the morning?"

"Sure. I'll go home and grab a couple of hours of sleep and then pick you up."

His mouth worked, but his feet wouldn't move.

"Dakota?"

He blinked. "I'm leaving." Still nothing.

She grasped his hand and tugged, freeing him from his stupefied paralysis. Lifting his other hand, he traced her lips with a finger. He couldn't help the emotion that sprang from somewhere he didn't know existed. "Thank you," he whispered.

A silent nod from her.

Then he left with a lingering glance that burned itself into his mind. She stood in the doorway watching him go, her expression hopeful, longing.

Which caused hope to rupture within him.

The night couldn't go fast enough, as far he was concerned.

Tuesday

Tuesday morning, his mind still unable to completely let go of the fact that Jamie had willingly kissed him the night before, he drove on automatic pilot back to the house he'd left only a few hours before.

One thought kept circling his mind.

She'd kissed him.

Wow.

He almost thanked God. Thought about it. Tried it out. *Thank you, if that was something you did.*

Arriving to the Wolfe residence, he barely had time to climb out of the car before

Jamie exited the house and walked toward him.

A slight blush covered her cheeks, and he figured she was a little embarrassed from the night before. Uncertainty swirled in his midsection. Should he say something?

How about hello? Good morning? He mocked himself into untying his tongue.

"Good morning."

She smiled and met his eyes. "Good morning. Thanks for doing this."

"Not a problem." Dakota held the door for her and waited until she was settled before he shut it.

He climbed back in the driver's seat and an awkward silence filled the car.

Road construction on one of the back streets to Jamie's house held them up about twenty minutes, and during that time, he kept shooting her looks, trying to read her expression.

"Are you all right?"

"Yes," she gave a little laugh. "I guess I just feel silly. I don't know what happened back at Sam's house last night and I'm embarrassed," she admitted. "I was just thinking about everything and remembering and . . ."

He took her hand, kissed her knuckles. When she flushed and looked up at him through her lashes, his heart thumped. "It's okay, Jamie."

"Thanks." She squeezed his fingers and left her hand in his. Finally, the road crew waved them through. Then they were at the house.

Jessica, the cop who'd been there the day he'd gotten conked in the head by the creep, sat out front. They still kept someone on Jamie's house at all times in case the guy decided to come back.

She waved as Dakota pulled into the drive.

Jamie climbed out, pulled her keys from her bag, and acted like she couldn't get inside fast enough.

"Hey, hold on a minute okay? I want to have a look around, all right?"

She jumped, nerves obviously back. "Oh, okay."

While Jamie sat in the car with Jessica, Dakota walked the perimeter. He found nothing out of place or any reason to be alarmed.

Back at the front door, Jamie joined him, opened it, and paused on the threshold.

He nearly ran into her. "What is it?"

"My alarm wasn't on."

"What?"

"When I opened the door, there wasn't any sound. There's always the long beep that warns you that you have forty-five seconds to punch in your code before the alarm sounds. That didn't happen."

Dakota pushed around her and pulled his weapon. "Wave to Jessica to get in here. Then you stay right on my back, all right?"

Jamie shoved down the familiar fear and waved Jessica over. The woman exited the car, frowning. Approaching, she placed a hand on her weapon. "What is it?"

"Someone's been here."

"That's impossible. I've been here since seven o'clock this morning." Even so, she pulled the gun from her holster.

"I know, but my alarm wasn't armed. Did you reset it after you got my stuff the other day?"

"Absolutely."

"I thought so but had to ask."

They entered the house and Jamie found Dakota in the den. "Come in here and see if anything seems off to you. We're going to sweep your house together. Be like glue on my side."

Jamie stepped in and looked around. She shook her head. "Everything looks fine."

"Do you have any gloves?"

"You mean like surgical gloves?"

"Those would do."

"Yes. I have a few more. Stitching you up only took one pair."

Surprise at her sassy comment in the midst of the serious situation made him blink.

She closed her eyes. "Sorry, I'm scared."

"I know, Jamie. Can you get them?"

"Sure." He led her through the house and into the bathroom, looking in every direction as they went, gun trained in front of him. She opened the linen closet door and pulled down the first aid kit from the third shelf. Slipping the gloves on her hands, she looked at him.

"Okay, let's go back in the den."

"No," she said slowly, thinking. "If he was in my house, he would have made whatever he was up to personal. Breaking in my house is personal. Invading my space at work. That's personal. Attacking my sister . . ."

"Personal," he nodded. "Okay. What's left?"

She looked at him. "My bedroom."

"Didn't he leave that picture in your Bible?"

"Yes. But if he came back, he had another message to leave me."

Dakota motioned toward the back of the house. "Let me check it first. When you go in, keep your eyes open for anything remotely strange." He looked back at Jessica. "Call Jake and Connor, will you? Tell Jake to rap three times on the door so I know it's him."

She nodded and got on her phone.

Jamie followed Dakota into what used to be her haven. Now, it just looked like any other room. A place she wouldn't feel safe sleeping in anymore.

Just one more thing he'd managed to take from her.

Clenching her gloved hands into fists, she tamped down the bubbling anger. Not now.

Dakota asked, "Well?"

She went straight to the end table near her bed and opened the drawer. Pulling out her Bible, she opened it. The well-worn pages crinkled under her fingers as she flipped through it.

"Nothing in here." Putting it back, she turned, went to her dresser and rummaged through every drawer, her skin crawling at the thought that *he* might have done the same thing only hours ago.

"I don't see anything out of place."

Giving a disgruntled sigh, she placed her hands on her hips and gave the room a three-sixty.

Everything in its place.

Then her gaze landed on the door to her bathroom.

Closed.

Now that was odd. She always left it open. Heart thudding, she approached it, and with trembling fingers reached for the knob.

"Wait!"

She stopped, breaths coming in hurried pants.

"Jamie, look at me."

Dragging her gaze from the bathroom doorknob took superhuman effort. She focused in on his eyes. Those intense blue eyes that seemed to see into her soul. "Why?"

"What is it?"

"The door's closed. I don't normally close it."

Jessica stepped into the room. "Jake and Connor are on the way."

Without taking his eyes from Jamie's, he asked Jessica, "Did you close this door after you packed up Jamie's things?"

"Uh . . . I'm not sure, I mean, I could have. If it was open, I don't think I would have, though." Her brows drew together. "I'm sorry, I just don't remember."

"Stand back and cover the door," Dakota said. "How far out is Connor?"

"He was at the hospital. He's probably in

341

the driveway by now."

Jessica slid sideways and Jamie moved out of the way, but made sure she could see what they were doing. Sweat slicked her palms. That familiar chest-tightening sensation closed over her. *Not now, not now.*

Three raps sounded on the door.

No one turned.

Breathing shallow breaths, Jamie kept the attack at bay. Focusing on Dakota and Jessica, she wiped her palms on her jeans.

Stance tense, nerves tight, Jessica held her gun pointed toward the door.

Connor entered the room, his steps silent, his presence bringing comfort. Glad Dakota and Jessica had backup, Jamie faded back against the wall next to Dakota.

Jessica stayed ready but allowed Connor to take her place on the side of the door. Dakota stood opposite.

The two men exchanged nods. Dakota reached out a hand to twist the knob.

With a shove he opened the door.

A blinding flash exploded from the room.

Connor, Dakota, and Jessica flung themselves backward and hit the floor. Dakota rolled and pulled Jamie down beside him.

"What was that?" he hollered.

"A camera flash," Connor grunted as he hauled himself to his feet.

"Stay here." Dakota's words filtered through the fog of terror. But she kept control. *Breathe.*

Connor disappeared inside the bathroom. Jessica followed. Her gasp, Connor's "Aw, no . . ."

Jamie stood on shaking legs. Dakota held her upper arm. She tried to enter the bathroom and pulled up short when Connor came back out. Jessica stepped around him and disappeared from the bedroom, phone tucked to her ear.

"What is it? What did you find?" Jamie knew it had to be bad. Connor's face looked like he'd dipped it in bleach. "What is it? Let me see."

Connor shook his head. "You're not going in there."

Dakota raised a brow, focusing on Connor's face. "It's . . ." He swallowed.

With a sudden twist, Jamie was out of Dakota's grip and past Connor before either man could move. "Jamie!"

At first she didn't see what had so upset Connor and Jessica. Then she moved to the tub and stopped, transfixed, horrified by the scene before her.

Maya, her friend, counselor, and prayer partner, lay in Jamie's tub, eyes staring at nothing, throat slashed. The note taped to the ceramic tile above Maya's head read "Stop trying to find me. I'll find you when the time is right. Enjoy the picture. Save it so I can add it to my collection."

Jamie's old cell phone sat on the back of the toilet.

It began to ring.

27

Dakota looked for something to pick the phone up with. He needed gloves. Before he could find something, Jamie had the phone in one of her already gloved hands and pressed the answer button.

Without him having to ask, she put it on speakerphone. The way her hand trembled, he was afraid she was going to drop the device, but her jaw had that determined set to it that said she was doing what she had to do once again.

He doubted she realized tears streamed down her cheeks.

He waited for her to speak. She said nothing, just stared at the phone.

Agitated breathing came over the line.

Still Jamie held silent.

He mouthed, "What are you doing?"

Her eyes flicked from his back to the phone. The stubborn set of her mouth didn't change. The tears had trickled to a slow drip.

A noise from the bedroom caught his and Connor's attention. Connor motioned he'd take care of it. Jake and Serena, no doubt. He turned his focus back on Jamie.

Why didn't she say something?

Rustling came over the speakerphone. Then a low-pitched noise. A growl?

"Hello, Jamie. Being stubborn like that sister of yours, I see." Dakota strained to hear the gravelly voice, wishing he could tape the call or trace it.

Jamie closed her eyes and clamped her upper teeth into her bottom lip. And still she didn't respond.

Then Dakota realized what she was doing. He remembered the conversation in the hospital with Samantha. An idea hit him. He pulled out his own phone, a Blackberry, and found the right button. Voice notes. He hit record and held it near Jamie's phone.

She looked at him, at his phone, understood what he was doing, and angled the phone closer to his.

"Speak to me, Jamie, tell me how much you miss your hero."

She turned the phone from her and gagged once. Took a deep breath and held still.

Voices in the background. Listening hard,

he tried to recognize the place, anything about the call.

Nothing.

"Speak to me!" the voice on the other end roared. Flinching, she pressed the other hand still encased in the glove to her mouth. A barely perceptible whimper escaped. Dakota doubted the person on the other end of the phone heard it.

"I know you're there." Although back in control, Dakota could hear undercurrents of rage in the words. "Well, if you won't talk to me, then I will talk to you. Tell your friends to stop their searching, their snooping into business that isn't theirs. Tell them that unless they stop, more people will die. People close to them. Like an Anabelle Richards in San Antonio, Texas. 126 Arrowwood Drive, I believe it is."

Dakota felt the bottom drop from beneath him. How had this guy tracked down his mother?

"Or maybe a young lady by the name of Jenna Wolfe? I believe she's staying with her grandparents at the retirement home."

Dakota shot a look at Connor, who'd returned from telling Jake and Serena to hold off for a bit. And to be quiet. The man looked furious. He was already dialing a number to provide protection for the people this guy had just named.

"I know you're there! I know you're all there! Stop looking for me, you'll never find me. I hide very well." A low laugh that sent shivers through Dakota. This guy really creeped him out. "And tell your bodyguards they're wasting their time. I can get to you anytime, anyplace. And I will."

A shudder wracked her body and Dakota placed a hand on her shoulder, squeezing gently, encouraging her. Letting her know he was there.

More breathing, a heavy sigh. "Talk to you soon, Jamie, very, very soon."

Click.

Jamie dropped the phone and sank to the floor, burying her head against her knees.

"No use tracking the number. It's either a stolen phone or prepaid."

"I sent it to Jazz. She'll take the recording from my phone and see if she can pick up any background noises that might help in pinpointing where this guy made his phone call from."

From a distance, their voices registered. Serena had already done her thing. Maya had been photographed and transferred to the black body bag. Jamie felt numb. She'd heard a conversation about protection for

Dakota's mother in Texas and then something about a car being sent to cover the retirement home where Connor's parents lived and then a shadow for Jenna.

Poor girl, Jamie thought absently. Jenna had already been through so much. Now, again, she'd have to put up with being threatened because of her father's job.

Then Jamie's mind jumped back to Maya. Smothering guilt pressed in on her from all sides to push away the numbness. Despair closed in, followed by a wave of rage so intense it bent her double.

"Jamie?"

A hand on her back. She straightened. Looked up at Dakota. He studied her, eyes widening slightly. She wondered what he saw.

Then he was guiding her from the room. "We're talking to the neighbors."

"How did he get in, Dakota?"

She almost didn't recognize her own voice. Low and hard, it grated. Clearing her throat, she waited for his response.

"We're hoping someone saw something."

"What about the person watching the house last night?"

Shifting, Dakota's eyes left hers for a moment, then came back to hers. "He left around five o'clock this morning. Some sort of family emergency. Got a call on his cell phone that his kid was in the ER. He didn't wait for a replacement."

"I don't blame him." She sighed. "So, sometime between five and seven, this guy got in my house, around my alarm system, and put Maya in the tub."

"Put her in the tub?"

"She was killed somewhere else. There was very little blood." Now she sounded mechanical, professional. She decided it was better than weepy or hysterical — or screaming at the top of her lungs.

"Yeah, Serena said something along those lines."

Serena stepped back inside. "I'll see you at the morgue?"

Crossing her arms, she gripped each bicep. "I don't know, Serena. I don't think I can handle this one. I'm sorry," she ended on a whisper.

Sympathy glistened in her friend's eyes. "No problem, Jamie, I'll call in someone else if I need to. I can probably handle it myself. This isn't your area anyway."

Jamie nodded and Serena left.

"Come sit in the den a minute." Dakota directed her to the sofa.

" 'For you have been called for this purpose, since Christ also suffered for you, leaving you an example for you to follow in His steps, who committed no sin, nor was any deceit found in His mouth; and while being reviled, He did not revile in return; while suffering, He uttered no threats, but kept entrusting *Himself* to Him who judges righteously.' "

"What?"

She'd whispered the words to herself so quietly, he hadn't understood her. She looked at him with deep, soul clenching sorrow and clarified, "First Peter 2:21. I have to quote it when the desire for revenge takes over."

Curiosity stared at her. "And it's wrong to want revenge?"

"It's not wrong to want justice, to desire to right a wrong or help put away the bad guys. But revenge, that's not right. It's not healthy and I won't have it in my heart."

She'd managed to render him speechless, she could tell. When he found his voice, he asked, "How?"

"How what?"

"How do you keep trusting him?"

"Because I can't *not* trust him. Because he is who he says he is and he hasn't let me down yet. Even when his ways aren't my ways, he hasn't failed me."

"Guys?" She turned to see Connor standing in the entrance to her den. "We may have someone who saw something."

Jamie stood. "What?"

"Around 5:45 this morning, a neighbor was up and happened to look out his window. He saw a car pull into your garage, then the garage door shut."

"What?" Disbelief slanted through her. "How? Only Samantha and I have garage door openers."

"This is how your guy's been getting in."

"But even if he got in the garage, the alarm . . ."

"He had the code. Only this time, when we changed it, he didn't have access to it, so he cut the phone line and dismantled it."

"Which is why it didn't work when I came home today."

"Exactly."

"But to open my garage?" She shook her head.

"We're working on that."

Dakota spoke up. "What kind of car was it, did the neighbor notice?"

"Yeah, get this. A light blue Honda."

All breath left her for a moment. Then, "That's the same car."

"Yeah." Connor looked at her. "Guess you're moving in with me for a while."

"It's not safe, Connor, you know that."

"I don't think it really matters, to be honest with you. I think this guy is someone you know and trust. That if you opened the door and saw him standing there, you'd let him in."

"No. No way. I'd recognize him if I saw him." She gave a nervous laugh. "You're crazy, Connor. Do you honestly think that I wouldn't know him? After what he did to me?"

Connor raised a hand. "Jamie, this guy is good. He's also mentally deranged. He's got to be criminally insane, which means he's capable of living a normal life while keeping his secret life extremely well-hidden."

"But . . . but . . . who?"

"I don't know, but I think the first place to start looking is someone you possibly work with."

"Do you know how many people that entails?"

"Yeah. I know. It's going to be like looking for a needle in a haystack."

Dakota drew in a breath and said, "Let's start back at square one."

"Square one?" Confused, she waited for him to finish.

"The girls the bones belong to."

Once the authorities were finished with her home, Jamie packed a bag and locked up, wondering if she'd ever be able to return. Not holding her breath on that one.

Back at Connor's house, Samantha let them in and the foursome settled into the den. Samantha claimed the couch to put her feet up. Dakota, Connor, and Jamie grabbed some drinks and the files of the missing girls and sat down at the kitchen table. Dakota propped his feet on the chair next to him and took a drink from the soda can.

Pushing her grief aside, she decided the best thing she could do for Maya was to find the person responsible for her death. Jamie said, "I've gone over and over these. The reports, the x-rays, the investigation notes. Everything. There's nothing that appears to be related — except the fact that all the girls seemed to be either going to a party or coming home from one."

Dakota's feet hit the floor. "What?"

She frowned at him. "What?"

"The link. You said they all either seemed to be on their way to a party or coming home from one."

"Yeah, why? Is that important?"

He shot a look at Connor. "I don't know, but it's definitely something we need to look at a little closer."

They spread the files out on the table

before them.

Jamie grabbed the first one and opened it. Dakota took the next and so on until they had them spread from one end of the table to the other. Samantha came into the kitchen, sat on one of the cushioned chairs, and put her feet up on the one opposite.

At her husband's look, she shrugged. "Sorry, I can't stay away. I need to help." She shifted so she could see the files.

Each report noted that the victim was returning home from or heading to a party.

"That's it. We need George to add this to his profile. Our guy doesn't like party girls? Or likes them too much?"

Jamie slapped the file. "That's crazy."

"But it fits."

She stood, paced to the window, and looked out. "Okay fine. But how would he know what they were doing? Surely, he's not one who keeps up with parties on a regular basis. There's no way he could."

"That's true." Dakota frowned and went back to the file. "That means there's another connector somewhere, something else linking these girls."

"Someone they all knew."

"A teacher?"

More file consulting. Jamie shook her head. "No, we have six or seven high schools around here in a thirty-mile radius. A couple of them attended the same one, but the majority of them went to different high schools."

"Church?"

"Sports team?"

They hovered over the papers.

Samantha sat up, two files clutched in her fingers. "Hey, guys?"

Connor looked up. "What do you have, gorgeous?"

Sam flushed and shot him a look. Jamie bit her lip on a smile. Sam looked anything but gorgeous right now, but Connor didn't see that.

"I've got a connection between these two. It may be nothing, then again . . ."

"What is it?" Jamie scooted closer.

"They were seeing a counselor."

"You mean like a shrink?" Dakota asked.

"Yeah, um . . . the group Eastside Psychiatric Therapists."

"I've seen their building," Connor noted.

Jamie grabbed the laptop from the coffee table, returned to the kitchen, and punched in her search in the Google box. It brought up the address and the names of the doctors. Five doctors in all, Jamie didn't recognize any of them.

She called them out, "Peters, Marshall,

Christianson, Paul, Berry."

The four looked at each other and shook their heads.

"Maybe George knows them."

"Maybe," Jamie muttered. "Do any of the other girls have that in their files? That they were in counseling?"

A search ensued.

Two minutes later, Dakota exclaimed, "Ah ha. Look here. Still a Missing Person, but she was receiving counseling at the group."

"Which doctor?"

"Peters."

"Keep looking," Dakota ordered, excitement seeping into his voice, "I think we've just found a huge connection with these girls."

Connor held up another file. "No mention of any counseling. I'm going to call her family." He snatched up the file and went into another room.

"I didn't have counseling," Jamie whispered. "So what's the connection there?" She blinked and shook her head. "Twenty-two files of missing persons matching the demographics. Plus four," Jamie paused, "*five* other victims that are linked together because of broken and healed bones and monogrammed handcuffs." She shuddered. "Could he have possibly killed that many people?"

Samantha sighed and leaned her head back against the chair. "It's happened before."

"But these aren't girls with no one out there looking for them. They have families, they're loved, they're missed . . ." She swallowed hard. "How is it he's been allowed to get away with this for so long? How has no one seen anything? It doesn't seem possible."

Dakota shook his head. "I don't know, but it's past time he was stopped." He looked up at Jamie. "We need to talk about putting you in a safe house."

Before she could respond, Connor reentered the room. "She wasn't in counseling. She's not an MP anymore either."

"What do you mean she's not a missing person anymore? She turned up?" Dakota tapped his file in his hand into his other palm.

"Yeah, she's now living in Missouri with an aunt."

"And no one thought to let us know so we could remove her from the system?"

"Guess not." He shook his head in disgust and picked up another file, then he looked at Dakota. "What's this about a safe house for Jamie?"

"I think it might be time."

"I can't go into a safe house," she protested. "We've already talked about this. He'll just back off and wait me out."

"Or escalate and start trying to kill off the rest of our family in retaliation." Samantha's words echoed throughout the room.

Jamie set her lips. "I'm not going into hiding. In fact, I'd like to set myself up as bait."

28

Dakota, Connor, and Samantha immediately nixed that idea. Dakota liked the idea of protective custody much better. He was about to mention it when his cell phone rang.

He snapped it up to his ear. "Talk to me, Jazzy."

Conversation ceased as everyone waited impatiently for him to finish listening to the woman. "Got it."

"What?" Samantha pressed.

"Jazz ran our suspect's phone call. It did come from a prepaid phone so no tracing it that way, but when she listened to it off the recording I did, she said she picked up an ambulance siren and someone paging a doctor."

"The hospital," Jamie breathed. "He called from the hospital?"

"Sounds like it."

Grim-faced, Dakota told Jamie, "This guy

is escalating big time. He's stepping up the stakes."

"And I'm the grand prize," she muttered.

"Not if we have anything to say about it," he reassured her.

Jamie watched the men leave to continue the investigation down at the police station. They both wanted to listen to the recording once more, focusing on the sounds Jazz heard. They'd call when they were done.

She and Samantha had the assignment of contacting each family of each missing girl to ask when and where she'd received counseling. Several of the files noted counseling, but didn't mention where they received it.

Alone with Samantha, Jamie studied the next file in front of her, but her mind wasn't into the task. "We have a sister."

"I know. It's all I've been thinking about. Well, that and the baby." Her hand moved over her stomach.

"Did you tell Connor? About our sister?"

"No, not yet. I haven't really had a chance to say anything. I think I'm still trying to process it all."

"I know. I want to see her."

"So do I."

Jamie rubbed her eyes. "Sounds like she wants to meet us too."

"I can't believe it." Samantha eyed her sister. "You have a twin. Not just a sister . . . a twin."

"I know. It's crazy."

"And you never felt like something was missing in your life? Like a part of you wasn't whole?"

Jamie snorted. "Nope, not even a twinge."

"I wonder what her name is. I was so in shock when Mom and Dad dropped this bomb on us that I never asked what her name is."

"I could call."

Samantha shook her head. "No, they'll get around to telling us shortly. I think we should wait to meet her until all this madness is over. I mean, it wouldn't be a good thing to bring her into this while we have a madman out there stalking you."

Tears filled Jamie's eyes. "Oh, Maya," she whispered, "I'm so sorry."

Wrapping her arms around her waist, she bent forward and sobbed. Samantha moved close and hugged Jamie until she was spent.

Jamie pulled away and scrubbed her face with her palms. "I'm sorry."

"It's okay." Samantha sniffed and wiped her own tears. "I loved Maya too."

"I know. Her funeral is tomorrow. I wonder if he'll show up."

Jaw clenched, Samantha stated, "Well, if he does, you can bet his picture will be taken."

A police photographer would be snapping pictures of the crowd the entire service. As soon as the funeral was over, the pictures would be studied, looking for the slightest clue that might lead them one step closer to the killer.

It was time for a subject change. "Tell me about Jenna."

"Huh?" Sam blinked at her.

"Jenna, how is she? Why did she sneak out that night, leaving the window in the garage open?"

"Ah." Samantha shifted. "Well, the girl is eighteen years old, going off to college in less than three months. I don't believe she needs to be sneaking out at night, but apparently she didn't want her father knowing she was going out."

"Who was she going to meet?"

"She went to a party to meet a friend."

Jamie gasped. "Oh, please tell me she's not reverting back to her days of rebellion."

Sam shook her head. "No, she got a phone call around two in the morning. Her friend Kara was drunk and stranded. She called Jenna, begging her to come get her and not tell anyone. She knew if Connor knew, he'd take her home and wake the neighborhood in the process."

"Oh my."

"Yeah. Anyway, she was very apologetic, admitted she shouldn't have done it, but also said she'd probably do it again if Kara needed her help."

"Stubborn."

"It's in the genes."

Samantha gave her belly a little pat. "Guess I'd better get used to it."

Jamie covered her sister's hand with her own. "I want to pray for you and him."

"Still a him, huh?"

"Yeah." She closed her eyes, focused her mind and reached out to her Father. "Jesus, you know what's going on. You know this little baby and Samantha need you. We all do, but Lord, if you would just put your protection around them, keep them safe and healthy, we would be so grateful." Sam turned her hand palm up to squeeze Jamie's fingers. "Thank you, Jesus, for loving us and knowing how all this is going to turn out. May it be for your glory, God. Only for you." Silently, she added, *And keep hatred from my heart.*

Wednesday Morning
"We got a hit on one of the cars." Connor

sprinted across the floor to Dakota, who was on the phone with his boss. Since Dakota worked out of the FBI field office in Columbia, he reported in on a regular basis. First thing this morning, he'd given the man a call.

Dakota held up a finger, nodded and said, "Yes sir, I agree. I'll stay in touch."

He hung up and turned to Connor. "What car?"

"The blue Honda. I had Jessica start keeping track of all the cars she saw coming and going from the neighborhood."

"Good idea."

"I figured if he's that intent on sneaking in her house, he's got to be monitoring it."

"And that means driving by it occasionally."

"Right. She's been feeding me plates over the last hour or so and I've been running them. When she said she had a light blue Honda . . ."

"Bingo." Dakota raised a brow.

"Exactly. Unfortunately, by the time I got the plate from Jessica, our guy had already disappeared. I've got a team out there searching for him and put a BOLO out on him, so we'll see if anything turns up."

"But we got the plate number. That's great. I bet he changes out cars, though,"

Dakota murmured thoughtfully. He rubbed the bridge of his nose, then pinched it.

"Like he only uses the Honda for his stalking and killing games but has another one for his daily life?"

"Yeah. Have you talked to George?"

"A little while ago. I asked him about the car thing and he agreed our suspect would take pleasure in driving by her house and watching it. He would also feel superior to the officer on duty guarding the house, because the officer has no idea the person she was looking for had just driven past her — or him."

"This guy is quite arrogant, isn't he?"

"Definitely."

"Did George have anything to say about the party angle?"

"He thought it was interesting, but didn't put much stock in it."

"What about the counseling side of it?"

"Again, he thought it interesting, but since not all the girls had that in their files, said it's probably a dead end and we'd better spend our time on the car."

Dakota frowned. "Huh. I don't think I agree with that."

"Yeah, I didn't either. But then George isn't a detective, so his brain isn't running along those lines."

"I think we need to push the counseling angle, find out as much as we can about that. George may be right and it'll lead us on a wild goose chase, then again . . ."

"I know. I feel the same way. We want to cover all our bases."

On his computer, Dakota clicked his way over to the screen that allowed him to open up the email that had been sent with the man's picture.

Immediately, a driver's license picture popped up.

"And we've got him," Dakota muttered.

"Maybe. Howard Wilkins. Six feet tall, mid-forties. I can't see what he really looks like with all that stringy hair and the beard."

"He's got the green eyes."

"Look at the acne on that dude's forehead."

Dakota gave a disgruntled sigh. "And the bump on that nose. He's had it broken at least once." He tapped the screen with his finger. "You know, that picture was taken almost nine years ago. He could look like anything by now."

"True."

"Let me Google his name and see what I come up with."

Dakota typed the name in the search bar. "Well, well, look here." A newspaper article from a little over twelve years ago popped up. "How is it that a newspaper article that old is on Google?" No one knew or cared. "Howard Wilkins was kicked out of his last year of med school after he was arrested for rape. Guy never made it to trial. Skipped town and apparently hasn't been heard from since."

"This has got to be the guy we're looking for."

"I can't believe he actually had the car registered in his name. Is he really that dumb?"

"Or arrogant, believing he won't be caught. Whichever, I don't care. It's a lucky break for us."

"Let me get Jazz to run him and find out as much information as she can. If anyone can find the dirt on him, she can."

He punched in a number.

"Hello, darlin'," she answered.

"Hi, Jazz, how ya doing this morning."

"Right as rain. What can I help you with?"

"I need you to find out as much information as you can on a guy named Howard Wilkins. I'm sending his license and last known address to you now."

Dakota clicked Send.

"Got it. Give me a little while and I'll call you as soon as I have anything."

"You're a peach."

"I know."

He hung up and turned to Connor. "All right, why don't we check on the girls and see if they've come up with anything new on the files?"

"Excellent plan."

Jamie snapped the file shut and yawned. She'd been up since 5:42 working on the counseling angle. Connor had waved at her as he headed out the door at 6:30.

Ignoring her rumbling stomach, she looked at the spreadsheet she'd made on Samantha's laptop. All twenty-two names, dates of disappearance, location last seen, and in the last column, she had an X if they had counseling notations in the file.

Then she added the names of the known victims and their information.

And last, she keyed in her name. The date she disappeared and the date she resurfaced.

She eliminated the girl who'd turned up with the aunt in Missouri.

Not bothering to consider that she was doing Dakota and Connor's job, she picked up the phone and started calling. Hoping she didn't offend anyone by calling so early, she decided it was worth it to catch people before they left for work.

Mrs. Spears, mother of Hailey Spears, answered on the second ring.

"Hello, Mrs. Spears, my name is Jamie Cash and I work with . . ." She didn't want to mention the morgue, not to a woman with a missing child, "I'm working with investigators on your daughter's disappearance."

"She disappeared over five years ago."

"Yes, ma'am, I know, but we've had some recent activity by the man we believe took your daughter."

"Oh no, he's taken another, hasn't he?"

Jamie gulped. "Yes, we think he's involved in several other girls' disappearance."

"How can I help?"

"I need to know if Hailey was in counseling with a group here in Spartanburg."

A sigh. "Yes, she was. She was seeing a doctor with the Eastside Psychiatric Therapists group. Hailey had some issues. She'd made several self-harm statements, and we felt she needed help we couldn't give her. But she'd only had two sessions before she disappeared." A short sob on the other end. "I'm sorry."

Heart clenched in sympathy, Jamie swallowed hard, yet excitement thrummed through her too. Another connection. "No, I'm sorry for having to bring it up again.

But this helps tremendously. Thank you so much for talking to me."

"You're welcome. I do hope you get him. I want to sit across from him at his trial and beg the judge for the death sentence." Anger vibrated with every word. Jamie couldn't blame the woman.

After she hung up, she picked up the phone and called everyone she could get. A couple of numbers had been disconnected, some people didn't answer, but the majority did, and each answer caused Jamie's blood to surge. She was definitely on to something.

Everyone she talked to had a daughter or sibling in counseling at the same location.

She'd found a definite connection.

But what about her? Jamie knew for a fact she'd never had a counseling session before she'd been snatched. Not that she couldn't have benefited from it at the time, but it hadn't happened.

And what about Karen Fuller?

She hadn't been to the counseling center either. She'd simply been visiting relatives from out of town.

But she had been to a party.

Jamie snatched the phone back up and dialed her mother just as Samantha came into the kitchen. She walked slowly, favoring the side where she'd been stabbed.

"You're supposed to be resting."

Sam let out a small laugh. "I just woke up."

Before Jamie could answer, her mother came on the line. "Hello?"

"Hi, Mom, it's Jamie."

"Hello, darling. How is everything this morning?" Her words sounded stilted as though unsure of Jamie and what she might be calling about. After all, they hadn't really had time to talk about the bombshell her parents had dropped on them.

"What's our sister's name, Mom?"

Sam went still, hand hovering over the coffeepot — decaf — and turned to look at Jamie.

A sigh filtered over the line as Jamie clicked the phone to speaker so Sam could listen in. "I never said, did I? Her name is Kathryn Kenyon, but she goes by Kit."

"Kit," Jamie repeated, seeing how the name felt on her lips. "Okay, thanks. Next question. Why did you give her up and not me? Why not both of us?"

Silence.

"Mom?"

The woman cleared her throat. "I just couldn't. Even though I was furious with your father for leaving and beyond depressed when I found out I was pregnant, by the middle of the pregnancy, I'd accepted it, was even a little excited about having another little one around even though I was scared to death at the same time."

"That's understandable."

"Then I went in for a checkup and they told me I was having twins. I was stunned. I also knew I'd never be able to handle two babies. For days, I wandered around in shock and then made the hardest decision of my life."

"You'd give one of us up."

"Yes."

Jamie closed her eyes on the sob echoing through the phone line, imagining a young mother's — *her* mother's — heart-wrenching decision.

Her mom drew in a shaky breath and said, "I called my best friend from high school. We'd kept touch over the years with the occasional phone call and a Christmas card every year. Other than that, we never really saw each other." Another sigh. "But, I knew she couldn't have children. I also knew how desperately she wanted a child, so I called her and told her my situation. She immediately agreed to adopt one of the babies, and Kit had a wonderful childhood."

"Did Daddy know?"

"Yes. After he came home when you were almost two, I told him."

"Was he mad? I mean, how did he react?"

"At first, I think he was a little angry, but mostly he was just sad. So very, very sad — and he felt so guilty. He's had a really hard time forgiving himself, but over time . . ." She trailed off, then added, "But he also understood why I did what I did. He said I did the right thing, the only thing under the circumstances. I had no help, nowhere to turn. I'd quit church by that time. My parents were dead, and his parents . . . well, you know his parents."

Jamie did. Into doing their own thing and definitely not into children, they were travelers, living the good life. Now, in their early eighties, they only recently sold their hundred-thousand-dollar motor home and bought a house. No, they wouldn't have put their lives on hold to help out with a couple of babies.

"Thanks for telling me all this, Mom. I'll pass it on to Samantha." She took a deep breath and changed her line of thought. "Okay, one more question, then I'll let you go. I never went to counseling, did I? Because I sure don't remember it if I did."

Silence.

"Mom?"

"No, you never made it to your first appointment."

"What?" Jamie nearly shrieked. Samantha's eyes went wide.

"Your father and I were afraid you were going to wind up dead. You snuck out at night, partied until all hours of the morning, and came home smashed or high. We were at our wit's end. So, we decided to get you into a place that could offer what we couldn't."

Her voice barely above a whisper, she asked, "Where? Where was I supposed to go?"

"A place on Henry Street. Um . . . Eastside Psychiatrics or something like that."

All strength seemed to leave her body. "Thanks, Mom, I'll call you later."

She hung up and looked at Samantha. "I think we need to call Connor and Dakota."

29

Delving into the history of Eastside Psychiatric Therapists proved to be a time-consuming endeavor.

When Jamie said they thought they had found something else in the files, Dakota and Connor had sped back to Connor's house. Just as they pulled into the drive, Dakota's cell phone rang.

He looked at Connor. "It's George."

"I'm going to go on in."

Nodding that he would fill him in, Dakota hit the green button. "Hello, George, what can I do for you?"

"I might have discovered something rather interesting."

"What's that?"

"I decided to enter the rest of the missing girls into the geographic profile data and came across some familiar names. I actually think I treated a couple of the missing girls."

Shock zipped up his spine. George had

his complete attention. "What do you mean?"

"Where are you? Do you mind if I meet you somewhere? This might be easier in person."

"I'm at Connor's house. Sure, come on over. What kind of car do you drive? I'll clear it with our watchdog."

"A black Buick. I'll be there in ten minutes."

"Hey, don't you need directions?"

A self-conscious laugh. "Yeah, I was just going to mapquest it."

"It'll take less time if I tell you how to get here." Dakota rattled off the directions and informed the officer watching the house that George would be arriving shortly and to be on the lookout for a black Buick.

Dakota headed into the house. "George is on the way. And get this, he thinks he counseled some of the missing girls."

"No way!" Jamie sat up straight in the recliner where she'd been curled up with the laptop. "Did he work at Eastside Psychiatric Therapists?"

"I don't know. He's on his way over. Said it would be easier to explain in person."

They waited on George. Twenty minutes later, he pulled up out front. Connor let him in and showed him to a seat. "Thanks for coming over."

"No problem. I would have been here earlier, but I took a wrong turn and got turned around. Then I got behind a semi on one of the back streets." He rolled his eyes and shook his head. "Anyway, I'm here now and wanted to show you something."

He opened the laptop he'd brought with him and powered it up. "Okay, I'll get to the part where I think I know some of the girls in a minute. First, I want to show you this. Dakota, when you and I were doing the geographic profiling the other day, we only entered the victims we had that were found. I went back and added the other twenty-one. I know we don't know that all of them are victims of this guy, but I put them in anyway, just in case."

A few more clicks. "Then I went back and numbered them according to the dates of their disappearances. Then I started thinking. This guy may have some kind of fixation on numbers."

"Numbers?"

"Yes. You said he branded his victims."

Jamie flinched and Dakota resisted the urge to go to her, but he conveyed his sympathy with his eyes . . . he hoped.

George went on. "Anyway, I figured if he has this thing about numbers, then maybe where they were buried could be numeric."

"Meaning?" Sam looked confused.

George waved a hand. "I'm going to skip the process because it took a long time to figure out and I don't want to waste time explaining it, but basically, the girls were buried according to where they lived."

He punched a few more keys and a 3-D diagram appeared. "Here, according to number and order of disappearances, are where the girls lived."

Scattered numbers in blue appeared on the screen. A few more taps and he said, "Here in green are where we found number 3, Jamie . . . ," he flicked his gaze to Jamie and she nodded, "number 6, Sandra — number 7, Olivia — number 8, Karen — number 10, Simone — and number 17, Lisa."

Dakota caught on quick. "The distance from where they lived to where they were buried is according to their number."

"Exactly." George looked like a proud teacher.

"So, I was pitched in the lake." Jamie looked at Samantha. "It's about three miles from Mom and Dad's house."

"Closer to four, but yeah. We couldn't believe you were found so close to home. Now we know why."

Jamie's cell phone rang. Serena. "Hello?"

"Jamie, I need you in the lab as soon as you can get here."

"What's wrong?"

"You had a package delivered to you. Knowing the trouble you've been having, I called in the bomb people. It's not a bomb, it's a set of bones. Old ones, recently dug up, I would say."

"What?"

"And a card signed 'Your Hero.' "

Sickness clenched her stomach. "Okay. I'll be right there."

When she hung up, four pairs of eyes stared at her. "I need to go to the lab. Apparently, I've received another gift from *him*. Jake's working on the box to see if there's any evidence."

Dakota stood and sighed. "All right, let's get over there and see what it is."

Connor looked at Samantha. "You sit tight. I'll call when we know something."

Frustration nipped at her features, but she nodded. Jamie knew she wanted to be there; however, her health and that of the baby's came first. "I'll be waiting."

Snapping the laptop shut, George stood. "I'll come too. We still need to discuss the girls that I think I counseled."

"That'll have to wait. Let's go." Connor

ushered everyone out of his house. They loaded into Connor's car, George into his, and headed for the hospital.

Almost before Connor could put the car in park, Jamie was out and running for the lab. Pounding steps followed her. She passed her office and saw Serena in Autopsy room two. Jamie burst through the door and stopped to catch her breath. "Where?"

"I hope you drove carefully. I think you set a record."

"Connor drove." Jamie nodded toward the innocent-looking brown box. Jake stood there snapping pictures. "Is that it?"

Serena arched a perfectly manicured brow. "That's it."

Trepidation clawing at her, she pushed it aside. But for the grace of God, that could have been her in the box. Anxiety shot through her.

No, she wouldn't panic here. This is where she felt safest, competent, in her element. Here, she was in control.

A quick glance at the clock told her Maya's funeral was in three hours. She would have to be done here in two and a half hours. She could do it.

Connor and Dakota entered the lab and took up residence in the far corner. George said he'd be in his office and to keep him updated.

Jake stepped back. "I'm done here. I've got a few things I can take a look at back in the lab, but I'm not making any guarantees."

Taking a deep breath, she reached for the box and opened the lid. "Thanks, Jake. Where's Dennis?" Dennis Carter, their resident entomologist.

"He's already taken samples. Said the body's been in the ground about six to eight years."

"Okay, who's been missing that long?" she muttered to herself. As much as she'd studied the files last night, she should be able to pull a name from her memory.

Nineteen-year-old Cristina Benini. From a wealthy Italian family. She'd disappeared eight and a half years ago.

"You'll want to take a look at this too." Jake pulled her from the box. He handed her an envelope. "It was taped to the lid."

With a gloved hand, she took it from him. "Guys?"

They approached. Absently, she noted Dakota's woodsy scent. It calmed her.

He asked, "What is it?"

"An envelope." She looked at Jake. "What's in it?"

"A couple of pictures." He shook his head.

382

"That poor girl. Just keep your gloves on."

Obediently, Jamie did as he asked and pulled the pictures from the envelope.

"Here's the note that came with it." Jake handed her a piece of paper with typewritten words on it.

Jamie read them aloud.

" 'A gift for you, my lovely Jamie. Yes, it's Cristina. A beautiful girl suffering so much angst. I helped end it for her. I'm her hero — just like I'll soon be yours once again.' "

It took all she had in her to remain poised, to ignore her impulse to crumple the paper, but if she did that, it would give him satisfaction that he got to her. She knew it would, and while he couldn't see her right now, she refused to close her fingers around the paper.

Instead she showed it to Dakota, then put it back in the plastic bag.

Next, the pictures.

Obviously already dead, her throat had been cut and she lay on a slab like the one in the morgue. Only it looked more like a wooden work bench than a stainless steel table. Bruises splotched the girl's body. Arms, legs, ankles. One knee looked twice as large as the one next to it. She shuddered. "Where does he do this stuff?" Jamie wondered aloud.

"He's got to have a pretty big place. Either a basement or an attic — or even a whole separate residence."

"He can't live near people and do it. They'd notice."

Connor blew out a sigh. "Not necessarily. People tend to mind their own business these days. The world's not like it used to be with everyone knowing their neighbors and their neighbors' business."

"That's for sure," Jamie grunted and looked at the next picture. A dark-haired girl who'd gone Goth, Cristina had an angry forehead. Whatever she'd been looking at in the picture, she didn't like it. Black-rimmed eyes and black lips. Multiple piercings in the one ear she could see. A ring through her nose. A young woman searching for her identity, her life cut short by a madman.

Emotion clogged her throat and Jamie swallowed. *It's not fair, God, it's not fair.* But she kept her cry inside.

"Was she branded? Can you tell?"

"I think so, get me a magnifying glass, would you?"

Serena handed one over. Jamie focused on the girl's upper arm. And spotted a 4. "We need to find her grave."

Connor got on the phone and asked for a team to search a four-mile radius from the girl's home. "You're looking for fresh dirt."

Dakota slapped a hand on the table, making Jamie jump. He stood. "Sorry, I'm going to talk to George about the girls he counseled and find all I can there."

Jamie nodded to the box. "I'm going to get started here."

"I'm also going to get busy tracing where the box was mailed from and see if we have a post office that may have caught this guy on camera."

Jamie huffed. "He probably didn't even mail it."

A shrug. "You're most likely right, but we've got to try."

"All right. I'm going to get busy on these bones. See what they have to tell me. Unfortunately, I have a feeling I already know the story they're going to tell."

Dakota headed down the hall toward George's office. He had one of the nicer offices on the hall, one that had its own entrance and exit.

Knuckles rapped on the door and George called for him to enter. He looked around. "How'd you get lucky with this place?"

"You mean the office?"

"Yeah." Blank walls stared back. Interesting.

"I requested a separate entrance. This was the only office on this floor that had one excluding the morgue and entrances into the halls. I felt like my clients might appreciate the privacy it afforded. This way they don't have to worry about running into someone they know. Or the coroner bringing in a body." His lips twitched. "That would totally freak a few of my clients."

He could imagine. "Good idea. So where are all your plaques and pictures and stuff?"

George laughed and waved to several boxes in the corner. "Right there. In the time that I've been here, I haven't had a chance to breathe, much less worry about hanging plaques."

Dakota smiled. "Right."

"All right, here's what I've got. I treated four of the girls. I used to work at Eastside Psychiatric Therapists."

"What made you move?"

"A doctor and I had a conflict on how to treat a client."

"Conflict about what?"

"He wanted to release her, considered her cured. I thought the kid needed rehab. I . . . uh . . . said a few things to him I probably shouldn't have, and then when the girl committed suicide, the tension around the office just got to be a bit much." He shrugged.

"I decided I wanted something different, applied for this position, got a contract with the police to do consulting work for them, and here I am."

Dakota stood and walked to the window. Looking out, he saw Connor's car, his own that he left here when he'd caught a ride with Connor, and various other vehicles.

And a light blue Honda.

30

The Hero laughed to himself. He was pleased with his plan. It was amazing that they were all really that stupid. He'd certainly led them on a merry chase all this time. When Dakota had bolted from the office, the Hero had stood silently and watched.

The FBI agent had pushed up his timetable a bit, but that was all right. He was quite ready for all of this to be over so he could move on. Yes, he had probably worn out his welcome in this town.

His mother's contorted features played in his mind. Her twisted snarl that had so terrified him as a child now looked sad and pathetic when he brought her face forward from the back of his deeply buried memories. "I stopped you from all your partying, your drunkenness and evil ways, I did." He had to whisper to her. No one else could see her, but the Hero could. Once, as a child, he'd gathered a flake of courage from a distant part of himself and asked her why she did the things she did. "Why, Mama, why do you do it?"

For once she hadn't slapped him or shoved him or burned him with her cigarette. Or worse, broken a bone. She'd simply looked at him, the pain in her eyes visible even to him, a young boy of thirteen with more rage in him than anyone should ever have. "Because it numbs the pain. There's always the pain and that helps it for a little while."

"What would make it go away forever?"

His little sister had slipped up beside him and tucked her hand in his. At the age of ten, she was tall and slender with a toughness that impressed even him.

His mother gave a harsh laugh, looked at the two of them standing there, and pushed herself to her feet. "Death, kid, death would make it go away forever. But suicide is a sin, boy, and don't you forget it. God don't forgive people who kill themselves. So you just got to live with the pain."

Then she gave him a shove and he lost it.

After he beat her, he cut her throat to make sure she was really dead. He'd hated her and loved her. He wanted her to hurt, to suffer the way he had, and in contrast he didn't want her to hurt anymore.

And so he'd made her pain go away, he'd rescued her with the voice whispering in his ear. "Make it stop, make the pain stop. Make it stop."

And so he had.

And found his purpose in life.

For a long time, he lived like everyone else. Only he and his sister knew his secret. No one ever connected him to the death, the *rescue,* of his mother, and he finished high school, made his way into college and medical school.

And then she had come along his senior year and he had to rescue her. Only he hadn't killed her, he'd been careless, and she lived to report him. He went looking for her. Showed up on her doorstep. When she answered the door, the look on her face had been priceless.

He chuckled at the memory. "Hi, Rachelle, I'm back."

At his words, her eyes flew wide with terror and she screamed while tears flooded down her cheeks.

She slammed the door in his face and he heard the locks click home.

The next day he read about her suicide in the newspaper.

He clicked his tongue. What a disappointment.

His next one, he'd done right, though. Then the next one, and the next.

And with his new identity, his new face, he'd eluded the law and become the man he was today.

He watched Dakota grab Connor from the lab, saw them consult in the hall, then take off.

No doubt to check out the blue Honda.

The car he'd parked there on purpose.

He checked his watch.

It was time.

Jamie leaned over the bones she'd been cleaning and placing on the table in front of her.

Dakota had retrieved Connor and they'd rushed out of there like the place was on fire. The only thing they'd said was to stay put. Then a police officer had shown up in the autopsy room and said he was there to protect her.

Something was going on and she didn't like being left out of the loop, but she also had to get these bones, Cristina Bellini, ready for release to her family. And then head to Maya's funeral.

The bones had spoken. She'd died the way of the others. Cut marks on her ribs. No slash mark on the cervical vertebrae indicative of a slashed throat, but Jamie knew. She had no evidence, but he just hadn't cut deep enough to hit the bone on this one.

Jamie never looked up when Serena left.

"Ma'am? Ma'am?"

Blinking, pulled from her work, her world, she looked up to see the officer gesturing toward the door. Someone stood behind him.

She walked over. "Oh, George, hi."

"Hey, can I borrow you for a minute?"

She looked back at the bones. "Um . . . sure. What do you need?"

"I just need you to look at something on my computer in my office. I was doing some more of that geographic profiling and thought I'd get your input."

"Okay, let me just get cleaned up here." She stripped off the gloves and tossed them into the hazardous waste bin.

He looked at the officer. "I'll take care of her if you want to just hang out here."

"No sir, I'm going with you."

George shrugged. "Whatever."

Dakota checked the license plate and excitement ran through him. It was the same one. They had their car. Which meant their suspect was here, in the same building as Jamie.

Dialing her cell, he closed his eyes in relief and said, "Jamie, he's here somewhere in the building."

She pulled in a sharp breath. "Where?"

"We don't know. Just stay alert. Don't go anywhere alone, even the bathroom, okay?"

"I've got my bodyguard, Chet, here," she said, referring to the officer Dakota had sent up to stay with her. "But how do you know it's him?"

"His car's in the parking lot. The license plates are a match."

"Okay."

He could hear the fear in her voice even though she attempted to hide it. "I'm going to talk to Jake, then I'll be right up and I promise I won't let you out of my sight until this guy is caught."

"I'll be waiting. George wants me to see something on his computer, so I may be in his office, all right?"

"Just take Chet with you and sit tight. I'll be there as soon as I can."

"All right. I will."

They hung up and Dakota clenched his fist around the phone. He so wanted this guy. *God, just let us get him, please?*

He wanted Jamie free of the past, of her

393

tormentor who kept turning up and knocking her world upside down. "I'm giving Jake five minutes, then I'm out of here. I'm going to be Jamie's shadow for as long as it takes."

"You know, Dakota, you might want to think about disappearing with her. It might be the only way she's going to have a normal life and be safe."

"You mean disappear as in new identities and such?"

"Unfortunately, yeah. And hopefully it wouldn't be forever."

Dakota nodded. "Already thought about it."

The only response Connor made was to raise his eyebrows and nod. "Come on, let's see what Jake has to say."

"Five minutes, Connor, that's it. Then I'm getting Jamie from Chet and taking her someplace safe."

"You got it."

Jamie followed George into his office. Chet stuck his head in the door and looked around. Then he stepped back outside. "I'll be right here, ma'am. I'm going to keep an eye on the hall."

She nodded and George told her, "Just have a seat over there by my laptop." He snapped his fingers. "Hang on a second, I need to tell Chet something." George slipped out and Jamie heard him murmur something to the officer before he pulled the door shut behind him.

She wandered over to look out of his window, telling herself to relax. Being alone with George didn't freak her out nearly as much now as it had in the beginning. It just took her a while to feel safe around a man. George had become one of the team, a fixture around the building. She spotted Dakota in the parking lot talking with Jake. Connor had his head in the blue Honda.

Distracting herself, not wanting to think that the car right outside her might belong to the man after her . . . or that he could possibly be in the building, she scanned George's bookshelf.

Psychology books, medical references, books on mental illness. A whole shelf dedicated to serial killers.

Jamie shuddered and clamped her arms over her stomach. She looked back toward the door. What was he doing?

Another look around. No pictures. Interesting. She realized she didn't know George well at all. Nothing personal about him, anyway. They'd been so focused on trying to figure out who was after her, she hadn't taken the time to get to know anything about the man.

The door opened and she spun around.

George smiled at her and shut the door once more.

Uneasiness curled in her. "Can you leave the door open, please?"

He stopped. Tilted his head. "Why?"

"I would feel more comfortable."

Moving toward the desk, he motioned to his laptop. "Let me just show you this. It's rather confidential and I'd rather not have Chet hearing it."

A reasonable request? Maybe. Still she felt weird, anxiety clamping down on her. She shoved it aside and moved toward the door. "I understand that, but I'd prefer to keep the door open. In fact," her pulse picked up speed, "I think I would rather just wait until Dakota and Connor can hear what you have to say, all right?"

For some reason her anxiety was reaching peak proportions. Her heart hammered in her throat and she reached for the door-knob.

"Sure, Jamie, no problem, just take a look at this, and if you still want to wait for Connor and Dakota that's no problem."

The Hero knew he didn't have much time.

She'd entered the office, and the officer had taken his position by the door, arms crossed in front of him, eyes alert. And while the car in the parking lot currently had Dakota's attention — just as he'd planned — he also knew it would throw a scare into the man and he'd be here within minutes to take Jamie into protective custody.

He fingered the syringe.

It was now or never.

Dakota bypassed the elevator headed to the stairs. The team still worked on the car, but he was anxious to get Jamie in his sights and keep her there. He knew Chet would protect her, plus she was with George, but that didn't stop him from wanting to be able to see her, to touch her and know she was all right.

He made his way to the morgue and down the hallway. Checking each autopsy room, he saw no sign of Jamie. Same thing with her office.

His ringing phone distracted him for a moment. Checking the caller ID, he answered. "Talk to me, Jazz."

"I got the picture from the post office. The person who delivered your box of bones was a woman. We're working on her identity."

"Can you send a picture of her to my

phone?"

"Sure."

"Thanks. And let me know when you get a name."

"You got it."

He hung up.

Jamie must still be in George's office.

Trekking his way back down the hall and around the corner, he saw George's office door open. No sign of Chet. Entering the office, he called out, "George? Jamie? Chet?"

No answer.

A bad feeling formed in his gut. He crossed to the window and looked out into the parking lot. Jake still worked on the car. Connor talked to an employee. The parking lot had been blocked off.

Had the Hero come into George's office to get Jamie and found her with George?

So where was Chet?

Dakota moved toward the bathroom.

Empty.

He rounded the desk and pulled up short.

"Chet, aw man. Hang on, buddy, help's on the way." Anger, frustration, and fear boiled inside him. Chet lay on his back, eyes blinking, desperately gasping, throat gushing.

Dakota ran to the door, down the hall a

little bit. "Hey! Where's Serena? I need some help in here!"

Two people stuck their heads out of offices. Serena came out of the break room, coffee cup in hand.

Dakota motioned her toward him. "I've got a man in here with a slashed throat. He needs help now!"

Serena tossed her coffee in the trash can near the door and raced toward him. "Call the ER, then hand me the phone, he'll need immediate surgery."

Snatching his cell phone from his pocket, Dakota got more help on the way, then while Serena did what she could for him, he focused his worry back on Jamie.

His phone buzzed and he pulled up the picture of the woman who'd delivered the box of bones to the post office. He didn't recognize her — then again, she looked vaguely familiar.

Odd.

A glance back down at the pool of blood left by Chet.

Cold terror splashed through him. He knew without a doubt Jamie was back in the hands of her tormentor from years ago.

He also knew if he didn't act smart and swift, Jamie would die.

■ ■ ■ ■

A sound buzzed in her ears. Annoying, persistent, she wanted to tell it to stop. But something held her still. A sense of self-preservation? What was wrong?

A headache pounded her temples, nausea knocked at the back of her throat. And still she made no sound and refused to open her eyes. Was she sick? Maybe. No, that wasn't it. She was moving. Bouncing in the back of something. A car? A truck?

Her eyes wouldn't cooperate, wouldn't open.

Familiar niggling jolted her. Clarity of thought came through for a brief moment. She'd done this before.

The memories hit her with the driving force of a jackhammer.

Familiar odors. Her nose twitched. So tired. She tried to open her eyes. Couldn't.

Something else registered.

Aching wrists clamped in steel.

Soon she would feel the soft mattress beneath her. Smell his putrid breath as he leaned over her . . .

Her breathing quickened.

Still, she didn't move. Didn't dare open her eyes. Didn't think she could force them open if she had to. So she just stayed still.

"I know you're awake, Jamie."

That voice. *His* voice.

And the terror claimed her. Her mind swirled, turned to mush, and she knew no more.

31

Dakota pounded out Connor's number on his phone. "Get in here. He's got Jamie."

Silence greeted him, then, "I'm on my way."

Two minutes later, face ash white, Connor rounded the corner and stepped into George's office. Medical personnel already had Chet on his way to surgery.

"There's no sign of George or Jamie, Chet had his throat slashed. Serena said the guy was lucky. Our hero," heavy on the sarcasm, "apparently didn't think to use more force on Chet than he does on the girls."

"Is he going to make it?"

"I don't know. Serena seemed to think so."

"Where's Jamie?"

Sick guilt covered him. "I don't know. There's no sign of her."

"He got her out of here somehow. I want to watch the video of all the parking lots around this building."

"Already got them being pulled."

"It should only take a few minutes, we know almost exactly when she was taken. You talked to her on her phone, what, fifteen minutes before you came up here to find Chet?"

"Yeah, something like that."

Connor studied the other door that led to the parking lot. "He went out this back entrance."

"You would have seen him come into the parking lot if he used that entrance."

"Right. And he knew that. So, since he couldn't go that way, he had to take a chance and go into the hall."

"I'll get video on that too."

His phone rang before he could dial the number. Jazz.

"What is it, Jazz? Make it fast, will you? Jamie's missing."

A swiftly indrawn breath. Then, "You'll want this. I kept fishing for information on this Howard Wilkins."

"Yeah? What'd you get?" *Oh, Jamie, I'm coming, darling, just hang on, baby.*

"Family situation was horrid apparently. He and his sister were taken from the home several times. They'd end up in foster care, then get placed back with Mom after she went through whatever therapy the courts assigned her. They dropped off the radar for a couple of years, then she died, was murdered when Howard was thirteen and his sister was ten. They were split up, placed in different homes. Nothing much after that on the sister. Howard was in and out of the court system until he was about sixteen, then became a model high school student, even graduated with honors. Went on to med school where his problems resurfaced. After he was kicked out of med school, I managed to track his movements. Found out he worked as an x-ray technician under the name of Howard Metcalffe."

"Why didn't we know this before?"

"He was very good at hiding. He acquired a fake ID and a new life. Besides, you were in a hurry before and this took some serious digging."

He shut up, knowing she was right. "What else?"

"I also pulled information on the girl he raped and left for dead during medical school. Her name is Rachelle Jones. She committed suicide not too long after the attack. I talked to her father and he said that after he was done with Rachelle, he went after her boyfriend — George Horton."

Dakota felt his stomach somersault. "Excuse me? Did you just say . . . ?"

"Yep. George. So, I pulled his records."

He had a feeling he wasn't going to like what was coming.

Jazz proved him right. "George graduated at the top of his class as a psychiatrist. Brilliant guy, really. Anyway, two days after graduation, he seemed to disappear. Then he surfaced a few years later working for Eastside Psychiatric Therapists in Spartanburg."

"Okay, that sounds about right. He now works here at the hospital."

"Right, or so the information says. I've got his college yearbook picture. I'm emailing it to you now."

"Thanks, Jazz, you're awesome."

"Of course." She hung up and Dakota waited for the email to come in.

When it did, his bad feeling grew to epic proportions.

She had a floating sensation. For some reason she didn't want to wake up. A bump, the squeal of brakes.

She was in a vehicle.

Moving again.

A turn.

Someone talking on a cell phone.

Nausea swirling. Terror returning. She should be afraid, but she couldn't think why.

A sharp turn this time, then bumping over something. Gravel? Grass? A back road?

She felt foggy, sleepy, groggy. She knew she needed to wake up but couldn't get her body to cooperate. Then she remembered.

And let the darkness close back over her.

Dakota, Connor, and Samantha stared at the video. When Connor had called her to tell her Jamie was in the hands of a madman, Samantha had left her bed and driven to the hospital. She now sat in a cushioned chair as the action went on around her.

Dakota could see Connor keeping a close eye on her. He hadn't wanted to tell her about Jamie but knew it was no use hiding it from her. She'd have found out anyway when Connor called to say he wouldn't be home.

No one would be sleeping until Jamie was found safe and in one piece.

"There," Connor pointed to the figure. "He came out of the side door next to his office."

Samantha leaned forward. "He put the mask on before leaving the office so we don't have a picture of his face." Connor pointed to the screen. "He shoved her into a red truck. I can't see the license."

Dakota stopped the tape and nodded to

Samantha. "Can you do your magic on the computer?"

"Sure." She scooted forward and took the mouse from him. A few clicks and a pop-up screen had a partial plate on the red Ford truck.

Dakota sent it to Jazz, although he had an idea who it was going to come back registered to.

Dakota's cell phone rang. He raised a brow and shot a look at Sam and Connor. "It's George."

The rage that had been building in him crested and nearly burst from him. But he couldn't release it. Jamie's life depended on him keeping a cool head. *Lord Jesus, give me the words to say and the composure to say them.*

He cleared his throat. "Hello?"

"Dakota, hi, I'm looking for Jamie, have you seen her?"

"No, I'm looking for her myself. We're pretty sure she's fallen into the hands of the guy who calls himself the Hero."

"What? You're kidding!" Shock resonated. If Dakota hadn't been suspicious of the man, he would have fallen for the act.

"I wish I was. We're watching the video of it now. She said she was going to meet you in your office."

"Yeah, she did, but then she said she wanted to wait until you and Connor could meet with us. She seemed nervous. So, I told her I had to take off and she said she and her bodyguard, um . . . Chet . . . would be in the autopsy room if anyone needed her."

"You're sure?"

"Positive. I left her in my office. Last I saw her, she was talking to Chet."

Dakota frowned. "All right. Thanks."

"No problem."

They hung up and Dakota dialed Jazz. "You get it?"

"Yeah. He's pinging off the cell towers between Arnett and Chowder Streets. Looks like he might be heading down 29 toward the Cowpens, Gaffney area."

"Get someone on him and keep tracking that phone. I don't know who he is, but he's definitely not George Horton . . . and he could be the Hero."

Shackled to the bed, Jamie heard him move across the room and waited for the pain to hit her. She wondered where he'd strike first. A leg? An arm? A shoulder? A toe? In preparation for the pain, she clenched her teeth, vowing not a sound would cross her lips.

When nothing happened, she cracked her eyes. He had his back to her. The familiar black mask covered his head.

Surprisingly, her fear had faded somewhat. Most shocking of all, she hadn't succumbed to a panic attack. Oh, she didn't look forward to what was coming, but because she knew what to expect, it was almost like his power over her had diminished.

A surge of triumph swelled.

Then he turned. And held up the knife.

Fear surged back full force. She pushed it aside.

Green eyes met hers. She refused to speak, narrowed her gaze, and lifted her chin.

She thought she saw the mask move right above his left eye. Had he raised an eyebrow? Surprised at her defiance? Or amused?

He flicked the blade of the knife with a black gloved thumb. "You know, your sister was a quick little thing. She moved too fast for me." The same raspy voice.

She remained silent, heart thumping. While she had the panic attack under control, she couldn't help the kernel of fear curling in her midsection.

Fear was all right. It was natural. Terror even. But this time, she'd start thinking faster.

"Oh come now, don't tell me you're going to give me the silent treatment."

"No." She hated the quiver in her voice, hated more the smile that curved his lips.

"Ah, good."

She recalled everything George had talked about and took a shot in the dark. "Who abused you when you were a child?"

He froze.

"Your father? Your mother? A relative?"

"Shut up." His voice was low. "I don't want to talk about her."

"Ah, your mother." Her breath came in short, soft pants. *Keep the fear away, Lord, keep it away.*

The cuffs felt tight around her wrists. She had to get him to undo them.

"Why?" she demanded softly.

He adjusted the mask. She wanted to tear it from his face, wanted to see him. Gaze upon the features she'd only imagined in her nightmares.

"Why what?" he asked, his words precise, bitten off as though he didn't want to say them but couldn't help himself. The knife dipped toward her throat and she sucked in a silent breath. Then it moved to the edge of her blouse.

And did away with the top button. She heard it ping on the floor. The hardwood floors she'd shuffled across so many times.

Jamie swallowed hard. *No fear, no fear, no fear.* The chant calmed her racing heart a fraction. "Why did you kill her?"

He stood. "I said don't ask me about her."

The voice lost its raspy edge and she froze. She knew that voice. A name tickled the back of her mind. She needed to hear him talk again.

"Who was she?"

He shoved his face near hers and trailed the knife down her cheek. She felt a sting, then a warm wetness trickle from the cut. "Shut up or I'll start with your tongue," he hissed.

Fury drove her over. She lunged forward, opened her mouth, and bit down hard.

He screamed and yanked away from her. The mask came off along with a chunk of his cheek. The metallic taste of blood seeped through the mask and she spit everything out, her eyes flying wide as she registered her attacker's identity.

Blood gushed from the wound on his face, and her last thought before his fist connected with her chin was that at least she'd have some of his DNA on her when they found her body.

32

Pain ricocheted in her head. Left, right, back, front. Everywhere. She wanted to moan. She didn't.

Jamie wondered if he'd hit her again after she'd blacked out. After the first punch, she'd known no more.

Surprise that she was actually alive shot through her. He'd moved her hands. They were now cuffed in front of her and linked to the chain that led to the bathroom.

Good move on his part. Nature called . . . urgently.

She cracked her eyes. They worked. She moved her jaw back and forth. It worked too . . . barely.

She winced at the shooting pain.

But at least it wasn't broken.

Scanning the room, she found it empty. *Thank you, God.*

And she still had her lab coat on. Another thank-you winged heavenward.

Sliding to the edge of the bed, she gradually made her way into a sitting position. When she moved, she gasped as shards of glass bounced inside her jaw to her head and back.

The mask lay on the floor to her right. Drops of dried blood trailed an intermittent pattern to the door that was now shut.

She had to get out of here. Her mind played scenes from twelve years ago. *Oh, God, please get me out of here. Please!* A sob escaped her, she couldn't help it. Stumbling to the bathroom, she made her way to the sink and stared in the mirror.

That was a mistake. Black and blue stared back. She averted her eyes and took care of her business. Her mind hummed, desperate to come up with a plan. She didn't bother to check and see if she could escape through the bathroom. If there'd been a way, she'd have discovered it twelve years ago. A window opposite the tub offered a little light, but no escape route.

The cuffs clanked against the sink as she splashed water on her face. Wincing at the sting, she ignored it and closed her eyes again. Memories flooded her, bringing terror and choking dread.

Think, Jamie, think.

Dakota and Connor would figure it out.

They'd do some research and eventually track her captor down.

The question was, would she still be alive when they found him? She had to be. She'd survived once against all odds, she'd survive again.

Sucking in a deep breath, shoving the terror as far away as she could, she knew she was on her own. She and God, once again.

"What are you doing?"

His voice froze the blood in her veins. Without turning, she said, "Praying."

He grunted. "Won't do you any good. Didn't help me any when I was a kid, isn't going to help you now. Get out here."

She spoke to the wall again. "I think I'm going to throw up. It'll be easier to clean up if I stay where I am."

Silence from behind her. Had she surprised him? She knew she wasn't responding as he'd expected. Twelve years ago, she'd just begged and screamed. But she was a different person now. A stronger one. One that he didn't know quite what to do with?

She could only hope.

A hand slapped against the wooden door frame, and she jumped, her breath hitching. A phone rang from the vicinity of the kitchen.

"Fine. I'll be back."

Relief wilted her shoulders as he spun and stomped away.

"Sam, you get the computer. Connor, you start with the files. I don't want a piece of dust undisturbed in here. I also need to know who that red truck belongs to."

Samantha settled herself behind George's desk.

Jake lifted a print from the phone. "I'll just run this and see what pops up. Be right back."

He left and Dakota hit the boxes in the corner. The ones he'd asked George about just the other day.

Connor got on the phone with a longtime therapist from Eastside Psychiatrics where George used to work.

The one-sided conversation hummed in the back of Dakota's mind as he focused on the awards and plaques all made out to George Horton. Uncertainty hit for a brief moment. Had he been wrong?

No, the picture Jazz had sent him of George Horton had been an African American.

The wrong George Horton?

Again, no, he was the only George Horton at the medical school at the time of the incident with his girlfriend and Howard

Wilkins.

I'm coming, Jamie, I'm coming. Just hold on, darlin', be strong.

His hands shook as he ripped open the next box. *Work fast, Jazz, Jamie's counting on us.* He switched over to prayer. *Please, God, I don't even know how to pray, but Jamie loves you. Keep her safe. Give her the smarts to deal with this guy. Please!*

Jazz was working on locating the African American George while the rest of them searched for the one who'd been using this office for the last few months.

Jake stuck his head in the door. "Fingerprints came up as a match to our guy. George Horton."

Dakota stopped what he was doing for a minute and thought. "The guy worked for the police. He'd have access to computer files. Could he have hacked in and matched up his prints in case they were ever run?"

A shrug. "It's possible. Difficult maybe, but possible. I would have thought they'd have run them before he was hired."

Samantha said, "He could have had someone he went to school with or an acquaintance hack in and change them before he applied."

"Wouldn't alarms go off like crazy that the system had been infiltrated?"

She raised a brow. "Not if you're good."

Dakota knew Samantha could do it. And if she could, there was probably someone else out there who could.

Or someone within the system itself. He snapped his fingers. "If George had a user ID and a password from someone who had legitimate access, he wouldn't have had to hack in."

"You're right." Sam nodded. "No alarms whatsoever to worry about then."

Frowning, Dakota wracked his brain. What was he missing?

"I've got an idea. Give me a picture of George . . . our George."

Samantha let out a whistle. "Guys, you're going to want to see this one."

Crowding around the desk, they looked over her shoulder to see the screen. She clicked. "This file contains articles on the missing girls." She scrolled through them. Each one, all the way back to Jamie.

Connor hung up. "I just got off the phone with one of the docs who remembers George. Said George treated a patient who later committed suicide. He was fired from the practice."

"He twisted the story around. Made it sound like he left because of another doctor's negligence. And I swallowed it, every word." Dakota slammed a fist against the wall.

"You had no reason to doubt him. None of us did. He was one of us." Connor shoved his phone back into his pocket. "All right, what else do you have, Sam?"

"A lot."

"Show us."

"Pictures. Tons of them. He must have downloaded them from a flash drive so he could get his jollies looking at them throughout the day. They're all pictures of the missing and dead girls."

"And look . . ." She drew in a quick breath. "A map."

Dakota muttered. "X marks the spot."

"Where all the graves are. Jamie's going to have her work cut out for her."

"If we get her back," Connor breathed.

"We'll get her back," Dakota said sharply, "there's no other option."

A few more clicks and Samantha said, "Here's his caseload. Let's take a look at who he treated." She scrolled through the names.

One made her blink. "Look at this."

Dakota read, "Evan Johannes. The guy we found dead in his house after delivering that package to Jamie!"

"Oh wow. Check this out. I just found our

418

link to Karen Fuller, the girl from New Jersey. Moira Fuller was a patient of George's. Look who she lists as next of kin and as an emergency contact."

"Doreen Fuller. Isn't that Karen's mother?"

"Sure is. Apparently Doreen and Moira are sisters."

"When was Moira's last appointment?"

Sam's fingers flew over the keys. "Look," she breathed in a ragged breath. "The day Karen disappeared."

"What you want to bet she came to the office with her aunt and that's when George got a look at her."

"She probably said something about a party that he overheard."

"We may never know. Doesn't matter anyway. But it does answer our question about the connection between this guy and Karen."

A knock on the door brought their heads around. Dakota gave a surprised, relieved cry, and rushed forward to gather the woman standing there in his arms. "Jamie! Where've you been? We've been so worried looking for you . . ."

The woman struggled from his grip. "Hey, back off, big guy. I'm not Jamie."

He pulled back and looked down. What

419

was she talking about? "What?" His hands went to her head. "Did you bump your head? How did you get away from him?" He blinked, then said, "Your hair's shorter."

Gentle hands pushed his away. "I'm not Jamie."

"You're Kit," a voice breathed from behind them.

Jamie's smile lit up the room. And yet it wasn't her smile. It curled up at the corner and the dimple was on the wrong side. Dakota grabbed her arm and shoved up the sleeve of her sweater.

No scars.

He jerked back as though touching her burned him. "Who . . . how . . ."

A hand settled on his back. "Dakota, meet Kathryn Kenyon, better known as Kit. She's my sister. The other one. It's a really long story." Samantha's voice sounded teary.

Dakota still couldn't find his.

In the back of his mind, he knew they didn't have time for this, Jamie was missing. He gathered his composure. "All right, you guys can explain all this later. We've got to find Jamie."

Kit stepped into the room and stared at Samantha. "I've waited a long time to meet you."

Samantha engulfed her in a hug, swiped a

tear, and looked at Connor. "I'll explain later."

He nodded and kissed her nose.

"What's this about Jamie being missing?" Kit asked, stepping into the office.

"A killer has her and we've got to track him down," Dakota muttered.

Concern creased the woman's forehead. "How can I help?"

Dakota and Connor exchanged a glance. "There's really nothing you can do. Better just let us do our job and we'll let you know when we find her."

"But I can help."

Now that he had a picture of George in his hands, Dakota was impatient to get moving. "You can't help, now just stay out of the way, please."

She crossed her arms and set her jaw. She looked so much like Jamie his heart nearly burst. "I might be in a position to help you more than you know. If Jamie's a hostage, you might be able to use my skills."

"Which are?"

"I'm a detective with specialized training in hostage negotiation. I work with the Raleigh, North Carolina, police department."

33

Jamie blinked her eyes. Slowly. Groggy, lethargic, and a mushy brain. He'd drugged her.

Nausea swirled and the room shifted. Shadows said the sun had moved and it was now late afternoon.

What had he done to her? She felt awful.

Taking inventory, she decided nothing hurt except where he'd hit her earlier. No new pains. No broken bones.

That seemed to be the good news.

The bad news? She was still handcuffed to the bed and her lab coat lay tossed over the chair in the corner. Panic nearly set in. She'd waited too long. She had to get to her coat. Pulling on the cuffs told her they were snug.

Just like before.

And she was cold. Shivers wracked her. Had he turned the air-conditioning up? Why was she so cold?

And burning up at the same time? How odd. Her face felt hot. It hurt to breathe.

Dakota, where are you? Please find me!

The door opened and she tensed. He stood there, the mask no longer needed. The baseball bat over his shoulder.

A scream gathered in her throat.

No matter what it took, she wouldn't release it. But she couldn't stop the terror from darting through her. *Oh God, please . . .*

Panting shallow breaths escaped. She licked dry lips. So thirsty. And so scared.

No fear, don't show him you're scared. Act like you don't care.

Another chill shook her and her teeth chattered.

She looked at him again and swallowed. "Just get it over with."

He cocked an eyebrow. She'd surprised him. "Ah, Jamie, why would you want to hurry?"

"You said it was your duty to release me from the pain. So release me." She shivered.

He frowned. "What's wrong with you?"

Jamie managed to choke out a little laugh. "If you have to ask . . ."

The bat swung down and cracked against the bedpost. She jumped, adrenaline surging.

But she didn't scream.

A hand shot out to touch her forehead and she couldn't help the flinch, then she stilled.

"You're burning up with fever." He sighed in disgust. Tapped the bat against a palm.

Then he reached up and unhooked the chain that kept the cuffs attached to the bed rail above her head. He pulled the cuffs down and hooked the other chain to the center link. "Here, you'll be more comfortable this way."

Shock rippled and she stared at him in disbelief. She would never understand this man. Why did he care whether she was comfortable or not? She kept her mouth shut.

He strode to the door. "I'll get you some ibuprofen for the fever."

Two minutes later he was back with two little orange pills and a cup of water. "Here."

She swallowed them, praying she could keep them in her system and that they really would reduce her fever. She'd give the pills as long as possible to work, then it would be time to act.

Dakota watched Samantha work her magic with the computer. The picture of George as he looked today had been scanned into the system.

Samantha pulled up the mug shot from fourteen years ago. Side by side they looked like two different people. Then she moved her mouse and snagged the first picture, dragged it over to the second, and released it.

A perfect match. Except for the nose. The bump was gone.

"He had plastic surgery on his nose," Samantha said.

Dakota punched a fist into his other palm. "Unbelievable. George Horton and Howard Wilkins are one and the same."

"He's got to have a contact in the police department somewhere," Connor insisted. "Someone who could fix his prints."

"Look up everyone who works here with the last name or maiden name of Wilkins."

Samantha tapped a few more keys. "Beth Wilkins. Works in the records department."

Dakota's phone rang again. He snatched it with an impatient snarl. "Yeah."

"The red truck is registered to a Beth Wilkins."

Thanking the woman, he shot a look at Connor. "Let's go get her." He looked at Samantha. "You stay put."

She waved them on. "I'm fine, I'm fine. Not even a twinge of pain."

Dakota didn't believe her, but the clock was ticking. Almost as an afterthought, he looked at Kit. "You coming?"

He didn't have to ask twice. She shot him a grateful look and waved goodbye to Sam.

Bypassing the elevator, the trio raced outside and down the sidewalk to Connor's car. Hopping in, Connor cranked it, and squealed from the parking lot before Dakota had his door shut. Kit had moved faster and was grabbing her seat belt.

Less than a minute and a half later, they were parked at the police station and headed inside the front door. Down the stairs, around the corner, and to the end of the hall.

Connor stopped at the door marked Records.

Dakota didn't. Shoving it opened, he charged in. "Where's Beth Wilkins?"

A woman jumped up. A mousy-looking thing with frightened eyes and pale skin. "I . . . I'm Beth."

Dakota could feel the vein jumping in his neck. Making an effort to calm his racing pulse, he could see the woman in front of him looked ready to bolt. "Ma'am, we need to ask you a few questions."

"O-okay. About what?"

"Let's go in the conference room down

the hall."

She pulled her white sweater closer around her neck, her eyes darted to each of them. Dakota, Connor, Kit. Back to the floor to follow her feet into the room.

Once inside, Dakota motioned for her to have a seat.

She did.

Her throat convulsed. "This is about what I did, isn't it?"

Dakota shot a look at Connor then back to the woman. "What is it you did, ma'am?"

"I . . . well . . . I . . ." Tears filled her eyes and she looked down. "I knew this job was too good to be true," she whispered.

"What do you mean, Ms. Wilkins?"

"Howard. He got me this job. Told me I should apply. That I was a perfect fit for it. He was right. I love it."

"He needed you on the inside, didn't he?"

Resignation slumped her shoulders. "I . . . I . . . guess. I've been here almost seven months." She twisted the edge of her sweater. "About a month after I was hired, Howard came to me and said there was the perfect opening in the psych department at the hospital and he wanted to act as a consultant to the police. He . . . he had all the documentation, credentials, everything."

Kit stood at the door taking it all in,

processing the information. Dakota's heart clenched as he noticed that she looked almost exactly like Jamie when she was deep in thought. *Oh God, please . . .*

He cleared his throat. "So, he wanted to work for the hospital and the police. But he had a record because of the rape and almost killing that girl in college."

She winced and nodded.

"And?" Dakota prompted.

"And," more twisting of the sweater, a glance above the glasses, "he knew they'd run his prints. So, I switched them with the name he gave me. If you run a search for George Horton anywhere outside of the police department, they'll come up with the real one. But in this system, Howard's face comes up."

"Why? What do you owe him?"

Her face crumpled. "He said he'd kill me if I didn't obey," she whispered. "He killed our mother. I knew he would kill me too. So I did it. I'm sorry, but I did it."

"Do you know that your brother is a serial killer?"

She gasped and looked up, meeting Dakota's eyes for the first time. "What? What do you mean? No. I mean, yes, he killed our mother, but she really deserved it." A humorless chuckle. "You never met anyone

428

so mean, she was beating me and beating me," she closed her eyes and more tears leaked out. "And he killed her." When she opened her eyes, they had an almost defiant light in them. "And I was glad. I was grateful and I thanked him over and over." She blinked, coming back from whatever memory she'd been lost in. "But Howard? A serial killer? I . . . I don't think so."

"Do you own a red truck?"

"Yes." A wary look. "Why?"

"Did you drive it to work today?"

"No, I took the bus. Howard said his car was in the shop and he needed to borrow my truck." She shrugged. "I let him."

Connor shifted. "Where would Howard go if he wanted to get away from things? A place to hide, maybe?"

She blinked, looking owlish behind the large round glasses. "I don't know. There's my place, I guess, but he doesn't stop by very often." She swallowed. "Just to let me know he's still watching me and for me to keep my mouth shut. I . . . I . . . wouldn't have said anything now, except I could tell you already knew what I did." She sniffed. "He doesn't tell me anything about his personal life and I don't ask."

"Any place else you can think of? A friend. Another residence?"

"No . . . no," she shook her head, "he doesn't have many friends. At least none that I know of. I can't think —" She stopped, sucked in a breath.

Dakota leaned in. "You've thought of something. What is it?"

"I don't know . . . I . . . it could be nothing."

"We'll take it. What is it?"

With the back of her sleeve-covered hand, she wiped a stray tear from her face. "Um . . . he might go to our childhood home. Maybe." She shuddered. "I wouldn't ever go back there, but he . . . ," another deep breath, "he said he sometimes goes to . . . think. To remember."

"Remember what?"

A shrug. "I really don't know. Maybe he feels guilty for killing our mother and goes back to think about it." She ran a hand down her face.

"Where's your childhood home?"

"About fifteen minutes from here. It's in Cowpens on a little farm area." She gave directions.

Nerves humming with the knowledge that they might actually know where Jamie was being held, Dakota called and gave the address to the backup that would meet them out there and looked at Connor and Kit.

"Let's go." He looked at Beth. "You'll face charges."

She nodded. "I know." Then fear flashed in her eyes. "You realize when you get there, he's going to know it was me that sent you. If you don't get him, he'll kill me."

Dakota felt his jaw become granite. "We'll get him."

Jamie felt the sweat break out across her forehead. Her shirt stuck to her back. All good signs that her fever had broken. She felt better, but weak, and that worried her. Would she have the strength to do what she needed to do?

She had to. It wasn't exactly like she had a choice. Not if she wanted to live.

Rolling to her side, she looked at her lab coat. She stood, stumbled slightly, then caught herself. The nausea she'd felt earlier returned full force and she made a dash to the bathroom.

The door opened just as she lost the contents of what little she'd had in her stomach.

"Still not feeling well, I see."

Jamie didn't even have the strength to flinch. Resting her forehead on the side of the tub, she ignored him and closed her eyes.

A cool cloth touched her head and she opened her eyes. Evil stared back. She swallowed. "Why are you being nice?" Her mouth tripped over the last word used in connection with this man. Wary, she watched him, waited for his next move, certain this was just another one of his psychological tortures.

He smiled, his lips parting in a way that sent a shiver through her. No, he wasn't being nice. He said, "You're no fun this way, Jamie, but that's all right, I have time to wait on you to get better. And if you don't get better soon, I'll just do what I have to do."

Her head lolled away from him. His hand shot out and grasped her chin in a bruising grip to turn her to face him. "You were so easy to take twelve years ago. So easy."

She tried to jerk out of his grasp but only succeeded in causing him to squeeze harder. A cry formed on her lips and she bit it back. Satisfaction at her success in not making a sound almost overshadowed the pain in her jaw.

"Why did you take me?"

He let go of her and stood. She flexed her jaw, wincing at the shooting pain.

He shook his head. "Because you were living your life all wrong. Partying, sleeping around. You might have become pregnant, then what would you do with the child? Lock it in a closet all day? Smack it across the room when it asked to be fed? Come home drunk or high and beat it until it falls into unconsciousness? Break its arm for digging food from the trash can? And more?"

Shock held her still. "Is that what your mother did to you?"

Eyes narrowed, muscles along his throat pulsed. "It doesn't matter now. What matters is the need to rid the world of girls and women like you."

"But I would never do that to a child," she protested.

Another hard, evil smile. "You're right about that, my dear. You sure won't."

34

Dakota pulled the van into a small side road across the street from their intended target. Connor rode shotgun, Kit had one of the back seats. Technology surrounded her.

The SWAT team had already arrived and taken their places around the isolated property. Dakota looked at the house, his gaze probing, desperately searching for a sign that Jamie was here — and still alive.

Not much to look at now, the ranch-style brick building had seen better days, had probably been a pretty nice house once upon a time. Grass and weeds grew as tall as some of the windows. An abandoned car with no wheels sat off to the side, rusting and home to all kinds of critters he had no desire to get up close and personal with.

"Better watch your step in there, could be snakes."

Connor lasered him with a look. "Thanks for the warning. You know how I feel about snakes."

"About like I do, I'm sure."

Kit's gaze bounced back and forth between the two of them. "I don't mind snakes. I'll take care of them if you'll take care of the spiders." She shuddered. "I hate spiders more than anything."

Connor offered a tight smile to his newly acquired sister-in-law. "I think we're going to get along just fine."

Dakota spoke into his microphone. "Everyone in place?"

"Copy that."

Squinting his eyes against the sun, he asked, "You see any kind of warning system? Alarm?"

"Negative, sir," came the response into his ear.

"Can we get some cameras in there? I need to see what's going on."

"Moving in now, sir. Blinds are covering all the windows. If I cut the glass, he might notice. I'll have to thread the line through the air vents or go up under the house. May take me a little bit of time." Two SWAT members crept forward, one would take the front of the house, the other the back.

"We don't have time. I want a running commentary when and if you can talk."

"Yes sir. Approaching the west end of the

435

house now, sir."

The man seated at the computer in the back of the van transcribed the dialogue.

"Camera one ready." Dakota flipped the screen on. "I've got eyes." What looked like a square cut into four pieces flashed on. Only one fourth of the screen was filled. The top left-hand corner showed a room that looked like a simple bedroom.

"Camera two ready. Easier than I thought, sir." The right-hand corner flickered, then came on. The kitchen. Fastidiously neat.

"Camera three ready." Left bottom corner. "Another bedroom. But look, what's that in the corner there?"

Kit leaned in. "A chain. It's hooked to the bed and is leading into the bathroom." It jerked.

"Something's on the end of that."

"Camera four ready." The last empty spot in the right-hand corner filled up with an image that made Dakota jerk.

Connor gasped. "Is that a . . . ? What is that?"

"It almost looks like a morgue, doesn't it?"

"But what's that machine?"

Dakota remembered Jamie's whispered words about a week ago. "I bet that's an x-ray machine."

"You're kidding. Wonder what this guy's power bill is?"

"Does anyone see our victim or the suspect?"

"Negative."

"Can we get a camera in that bathroom?"

"Negative. I tried. There aren't any blinds, but I can't get a good visual."

"Try again. At least get me some audio."

"Yes sir, trying again."

The second screen, identical to the first, sat waiting for the images. A minute and a half later, a swiftly indrawn breath and low, whispered voice came through Dakota's ear piece. "I have a visual on the victim. Stand by."

"Standing by."

A picture popped up and Dakota's heart fell to his knees. "Oh my . . . Jesus, please," a whispered prayer, not a curse. Jamie sat on the floor of the bathroom, hands cuffed in front of her, knees drawn up to her chest, eyes staring straight ahead. She looked like death. A black-shod foot stood near her.

"Dakota . . . ," Connor breathed his name, his face stricken. "We have to get her out of there now."

"I know." He looked at Kit. She stared at the image of her sister, two tears silently streaking her cheeks. He squeezed her shoulder and she jumped.

"Who is this sicko?" she breathed.

"Someone whose reign of terror is coming to an end today."

She palmed her cheeks to swipe the tears, then said, "Tell me what to do."

He looked around and didn't see the department negotiator. He was still working another case and hadn't arrived yet. May not arrive in time. "Hone your negotiating skills, we may need them."

Nodding, she turned back to the screen.

Just then, the booted foot disappeared — then came back to catch Jamie in the ribs.

Kit cried out and jumped to her feet. Connor whispered a word he hadn't used in a very long time — and Dakota headed for the door.

A hand grabbed his arm. Connor's voice low and soft penetrated the red haze of murderous fury that had overtaken him for a brief moment. "Don't, Dakota. He'll kill her before you get to her. Right now, she's alive."

His partner was right. Dakota closed his eyes and drew in a deep breath. "Pray for her, Connor."

"I have been."

"For me too, because I want to kill this guy." He made a conscious effort to uncurl his clenched fists.

"I know."

Sanity settled back in. He pulled away from Connor to see Kit watching him, her eyes lit with an inner fire that reminded him of Jamie when she was determined to get something done. "She didn't cry out."

"What?"

"He kicked her and I don't think she made a sound."

Dakota moved to see the picture once more. Jamie had her eyes closed, her chest heaved, but her lips remained clamped together.

"As soon as he leaves the room, we're through the window, got it?"

"Roger that, sir."

Dakota passed the information on once more. "Wait on me."

Receiving affirmatives from each SWAT member, Dakota checked his weapon and made sure he had the safety off.

Connor did the same.

"What's this guy's story?" Kit asked. "I need some background on him."

Dakota told her of the man's fascination with Jamie. The history of childhood abuse they'd gotten from the sister, Beth, and his need to be the Hero, to rescue his victims from their pain.

"So, he causes their pain so he can rescue them from it?"

"Something like that. He's a sick, twisted son of a gun."

"All right, that helps. Anything else?"

"You've already gathered he's smart, maybe even genius-level IQ."

"Which might make him even more dangerous. From your observations, is he cocky? Arrogant?"

Dakota looked at Connor, thought back to all of their meetings with George, his attitude as he'd laid out his profile of this guy. He'd been talking about himself. "Yeah, I would say he's arrogant." He leaned forward. "In fact, looking back, every time he gave us a 'profile' on the guy, he was smug, rubbing our noses in the fact that we couldn't catch him. He even said something about the perfect crime one time."

Connor nodded. "Yeah, arrogant. Absolutely. Thinks he's smarter than any of us."

Looking thoughtful, Kit nodded. A curl escaped her clip and bounced over one eye. A sucker punch to his gut would have affected him less. Dakota had to look away. He turned his gaze to the screen. The guy was still in there with her, but at least he hadn't touched her again. And now he had audio.

"— back, Jamie. I have something to take care of first, then it'll be your turn."

Then he was moving, his feet disappearing. Only then did Jamie open her eyes. She stayed on the floor unmoving for several seconds, then Dakota saw her jaw firm, watched her wince with the pain of it, then push herself to a standing position.

A hand went to her side where the guy had kicked her. She had a cut on her cheek and bruises along her jawline. She was beautiful. She was alive.

"Location of suspect?"

Just as he asked, George appeared in the kitchen. "Take him out, now."

"No viable shot, sir," came the response.

George shifted, checked his cell phone, and put it back down.

Not taking his eyes from the man, he asked Connor, "Did you get a look at his face?"

"Yeah, he had a bandage on it."

Satisfaction tingled through Dakota. "Jamie got him pretty good. Can't wait to ask her about that."

"Let's get her out of there and make sure we get to hear it," Connor said.

George then strode from the room only to reappear on the screen in the room that held the suspected x-ray machine.

441

"Do you have a shot?"

"No sir, not yet. He keeps moving in front of objects, obscuring my view."

"All right, guys, get ready to move."

Then George disappeared from the screen once again.

Dakota looked back at Jamie. She'd moved into the bedroom, was rummaging with the lab coat on the back of the chair. Her desperation reached out and grabbed him by the throat.

It was now or never. Ignoring her nausea and all of her aches and pains, Jamie had bolted from the bathroom the minute the door closed behind George to shove her hand in the pocket of her lab coat. Her fingers closed over the object just as the door to the bedroom opened once again.

George stood there, syringe in one hand, baseball bat in the other.

Jamie thought she just might throw up again.

"You can make this easy or we can do it the hard way."

Her eyes flittered back and forth between his hands. "What do you want?"

That evil smile slithered across his lips. "It's time to end the pain, Jamie."

Her heartbeat kicked up a notch. Deep

442

breath, control. Her lungs started to feel tight. *Breathe, Jamie, breathe.* She couldn't. Her palms slicked and she squeezed her fingers tighter into her fist. "Why now?"

"Because the fun is over. They'll be looking for you and I have to get back to the office for an appointment. Can't miss that, you know. That might tip someone off that something isn't right."

"They already know it's you," she blurted.

His brows fanned down. "What do you mean? Of course they don't."

She bit her lip. She didn't know if they knew or not. Would saying they did encourage him to kill her faster? Or hold her as a hostage until he knew for sure?

Jamie wasn't a gambler and couldn't decide which way to hedge her bets.

"What do you mean?" he yelled. "Tell me what you know."

Please give me the right words, Jesus. "Just that they'll be looking for you too. Dakota knew I was with you in your office. You think he won't put two and two together? They'll watch the tapes. They'll see your car in the lot and wonder why you're not in the building. And Chet. Did you kill him? They'll wonder about that too."

"I'll come up with something," he muttered, yet indecision played across his features. She had him thinking, wondering. "Come with me," he snapped.

Jamie held her wrists up. "These might be a problem."

He tossed the syringe on the bed and stomped over to release the cuffs from the chain. Her hands were still shackled, but she could now move freely. He shoved her in front of him. She wondered if she'd feel the needle plunge into her back or if he'd decided not to use it.

She prayed he wouldn't as she needed all of her senses about her if she were going to make this work.

Dakota watched George usher Jamie out of the bedroom. A minute later, they appeared in the x-ray room, as he'd dubbed it. The man placed a syringe on the counter alongside the baseball bat.

He said something and Jamie shook her head. He grabbed her cuffed wrists and jerked her to the table. That was enough for Dakota.

He gave the location of Jamie and George, going with his gut that it was now or never. "Move into position. On three."

35

By the time he cuffed her to the table, hands together and above her head, and turned his back, Jamie had her terror under control and itched to put her plan into practice. Scared, knowing this was a one-shot deal, she grasped the handcuff key she'd pulled from the pocket of her lab coat — the key she'd carried with her ever since being released from the hospital twelve years ago — and inserted it into the lock. Her hands shook so hard, she nearly knocked it from the hole.

Her breath came in raspy pants, but she couldn't help that now. What was he doing? Over by the floor vent, he crouched down, staring at something. Whatever it was, it gave her more time.

She started on her right hand just about the time George let loose a string of curses. She jumped and the key fell from her fingers to rattle on the hardwood floor.

He whirled and she jumped from the table, one arm still held captive by the other cuff attached to the table. She could see the key, stretched her hand out to grab it — and got her fingers smashed in the process. The rocking pain shot through her hand and up her arm.

The door burst open and three men with guns forced their way in. "Freeze! Drop the knife!"

Connor and Dakota followed.

A hand grabbed a fistful of curls and yanked her to a standing position. She gasped and saw flashes of stars as he jerked her neck into an awkward position.

"Let her go, man." Dakota inched forward, gun trained on George's head.

"Not a chance," George snarled. He gripped the knife and held it against her throat. She didn't dare swallow. Still attached to the table, he couldn't drag her anywhere.

"Get them to let my hand go and I'll get you out of here," she said in a low voice, not daring to do or say anything to set him off.

"Right." She could hear the fury in his voice.

"I mean it," she promised.

"Why?"

"Why what?"

"Why would you help me?"

She thought, fought, prayed, for the right words. "Because you stopped the pain, George."

He paused, the knife shifted, and he snarled at Dakota. "Get her uncuffed."

"No way, man."

Jamie looked at Dakota. "Do it."

"Sorry, Jamie, not going to happen. If I uncuff you from that table and he gets out of here, we might never be able to find you."

She stared hard into his eyes. "Dakota, I need you to release my other hand and do it now. Do you understand?"

He and Connor exchanged a glance. Dakota's face twisted with indecision. Finally, he gritted, "Fine."

What do you have in mind, Jamie? She read his question without difficulty as he slipped the key into the hole that would trigger her release.

The cuff opened.

Her hand fell free.

Immediately, George backed up, the knife still held against her throat. "Okay," she panted, doing her best to ward off the panic attack. "Okay, I'm free. Where do you want to go?"

"I'm never going to get out of here alive,"

he muttered.

She wished she could see his face. If he would just turn a little, she would have a view of it in the mirror on the opposite wall.

"Sure you are, George." The voice came from the door to the room.

A woman stepped in and Jamie couldn't help the gasp that flew from her lips. The knife jerked against her throat and she automatically reared up on tiptoes even as she stared into a living, breathing mirror image of herself.

Dakota heard Kit's voice before he saw her step into the room. When he turned in her direction, she stood, unprotected, and facing the man with a knife at her sister's throat. He noticed another thing. She'd pulled her hair into the exact same style as Jamie's — a ragged ponytail.

George's eyes flew wide as he stared at Kit. His mouth worked but no words came out.

"Hello, George."

"Who . . . who are you? What are you? Where'd you come from?"

All of George's previous bravado had fled, leaving the man pale and trembling. A negative situation seeing that the man held a very sharp knife to the throat of the woman

448

Dakota loved.

He prayed Kit was very good at her job.

She stepped forward, voice low, hypnotic almost. "Do you really want to hurt me?"

George blinked. "You? No, Jamie."

"But I am Jamie."

What was she doing? Anxiety thrummed through him as he watched the scene before him. *Come on, man, move Jamie just a little to the right so I or one of my guys can drill you in the head.*

George's eyes blinked rapidly. "No, you're . . . you . . . can't be. I have Jamie right here."

"Jamie's gone. She died. I'm the one you've been looking for all this time."

Perspiration oozed from the man's head. His eyes had a frantic dart to them. "Then . . . then who . . ."

"Push her away, George. Look at her face. It's not Jamie."

Admiration for Kit swelled inside him. He looked at Connor and saw he understood what she was trying to do. As soon as George turned Jamie to face him or pushed her far enough away to get a good look at her, either he or Connor could put a bullet in the man's head in less than a second.

But George didn't respond. He just stared at Kit. She didn't show any emotion other than soothing friendliness. She continued her end of the conversation. "Did you take your medicine, George? You haven't been taking your medication, have you?"

His eyes flared. "How did you know? No one knows about my medicine, no one!"

"But you had me here for a long time. I know a lot of things about you." She sauntered forward, careful to stay out of the line of fire, and held out her wrists. "Want to put the cuffs on? You have them, don't you?"

"The voices, I want them to stop." He continued to blink rapidly, his breathing turned into pants.

Dakota kept his eyes on Jamie. She kept hers on Kit. Alert, focused, looking for an opportunity to escape. *Be careful, darlin', be careful.*

Kit moved a step closer. George screamed, "Stop! Don't come any closer to me! I killed you! You're dead! See?"

For a fraction of a second, the knife dipped as he tried to get a look at the woman in his clutches.

A shot rang out. The bullet caught George in the shoulder instead of the head because he'd shifted at the last nanosecond. But it was good enough.

Blood spurted, the knife flew up, then down. Everything seemed to move in slow motion. Kit grabbed Jamie's hand and yanked. Dakota dove for the two of them. They went down together and he rolled, taking the women with him and covering them with his body.

Another shot, the thump of a body hitting the floor.

A gurgling, bubbling, horrific noise.

It all registered in surround sound.

Then silence.

Jamie pushed against him. "Let me up, Dakota."

"Yeah, big guy, you're kind of heavy," Kit grunted.

He rolled once more and took in the scene. SWAT members swarmed George, but one look told Dakota it was too late. The man was dead.

They rolled him over and Dakota pulled in a deep breath. He heard Jamie gasp and Kit muttered under her breath.

George's knife, the one that had killed so many, taken so many innocent lives with one violent slash, now protruded from its owner's throat.

Jamie stood on trembling legs. She forced them to carry her over to the man she'd known as George. Looking down at him, she whispered under her breath, " 'For you have been called for this purpose, since Christ also suffered for you, leaving you an example for you to follow in His steps, who committed no sin, nor was any deceit found in His mouth; and while being reviled, He did not revile in return; while suffering, He uttered no threats, but kept entrusting *Himself* to Him who judges righteously.' "

Dakota squeezed her hand. " 'You are my hiding place; you will protect me from trouble and surround me with songs of deliverance.' "

At her surprise, he shrugged, "I've been doing a little reading in my spare time. Psalm 32:7."

Tears flooded her eyes and she threw her arms around his neck.

He gathered her to him and buried his face in her hair. "I love you, Jamie," he whispered.

She took a breath to respond, felt the world tilt, then stepped into the blackness.

Friday

Jamie breathed in the smell of hospital antiseptic and musky cologne. Dakota sat to her left. She tried to process the fact that she was safe. It didn't really register, and yet the constant fear that had been her companion for so long was finally gone.

She waited, thought about it, and decided her major feeling was one of grateful relief.

A knock on the door told her she needed to wake up. Opening her eyes, she watched Dakota usher in her visitors. Jamie scooted painfully into a sitting position, in spite of Dakota's hushed protests that she remain still.

Connor, Samantha, Kit, and Jamie's parents flowed into the hospital room to crowd around her bed. Jamie's mother took her hand and kissed it. Her dad bussed her forehead.

"How are you feeling, sweetie?" her mother asked.

"Mmm. Better than I was . . ." She frowned. "What day is it?"

Dakota chuckled. "It's Friday. You've been in and out for about two days."

"Really?"

"Yeah," Sam chimed in. "Look around you. You have enough flowers in here to start your own florist shop."

It was true. She had arrangements sitting on every available space, including the floor and the windowsill.

"What happened? I mean, I remember everything up to the point where George died, but after that everything is hazy."

"You passed out," Sam offered.

"Oh."

Connor leaned around Samantha. "You had a whopping case of the flu, were dehydrated and just plain sick."

"The flu, huh?" she sighed and smiled. "God sure does take care of us in the strangest ways, doesn't he?"

Dakota cocked a brow and shifted. "What do you mean?"

"My having the flu delayed George's intentions long enough for you to find me and get me out of there." She looked at Kit and again experienced the strangest sensation of looking at herself in a mirror — and yet it wasn't her. "Thank you for everything." Kit smiled and Jamie laughed. "Your dimple is on the wrong side."

Kit arched a brow. "Nope, yours is."

They shared a grin, and Jamie's mother sniffed, tears standing in her eyes. She whispered, "I hope you two can forgive me one day. I didn't realize what I was taking from you when I . . ."

Jamie clutched her mother's hand. "Don't, Mom. You did what you had to do. Let's not dwell on it, okay?"

Her mother searched her eyes. "Do you mean that?"

"Of course I do. It does no good to harbor bitterness in your heart. It does a lot of destruction, but no good. I learned that a long time ago." She glanced at Kit, who had a tight jaw, and got the impression that Kit didn't share her sentiments, but that was something the young woman was going to have to come to terms with herself. As for Jamie, she'd move on, accept it and not judge. "It doesn't mean I won't mourn the lost time with Kit, but I won't let it interfere with my life."

Grateful wonder shone in her mother's eyes, and she leaned down for a hug. Then traced Jamie's face. "He got you good, didn't he?"

"Yes, but the bruises will fade. I'll heal. He's dead and has no more power over me."

"He hasn't had any power over you for a while now. I admire you very much and your dad and I are so, so proud."

Tears sprang to the surface and Jamie blinked them back. "Thanks, Mom."

She looked around and gave a little chuckle. "Okay, fill me in on everything."

Dakota and Connor looked at each other, then Samantha launched into the explanation of how they'd found her. And that George Horton was really Howard Wilkins.

"What happened to the real George Horton?"

Dakota took over. "He's disappeared. Apparently, he's got few relatives and has been pretty much a recluse all his life, even through medical school. When his family got a note saying he was moving to Europe to live abroad, they didn't think much about it."

"Howard killed him, didn't he?"

Connor nodded. "Yeah, we figure he did. But he sent the family emails over the years and they bought it. Never even questioned it."

Jamie shook her head. "Poor George."

"And Howard simply adopted the man's identity, credentials, licenses, and all."

"So, somehow George, I mean Howard, found out you were still alive and engineered all this to get close to you." Dakota rubbed his eyes and sighed. "Unbelievable."

"Yes, exactly."

A frown knit his brows. "Okay, I've been in law enforcement a long time and I've seen a lot of characters — the crazy ones, the guilty ones, even a few innocent ones — but I have to be honest, I don't think I've ever come across one like Howard Wilkins. He seemed absolutely normal to me. I never got a weird feeling around him."

Connor nodded. "Same here. And all that profile information? He was just describing himself. It was easy for him."

"But he actually helped solve some other cases."

Dakota shrugged. "The guy did almost make it all the way through medical school. He was an intellectual, smart and devious. He used that to further his goals."

"Which was to get close to me," Jamie whispered and shuddered.

Dakota squeezed her hand. "He can't hurt you anymore."

"I know. Okay," she took a deep breath and put on a smile, "when do I get to get out of here and go home?"

"This afternoon, it looks like."

"Good." Her eyes felt heavy and one by one her visitors filtered out until she was left with Dakota. Then she remembered. "Chet! What happened to him? Is he okay?"

Dakota's eyes narrowed. "He's going to be fine. Came through surgery like a champ. His wife is with him now."

Shocked, she stared at him. "Surgery? What happened?"

"What do you remember?"

"George . . . Howard, drugged me. I remember that much now, I just didn't know it at the time. He got me to look at something on his computer, and when I leaned over, I felt something prick my arm. I started feeling woozy, dizzy. Then I remember him calling to Chet, saying I was in trouble and needed help. Chet came through the door and then . . ." She squinted, "I don't remember much after that. Why did Chet need surgery?"

Dakota looked at the window, then back. "Howard slashed his throat. Luckily it wasn't very deep and he got help fast."

A gasp escaped her as well as a few tears. He brushed them away, then picked up her hand. He pushed one of her sleeves up to reveal the ugly scars on her wrist. Jamie tensed, wondering what he was doing. When he raised it to his lips to place gentle kisses along each one, she thought her heart might bottom out. She couldn't move, couldn't speak — couldn't think.

Finally, her voice barely above a whisper, she asked, "What are you doing?"

"You're so brave."

Closing her eyes, she turned her head away. If he knew . . . "No, I'm not very brave."

An incredulous chuckle reached her ears. "Jamie, I've never met anyone with more courage than you. Or more faith."

She had to tell him. Agonizing over the decision, she looked at him. His face changed when he saw her expression. "What is it, Jamie? Tell me. Tell me everything."

"The scars?"

"Yes?"

"They don't represent bravery, they're there because I'm a coward."

He frowned and she hitched her breath on a sob. On her shame. "I tried to kill myself."

Silence.

Then a low voice. "You wanted out of those cuffs one way or another. Isn't that what you said?"

She couldn't speak. But she nodded. Staring into his eyes, she confessed. "I sawed my wrists back and forth, over and over. I was beyond rational thought. My goal was to either bleed to death or cut my hands off." She gritted her teeth. "But I was going to get away from him. I was going to be in charge of my death. Not him."

He gasped, his fingers tightened around her wrist.

She felt wetness slide over the scars, then his lips pressed another kiss to them. With a start, she realized he was crying — for her. "I'm so sorry," he rasped.

"For what?" She couldn't fathom his reaction. He didn't think less of her? He didn't condemn her cowardice?

"For all that you had to endure. For everything you . . ." His throat worked, choked on the words. "You're amazing."

Her self-esteem notched up a bit. "You can still say that? Now that you know?"

"Jamie, one day, I pray you realize just how incredible you really are. You've changed my life. Watching you and Connor and Samantha, seeing your faith in spite of everything that's happened, I finally had to admit I wanted what you have."

"I'm so glad." Her hands cupped his face, his bristly whiskers scratching her palms. "Thank you for saving my life," she whispered.

"No, I think it was actually you who saved mine. I can't imagine my life without you in it."

Beyond words, she traced the tracks of his tears, brushed them away, and leaned forward to bury her face in his neck. His arms encircled her. She winced when he squeezed a little too hard, and the rib that had taken Howard's kick protested.

Easing his grip, he settled her back against the pillow. "Get some rest, Jamie. We'll have a long talk after you get out of here."

Then his phone rang, and with the promise to be back soon, he left to take the call.

Jamie sat there, absorbing everything, taking to heart the fact that Dakota didn't seem affected by her confession. At least not in a negative way.

A knock on the door pulled her from her musings. "Come in."

Kit pushed her way in and smiled. "Hi."

Jamie could only stare. She blinked and Kit laughed. "I know. It's going to take some getting used to, isn't it?"

Jamie finally found her voice. "Yeah. I guess so." She paused. "Thank you for everything you did."

A scowl crossed her sister's face. "I didn't do much. I wanted the creep alive so he could rot in jail."

"No. I think it's better this way."

A shrug. "Maybe."

"Have a seat."

"Thanks."

Jamie twisted the blanket through her fingers. "So, tell me about you."

Kit laughed. "Where do I start?"

"Where else? The beginning."

Four hours later, Jamie lay on her couch, a quilt tucked around her legs, the remote held loosely in her left hand.

Her mind couldn't seem to shut off. Kit brought her home and Dakota and her parents had met them there. Once settled, she'd sent everyone away. Including Dakota. She just had too much to process and

461

needed space to do it. Once again, she'd defeated the odds and survived a serial killer.

Her new Blackberry pinged and she looked at it. A text message from Dakota. "Are you okay?"

She smiled. "Yes," she typed back. "I'll call you soon. Let's do dinner."

"Great! You're on."

She flipped the channel. Media had swarmed her as she'd exited the hospital earlier today. She'd stopped to talk to them, to give them answers to their questions, both as a victim and as the anthropologist on the case. She talked to them for an hour, giving an impromptu press conference. She had hopes it would keep them off her lawn.

A glance out the window proved her true. No reporters, no psychos . . .

The television flashed again.

Maya's picture filled the screen along with pictures of the other suspected victims and grief hit Jamie hard. She caught her breath on a sob. "I know in my head it wasn't my fault, God. Help my heart believe it."

Dakota stuck the phone in his pocket and headed back to the crime scene. He hadn't told Jamie he was going to be working there today. No need to bring up that unpleasant fact.

He'd been here every day since the confrontation with George, going over evidence. One thing had him stumped.

A two-way mirror.

With two chairs facing the room.

At first he hadn't thought anything about it, he just figured it was one more way George let his victims suffer. Leave them alone on the table and watch them squirm. But then things began turning up that didn't make a whole lot of sense.

In the kitchen, they'd found a pair of sunglasses with a hair caught in the crease of the arm. It had been sent off for DNA testing against George. It looked a little long to be his, though. Plus the glasses seemed odd, but Dakota couldn't put his finger on why. They were simply dark-colored sunglasses.

Several pairs of brown, almost black contacts had turned up in Howard's bathroom. To cover up the green eyes he knew Jamie would recognize the first time she saw him. Eyes that had an eerie otherworldly quality to them. Dakota didn't know if that had been the mental illness affecting the way his eyes looked or just plain heredity.

Whatever, those eyes were now closed forever.

Now, back in the x-ray room, he looked at the machine that techs were in the process of dismantling. Dakota squatted next to Brad, one of Jake's CSIs. "What *is* all this stuff?"

Brad looked up. "I'm shaking my head because it's a fairly simple machine to build if you have all the right parts." He waved a hand toward the stack on the floor. "Nothing there you couldn't get off the internet. I bet he got on there and googled 'homemade x-ray machine' and the directions just popped right up."

He lifted a brow. "Can too much information be a bad thing?"

Brad rubbed an eye. "In this case, I'm going to say 'yes.' "

Dakota clapped the man on the shoulder and rose to his feet. Looked at the two-way mirror again. Thought about the other evidence gathered. The pictures from the book. Every girl the man had taken had been portrayed in that book, and they'd already started contacting families.

And locating graves.

They'd found two remote control garage door openers. One belonged to Jamie's garage. Soon enough, they'd know who the other one belonged to.

The mirror really bothered him.

And why would you need two chairs?

Dread curled in his midsection.

"What if there's someone else involved in this?" he muttered to himself. "What did we miss? *Who* did we miss?"

When the doorbell rang, Jamie jerked from the doze she'd just managed to fall into. She didn't know whether to grumble or laugh. Her family sent her home to rest — and called every five minutes to check on her to make sure she was resting.

Now one of them had decided to visit?

She threw the blanket off and stood. Checked the time. She'd slept a few minutes. She looked at the blinds on her window and smiled. They were open. Barely, but just enough to let a little daylight in and to remind her that she was safe — and continuing to heal more and more every day.

Her bell rang again and she frowned. "All right, all right. I'm coming."

A glance through the peephole had her brows lifting. A stranger. Unease flickered and she squelched it. Dragged in a breath. She was safe now.

Opening the door, she smiled and said, "Hello."

"Hello, Jamie."

The woman stood about two inches shorter than Jamie's height and wore a shapeless brown dress with a lightweight white sweater. Plain brown sandals covered her feet and her toenails needed polish.

Jamie blinked. "Do I know you?"

"No, not really, but I know you."

That twinge of uneasiness returned. Jamie kept her hand on the doorknob and her body blocked the opening. "I see. Well, do you need something?"

"Yes, actually, I came to see you because . . ." The woman's eyes flickered up the street, back to Jamie.

The urge to slam the door in the woman's face nearly overpowered her. What was going on?

The gun appeared almost as quickly as the woman moved. Stiff-arming a shocked Jamie with a hand to her chest, the stranger pushed her back into the house, shut the door behind her, and leveled the weapon at Jamie's head.

". . . you killed my brother."

36

Dakota got Connor on the phone. "We missed something."

"What do you mean?"

"There are two chairs."

"Huh? Make some sense, Dakota."

"In that little x-ray room, there was a two-way mirror, remember?"

"Yeah, he probably liked to watch his victim squirm before he . . ."

"Right. But behind that mirror, there were two chairs. Who was the other chair for?"

Silence. Dakota could feel his heart pounding.

"I don't know, man." Connor's words came over the line, slow and thoughtful. "Why would he need two chairs?"

"Exactly."

"Did we get the DNA back on that hair from the sunglasses yet?"

The lightbulb went on. "A woman."

"You lost me again."

"The sunglasses bothered me. That's because they were so out of place with everything in the house. They were feminine. Not overly so, but the arms had some very slight bling on them. That's what bugged me. They look like sunglasses that would belong to a woman."

"The sister," Connor whispered almost to himself.

"Beth."

"Yeah. She's been fired from her job and arraigned with various charges involving fraud, identity theft, and a couple of other things."

"Where is she now?"

"I don't know, but I think we'd better find out."

Heart in her throat, Jamie couldn't process the events unfolding. Would she never be safe?

The phone rang in the background. She glanced over her shoulder at it. The handset lay on the end table next to the couch.

Beth used the gun to jab her in the shoulder and move her back. Jamie stepped sideways toward the kitchen opening. Her phone on the wall rang again. There was no way she could get there fast enough, so she did her best to ignore her only hope of rescue. She focused on the woman in front of her. "What are you doing?"

"Something Howard should have done months ago."

"So, you're going to kill me." Then it clicked for her. "You," she whispered. "You're the shadow."

Beth's brows knit. "What?"

"I never really knew what was real and what I'd dreamed. But I kept seeing this . . . shadow. Sensing . . . movement. I just never could see it. And it was you, wasn't it?"

"I liked to watch him put people out of their pain. Every day when we were kids, she beat us, broke our bones, starved us." Her eyes took on an otherworldly glaze. "I hated her, but I was small, I had no power, could do nothing except take it, day after day after day." A deep breath, back to reality. "I begged him to kill our mother, you know." In a singsong voice, she chanted, "Stop the pain, please stop the pain. You have to stop the pain, Howie."

"And so he did," Jamie finished for her, desperately holding on to her sanity, controlling her fear, refusing the desire to give in to the tight panic pounding in her chest. She sidestepped the gun, her back now toward the sunroom.

"And so he did," Beth echoed, eyes widening with the memory. "I don't think he actually meant to do it at first, but then when he realized she was dead . . ." Deep breath then, "He was my hero. He did anything I wanted him to do."

"And every time he killed another girl —"

"A party girl, a bad girl," Beth interrupted. "A girl who didn't deserve to grow up and have children that she would one day abuse and leave all alone while she drank away what little money she had."

Jamie swallowed hard. She'd been on that path. The party girl who drank too much, didn't care who she hurt or who was affected by her carelessness. Who knows where she might have ended up if she hadn't been snatched by this woman's brother?

"I would never hurt a child," she whispered.

"You don't know what you would have done twelve years ago." Flat, dead, cold words that told Jamie that Beth was moving beyond caring about the conversation. She'd come here for a reason and was getting ready to carry it out.

"Howard's dead," Jamie blurted, moving back another step into the den. "Why kill me now?"

"Because I have nothing left. You took the

only thing in my life that I loved. I owe it to him to finish his work."

Jamie could tell it would do no good to argue with the woman. She wanted to shout, "If you hadn't taken me in the first place, we wouldn't be in this position!" Instead, she kept her mouth shut, stamped down her raging fear, and engaged her brain. There had to be a way out of this. *Oh Lord, show me.*

The gun in Beth's hand trembled. How did such a meek-mannered woman like Beth get up the guts to come to Jamie's house and confront her?

Or was that really her personality? Was it just for show? A game?

"I don't get it," Jamie sputtered, grabbing her fear and controlling it, refusing to give it free reign. She had only one thought in her mind — to keep Beth talking until she could figure a way out. "You gave him up to the cops."

"What?"

"Dakota said when they questioned you, you sent them straight to Howard."

A sigh. The gun lowered a fraction. Movement caught the corner of her eye from the open blinds and her heart leapt into her throat. A uniform? Had someone figured out she was in danger? When she didn't answer the phone, had someone decided to come check on her?

She ignored the window, kept her eyes from straying there and giving away the fact that she might have help.

Her goal now consisted of focusing all of her energy on keeping it together, staying calm — and breathing.

"A strategy that got him killed, unfortunately. I planned to call him after the police left, but they kept me in custody." She frowned. "I didn't expect that. I thought they would just . . ." More frowning. "I don't know what I thought. But I did believe that if I gave them what they wanted, they would leave me alone. At least see that I was trying to help." A bitter eye roll. "I knew that if I covered anything up, it would only be a matter of time before they had every ounce of information available on me. Including where I grew up. I thought if I helped them, they would let me go and I would have enough time to warn Howard. But it didn't work, they arrested me. It took forever to get out of there."

Jamie was familiar with the process. By the time Beth would have gotten free, most likely Howard was already dead. Maybe if Jamie tried to sympathize with her, it would reach her on some level. "I'm so sorry you had such a terrible childhood. I can't even imagine —"

"No, you can't," she hissed as her eyes sparked with anger. "No one can imagine. Even the social workers and foster families didn't have a clue how bad it was."

Sympathizing wasn't going to work. Jamie held her hands up, looked around. Fighting back was her only option. She needed a weapon.

Beth's finger tightened on the trigger.

Dakota couldn't hear Jamie talking, but he had a good view of the den from the corner of her blinds. When he'd realized there'd been a second person involved, the only individual that came to mind was the sister.

His gut told him that Beth Wilkins had known exactly what her brother had been up to. When he'd called to check on her whereabouts, he'd been informed that she'd bailed herself out and left the station. A cruiser had been a minute from her home. The officer had swung by and reported no activity at the residence.

Which meant Jamie's safety immediately became Dakota's first priority once again. Putting it all together, the two chairs, the feminine sunglasses, Beth delivering the package to the post office.

When confronted, she'd lied.

Big-time. Gave an Academy Award–winning performance.

He sent a car to cover Jamie's house, asking for the officer to report back anything suspicious — and to run the tags of any vehicles not parked in a driveway. The officer stated that there was a red truck sitting across the street and down two houses. The only vehicle on the street. He was waiting for the tag report.

The minute he heard the words "red truck" Dakota had immediately asked for a team to head to Jamie's house. He knew who it would belong to.

Now, he tried to picture how this was going to go down. What the situation would look like from every side. And how best to handle it. Because he had no doubt that there was a situation.

He spoke into his microphone. "I need eyes and ears, people."

"Copy that," came the voice in his ear.

He wondered if he had time to wait. Scooting forward, he took another look through the blinds. Jamie backed into the den, then he caught a glimpse of the gun that followed her. Beth Wilkins stepped into view.

Jamie was saying something. Beth wasn't

474

having any of it, shaking her head and waving the gun.

"Is the alarm deactivated?" he asked into his microphone.

"Copy that."

Connor shot him a look as though asking if Jamie was all right. A thumbs-down from Dakota brought a frown to his face.

Then Dakota said, "We're going to have to get in there. The woman is unstable and she's got a gun on Jamie."

He called her number one more time, watching through the slits of the blinds.

The ringing phone made her blink. "I need to answer that."

"No!" Beth's hand shook.

Jamie took a deep breath. "Okay."

The phone rang through to voice mail. Jamie backed up more. Beth followed.

Keep her talking.

"What do you want?" Another step back.

Evil settled on the woman's face. Malice glinted, and any ounce of sympathy Jamie had lingering for the children who'd suffered such a horrendous childhood disappeared in the presence of the twisted adult. She had to do whatever it took to get away from this woman or she was dead.

Jamie took another step back and ended

475

up in the sunroom. Could she get to the door and get out before Beth shot her?

The gun tilted and Beth's eyes widened as though she just realized where they were. "Stop moving."

Jamie stopped, having accomplished her goal of moving the woman away from the door.

Beth shifted closer. Jamie tensed.

"What do I want?" she asked calmly, as though the two of them were sitting down and sharing a cup of coffee. "I want a normal childhood with parents who loved me. But that's not going to happen. I want my brother back." A scowl, then grief twisted her face and tears appeared. "But since that's not going to happen, I want to finish his work."

"You're crazy," Jamie whispered.

"Crazy!" The tears stopped, the face hardened. "I'm crazy?" A pause. "Well, I might be, but it's only because people like you made me this way."

"Beth —"

"Shut up."

The back of Jamie's thighs hit her paint supply table. An idea formed and her fingers felt behind her. Groped. Closed around the can.

Beth motioned once more with the

weapon. "Now, we're going to get in your car and we're going to leave."

Heart thumping, adrenaline rushing, Jamie kept the can behind her, waiting, watching for the right moment. "Where are we going?"

"Back to the house. No one will look for you there."

"They're still processing it as a crime scene. There are people still there."

Indecision creased her forehead. Jamie could see she'd confused her, blown her plan out of the water, and now she didn't know what to do.

A lilting whistle came from behind Beth.

The woman whirled.

Jamie grabbed the can and hurled it toward Beth's face.

Turpentine splashed, Beth screamed and the gun fired. Some part of her brain registered the sound of a window breaking.

"Jamie!"

Dakota's voice came from the door. Jamie threw herself past the woman who swiped frantically at her eyes and gasped for breath.

Strong arms pulled her behind him and uniforms swarmed the house.

Beth's screeching protests rang in her ears, but all she could do was hold on to the man who'd saved her life once again.

37

Jamie looked down at Maya's grave, grief twisting her insides. "I miss her so much, Dakota. She was there with me, from the moment I woke up in the hospital until . . ." She thought. "Well, just until. A twelve-year friendship that was so much more than a friendship. She was my sister in Christ, my confidante, my spiritual mentor, my encourager . . ." Her whispered words trailed off.

"She loved you like a sister."

"I know and it's funny that we hit it off as well as we did. She was about ten years older than I. The same age as Samantha, and yet for some reason," she shrugged, "we clicked." A laugh. "I think I got the better end of the deal. I'm not so sure I did much for her. I was very needy, you know."

The arm he'd settled over her shoulders pulled her closer to him. She let him, relishing the feeling of trusting him completely.

His voice rumbled above her head. "She didn't expect you to. Maya spent her life helping others, wanting to make a difference in the world."

"You got that from her just from the few times you saw her?"

"Yep. And from observing your relationship with her."

A tear trickled from the corner of her eye. "I know she's with God, Dakota, but I *miss* her."

"I know, hon." He planted a kiss on top of her head.

"I don't want to hate them," she whispered in reference to Howard and Beth Wilkins, the brother and sister who'd suffered so dreadfully as children, warping their perception of the world and of people in general.

"No one would blame you if you did."

"I would. I often think about what if someone had intervened sooner in their lives. What was wrong with people? Couldn't they tell something was incredibly wrong in those children's lives?"

Another hug. "We've been over this. Things were different forty years ago, Jamie, you know that. Unfortunately, we can't change it."

"I know." She knelt down and placed the flowers on the mound. She patted the headstone. "Bye, Maya. I'll be back."

Dakota took her hand. "Maya really made a difference in your life, didn't she?"

Jamie looked up at him. "I wouldn't be where I am today if God hadn't placed her there for me. Even when I was rejecting him, he was taking care of me."

"Makes you wonder why he'd let her be killed, doesn't it?"

She shrugged. "Sure, it does. But I don't question his goodness, his overall plan. In spite of my grief and shortsightedness, I still believe he knows best." She thought for a moment. "And if Maya thought her death would further his work, then she wouldn't regret the cost to herself."

"I'm still processing all that."

She grinned up at him through a sheen of tears that still lingered. "You're praying and seeking God, Dakota. You've given him your life. That's all he asks. He'll take care of the rest."

As they walked back to the car, Dakota watched Jamie. She had a newly relaxed attitude. She smiled more and didn't jump when he touched her anymore.

He heard her phone ring and she grabbed it. "Hello?"

As she listened, her eyes widened, then

she swung around and grabbed his hand. "Come on, it's time. Samantha's on her way to the hospital!"

The moment they'd all been waiting for.

He felt just as eager as Jamie. He was going to be an uncle. Well, almost an uncle. If Jamie would marry him, she'd make him an uncle.

He reached over and clasped her hand. "Are you ready yet?"

"Ready?" Confusion clouded her gaze.

Dakota rubbed her ring finger. "Ready."

"Oh." The light went on and she flushed, then looked up at him from beneath her lashes. "Yeah. I think I am."

Joy exploded in his chest. To cover it, he started the car. "Okay, we'll address that issue later."

"Okay."

"And definitely soon."

The hospital never stilled. Jamie sidestepped a mother and two toddlers to make her way over to the elevator. She punched the button with a shaking finger.

"Hey, you left me in the dust back there."

Whirling, she threw her arms around Dakota's neck and squeezed. "I'm sorry, I'm just so excited."

He hugged her back and laughed. "I know."

The doors slid open and she darted in, pulling Dakota in after her. Everything seemed to move in slow motion. "Come on, come on," she muttered.

"Jamie, chill. They're not going anywhere."

She slanted a look at him. "Laugh all you want, Richards. I'm ready to meet my nephew."

"Might be a niece."

"He wouldn't dare."

Dakota just shook his head at her and she smiled. "I'll still love her if she's a girl."

The car finally stopped on the right floor and they stepped out. Jamie spotted her parents in the hall. "Mom?"

The woman turned and grinned. "He's here!"

Jamie squealed and gave Dakota's arm a light punch. "See? I told you."

Her dad grinned. "An eight-pounder."

"He's not a fish, Charles," his wife reprimanded him.

Jamie let the laughter peel from her. Connor chose that moment to stick his head out the door. "Come on in, everyone."

He didn't have to ask twice.

They all crowded into the room.

Jenna stood holding her little brother,

beaming down at him. Jamie pulled the blanket aside and reached out a finger to touch his perfect cheek. "He's just beautiful," she whispered. Awe filled her. *Thank you, God, for bringing us here.*

"Amen," Dakota whispered in her ear as he gazed down at the newborn. "You were praying again, weren't you?"

"Yeah."

Jenna grinned. "You want to hold him?"

"Uh-huh." Jamie held out her arms and Jenna placed the precious bundle in them. A perfect fit. She inhaled his clean baby scent and her heart clenched as though he'd reached through her chest and grabbed it in his tiny fist.

"Hey, Jamie, I'm the one that did all the work. You wanna speak to me?"

Everyone laughed at Samantha's affected outrage. Jamie crossed the room to lean over and kiss her sister's cheek. "You did good, Sam."

Sam's eyes flooded with tears. "Yeah, I did, didn't I?"

Connor didn't seem to know where to look. His eyes flitted from his wife to his son, then back to his wife. Dakota punched his buddy on the arm. "Good job, man."

Connor grunted. "I better not take any of the credit if I know what's good for me."

A knock on the door brought their attention around. Sam called out, "Come in."

Kit pushed open the door and stepped inside the room. "Hey there. Thought I'd come meet my nephew."

Jamie passed her bundle reluctantly to her twin. "What's his name?"

Samantha and Connor exchanged a look, then Sam said, "Connor Andrew Wolfe. We're going to call him Andy." Andy let out a squawk as though approving the name.

"For Connor's partner, Andrew, who was killed," Jamie whispered.

Sam nodded and Conner cleared his throat. "He would be proud."

Dakota gripped her hand and looked her in the eye. "Soon?"

She nodded. "Real soon."

And in front of everybody, he leaned down and kissed her. As the sound of clapping penetrated her fog of bemusement, she grinned against his lips. "Real, real soon."

EPILOGUE

One, two, three,
You laughed at me,
You tapped your feet,
You rolled your eyes,
The time has come for you all to die.

The Judge clutched the pen so hard, it snapped in two. Blue ink dripped onto the paper in front of him. He ignored it. Not the best poem he'd ever come up with, but it would do. The Judge pulled the last picture in front of him, then placed it into the box. One by one, he'd gathered their pictures, their photos, their schedules. He'd learned everything there was to know about each and every one.

Glancing up, he caught his father's empty stare, watching. Always watching. "What are you looking at, old man," he snarled.

The man remained silent.

"What?" the Judge snapped. "You've got

485

nothing to say now?"

It drove him crazy how the man could just sit there for hours on end saying nothing. Then other times he would talk until the Judge wanted to run screaming from the house.

"Aw, why do I waste my time on you?"

He gathered up his treasures and carried them from the room. It was time.

Time to take care of those who'd mocked him.

Yes, he decided as he drew in a deep, calming breath. It was a good day to kill.

ACKNOWLEDGMENTS

This is always the hard part. I'm always so scared to thank anyone because I'm sure to miss someone. However, I'm going to give it my best shot.

As always, thank you to my **very understanding** family, my husband, Jack, daughter, Lauryn, and son, Will. I don't cook — much. I don't clean — often. I do laundry — occasionally. And I have Chinese takeout, Pizza Inn, and for the guilt-induced vegetable night, Wade's Family Restaurant, on speed dial. (You know it's bad when they recognize your number from the caller ID, and instead of "Hello, how can I help you?" your greeting is, "It'll be ready in 15 minutes, Mrs. Eason.") 'Nuff said.

Major thanks to Wayne Smith, retired FBI agent, who read my manuscript and said, "It's a great read that even a macho male would enjoy." Whew! What a compliment! Thanks, Wayne, you rock.

Mega thanks to the Revell staff. Thanks to everyone who had a hand in the book. Even though I haven't met you, I appreciate you!

And to my faithful, loyal readers, thank you SO much for being first in line to purchase my stories. I hope you enjoyed this one as much as the last.

ABOUT THE AUTHOR

Lynette Eason grew up in Greenville, South Carolina. She graduated from the University of South Carolina, Columbia, and then obtained her master's in education at Converse College. Author of ten inspirational romantic suspense books, she is also a member of American Christian Fiction Writers (ACFW) and Romance Writers of America (RWA). In 1996, Lynette married "the boy next door," and now she and her husband and two children make their home in Spartanburg, South Carolina.

Visit Lynette at www.lynetteeason.com.